FOOTBALL
Royalty

EDEN FINLEY

disclaimer

This is a work of fiction.
While I stuck as close as I could to the NCAA guidelines and rules in regards to football, I took creative freedom with some small details. Plus, football is, like, really confusing. It hurts my brain. And if I'd let Peyton become a hockey player instead, Talon would've had a stroke.
Names, characters, businesses, places, events, and incidents are either the products of the authors' imaginations or used in a fictitious manner. Any resemblance to actual persons, living or dead, or actual events is purely coincidental.

CHAPTER ONE

THE HOUSE PARTY scene of Montgomery Preparatory in Chicago is always extravagant and insane. Rich kids in mansions with no parents. I've thrown many of my own over the years when my dads have been away, but this one is different. Not only because it's not my party but because there's a vibe to it that doesn't sit right with me.

It's weighted with a sense of finality, which makes sense—it is a graduation party—but I shouldn't be feeling it. I'm not the one graduating.

The walls sink in on me, like they're pulsing in time with the bodies and music that surround me. The living room is a little too hot, and my panic is a little too real. No matter where I go, I can't get away from it. I lost my brother, Brady, somewhere along the way. I'm edgy and sweaty, and it's hard to breathe.

I need air.

I find the nearest exit and stumble out onto the terrace of Levi Vanderbilt's penthouse that overlooks Lake Michigan on one side and the city on the other.

This place, all eight thousand square feet of wood-paneled halls and limestone staircases, screams old money. Mine screams famous family. Levi and I might be in the same world, but we're billions of dollars apart.

The pumping music is muted out here, enough to keep the neighbors below us from complaining but still not enough to stop the throbbing in my head, so I cross the lawn, ignoring the thought process of how they got grass to grow twenty floors in the air.

They even have a fountain in the middle.

Definitely old money.

Levi and I haven't had a whole lot to do with each other. He's in the grade above me, even though I'm his age.

My dads decided when Brady and I were little that I wouldn't start school until Brady did so we could go through school together like we were twins. Which we're not. Far from it. We don't even look like *brothers*. I take after Dad with my blond hair, blue eyes, and the perfect quarterback physique. Whereas Brady is filled out like Pop, with the kind of wide body he needs to be a center on the field with me, and has brown eyes, but he has a lot lighter hair than Pop. Somehow. It's a darker shade than mine, like an ashy-brown color, but we can only speculate the egg donor they used must have been blonde. Black hair, plus blond, equals brown ... or something. When we were younger, he used to have blond hair like mine, but as time's gone on, it's gotten darker. Genetics are weird, and it's not really talked about in our house.

Unlike the reason my dads say they kept me back a grade, which is talked about constantly. They claim it's so by the time I graduate college and enter the draft, I'll be the strongest I possibly can be, but they say it so much I think it's an excuse to hide the truth. They didn't want Brady or me to be lonely. They knew we would grow up to be each other's only friend we could trust wholly.

And maybe they had a point because technically, this party should have been my graduation celebration too, and I'm out here by myself, trying not to hyperventilate.

I go over to the balcony and sit on the edge, swinging my legs over the side. The railing is short, and the fall is big, but I anchor myself by wrapping my arm around an ugly-ass stone lion statue. I guess safety measures for balconies weren't a thing when this place was built.

I can finally breathe out here … so long as I don't look down.

But then a voice comes from behind and scares the shit out of me. "You don't have to do this."

I flinch so hard I have to grip onto the lion tighter. I turn to see Levi himself, standing a few feet away with his hand out and a concerned look on his face.

He's your typical privileged white kid. Not that I can talk. His chestnut-colored hair is shaggy and sits around his neck, but that's probably the only thing about him that says he's unkempt, and if I had to guess, I'd say he keeps it that way to piss off his parents.

I remember one year when Brady was eleven, he told our dads he wanted to play baseball instead of football just to annoy them. He can't hit a ball with a bat to save his life.

We love our dads to death—they're the best parents anyone could ask for—but growing up as the sons of the first ever queer couple to win a Super Bowl, we haven't had a normal childhood. They're not to blame for that, though. It's all the media wanting to pry into their relationship. Two bisexual football players? Together? Clutch your pearls and pray to Jesus.

"Are you okay?" Levi asks.

I snort. "You know a good way to get someone to fall off your building is to scare them half to death?"

Levi smiles and drops his hand. "Or, you know, a good way to fall off yourself is to climb the damn railing."

"Touché."

"So, to be clear, you're not thinking about jumping?"

I point to my face. "This is too pretty to be splattered all over the sidewalk."

"That's ... disturbing."

"Disturbing but true."

Levi comes closer and takes the spot next to me, but he puts his back to the water, refusing to dangle his legs off the side of the building like I am. "I'm Levi."

"No shit."

"You're Peyton."

"Yep. We've been going to the same school since pre-K. We know who the other is."

Levi rubs his chin. "Been in the same circles for the majority of our lives—"

"Our long, long eighteen years of life. Sure."

"But this is the only conversation we've ever had."

I shrug. "Different grades. Different interests. I don't see your scrawny ass trying out for football, and if you ever find me in debate club, just know I'm being held against my will and I urge you to call 911."

Levi laughs. "You say that like I wanted to do that shit. Also, my ass is not scrawny."

"So why did you do debate club if you didn't want to?

Also, it's very scrawny."

"Because my dad made me. And it is not." He stands and grabs his ass with both hands.

I admit his ass might be the only thing not scrawny about him and that my definition of scrawny might be skewed. I'm on a field with guys who are jacked up to their eyeballs every day. Everyone is scrawny in comparison.

"I relent."

"Thank you." He sits back down beside me and gives me this weird smile that makes my gut flutter in a way that's familiar but also foreign at the same time.

It's happened with girls countless times, but Levi's the first guy that's made my stomach do a backflip.

My dads taught me not to ignore these kinds of feelings. That it's completely normal, they'll accept my brother and me however we identify, blah, blah, blah, so it's not like I'm scared to act on it. Well, other than putting myself out there and getting punched in the face.

Levi's gaze is still on mine, his gray eyes shining, and I'm locked in his stare.

He's the first to break eye contact. "So why is football royalty sitting out here by himself during the biggest graduation party the school has ever seen?"

"Why are you out here talking to football royalty when this is *your* party, King Vanderbilt?"

"Mmm, King Vanderbilt has a nice ring to it, but to answer your question, I saw someone out here and didn't want another death on my hands."

I pull back. "Another? Okay, should I be worried about you shoving me off the side?"

"That was a joke. I make them sometimes."

"Aren't jokes supposed to be funny?"

"I dunno. Why don't we ask your face?" he quips.

"*So* mature."

"Hey, I'm riding the immaturity train for as long as I can before …" He flicks his gaze away.

"Before what?"

"Before my future slaps me upside the face."

Shit, don't I know what that feels like. I'm excited for the future. Brady might not want to follow in our dads' footsteps, but I sure as fuck do. I'm NFL-bound no matter what. But … it's always been a future thing—something that has always seemed like a million years away. But now …

"The reason I'm out here is *because* it's a graduation party," I admit.

"Uh, I get football players are known to be slow, but you know it's not *your* graduation party, don't you? You still have another year of Mr. Collin's torturous science classes to sit through."

"Don't remind me, but no. Being here, it's cementing that I have one year of high school left, and then I'm starting my college football career."

"You don't want that?"

"I want it so bad," I whisper.

"Then why do I get the feeling you're freaking out about it?"

"Because I am. I've been training for it my whole life, and I love the game, but the pressure …" I shake my head. "It's so much pressure."

"I get that. My dad is the same."

"Except it's not my dads that the pressure comes from. Sure, *the* Marcus Talon wants his kids to play football, but our pop has always said whatever we want to do is fine, and I know Dad would come around if I didn't want it. It's the outside pressure that's already building, and I'm nowhere near being drafted yet."

"I bet the comparisons are hard."

"*So* hard." And as if the word *hard* granted my dick permission, it so valiantly answers the call.

Down, boy.

I shift where I'm sitting, inching away from Levi and closer to the lion.

"Having the second-best quarterback in history as a dad? I can only imagine," Levi says.

"Eh. If you ask Dad, Tom Brady cheated."

Levi cocks his head. "Yet, your brother is named after him."

"I think after naming me Peyton, they thought they had to stick with the football theme when it came to Brady. And no one wants to name their kid after Brett Favre."

"Who?"

"Exactly."

"So, where exactly are you planning to have this amazing yet pressure-filled college football career?"

I don't answer him right away. I get caught on his hand that reaches inside his jeans and pulls out a cigarette. Oh. Nope. That's a joint.

"Pey?"

I shake it off and meet his stare. No one calls me Pey except my family, so it's weird but also kinda cool to hear it from someone who's taken it upon himself to give me a nickname. "Uh, we haven't decided yet."

Levi puts the joint to his plump lips and lights it. "We?"

The joint bounces in his mouth as he talks, and then he wraps his lips around it and inhales.

"Brady and me. And our dads, I guess. They want me to go to USC, but Brady doesn't want to go there."

"Ah, West Coast. I *wish* I could go to a school at the beach."

"Brady and I think Franklin U in San Luco would be a good fit for both of us, but we haven't told our dads that yet. We are not looking forward to that day."

"You and your brother do everything together?"

"Yep. It kinda comes with the territory of having the last names Miller and Talon."

"Why *do* you have different last names?" he asks.

"It's a long story." One I hate explaining because it's nobody's damn business.

"I haven't got anywhere to be."

It's a pain getting into it because most people don't understand, but there's a method to my dads' madness. "Everyone assumes Shane Miller is my biological father because I have his last name, but that's not true at all. I have Talon DNA but am a Miller by name. It's the opposite for Brady. Our dads wanted us to have a piece of each of them. I also think they were under the impression no one would get confused or even care. They were wrong."

"Want a hit?" Levi holds out the joint.

"I shouldn't."

"Come on. Football season is over."

"You say that like there's an actual football season in my house. Every day is football season." Every minute. Every second.

"Do your dads drug test you?" he asks.

"Well, no. But ... I've never done it before."

Levi leans in. "There's a first time for everything. Why don't you live a little? Now's the time to do it." He brings the joint to his mouth again, inhaling deep.

He keeps moving closer, so close that I don't want to say no at this point because I don't want him to move away. My gut flips again and fills with butterflies to the point that when the word "Okay" falls from my mouth, I don't know if it's to the weed or *him*.

I'd probably take both at this point.

Levi moves in, his lips almost touching mine, and I instinctually open for him. He exhales at the same time I breathe in.

I'm trapped, looking into his gray eyes, wanting to move that tiny bit closer and press my lips to his to see if I react the same way to him that I do to girls. My heart thunders in my ears, but unlike when I was inside trying to find an escape, I want to savor this and embrace it. I want to feel the thrill thrumming through my veins.

But Levi moves away, not closer, and glances over my shoulder, back inside at the party.

We both speak at the same time.

"If you need to get back inside—"

"Want to finish this in my room?"

I don't know if he means the joint or more. Either way, the answer is yes.

When he stands, I swing my legs back over the railing and follow him. He doesn't go toward the door I came out of, where I can see the party still in full swing, but to a different entrance at the other end of the house that opens to a hallway.

We take the first left, entering a room with royal blue walls, arched windows that overlook the lake, and the most modern furniture I've seen in this house so far. Every other room I've been in has had wooden and ornate things that look like they're from the 1800s.

He goes over to the window and opens a panel. "Not supposed to smoke in here." He lifts his chin for me to join him, and I'm quick to obey.

Levi takes another drag, and I step closer, wanting him to repeat what he did outside, but he doesn't. He lifts the joint between us instead.

Hmm, guess that answers my question. This isn't a more … thing. It's just the pot.

I take it from him and lift it to my lips, sucking in as much as I can. *Oh, shit, bad idea.* It would be embarrassing to cough all over him, so I take a step back and hold it in until my eyes water and I can't help breathing out. Luckily, the stinging and tickle in my throat is weaker, and I only let out a single cough instead of the string of barking trying to escape me.

"You okay?" Levi smiles again, and I get the impression he's mocking me on the inside.

"Wrong pipe," I croak.

"Fuck, you're cute."

Okay, the mixed signals are giving me whiplash. "I am?"

"You know, in a jock kind of way."

"Oh, then in that case, you're cute too. In a white-privi-leged, *will own the world one day* kind of way."

"Then I really could be King Vanderbilt." Levi steps forward. "Wanna see if this toad can turn into a prince?"

Is that his way of asking me to kiss him? "I thought you wanted to be king."

"Have to work my way up. You want to help me get there?"

Okay, I have to ask. "A-are you asking to kiss me?"

Levi laughs. "Yes. That's me asking to kiss you. I mean, your dads are—"

"They're my dads. It doesn't mean we're all queer."

Levi's gray eyes darken like storm clouds rolling in, and there's an edge to his tone when he says, "Are you? Uh, *that*?"

"Queer? Yesterday, I would have said no, but I really, really want to kiss you."

"Then it's settled." He takes the last drag of the weed and then puts the remaining bit in a glass on his desk. There's only a little water left, but it makes a distinct hissing sound as the joint dies out.

"What's settled?"

Instead of answering me, Levi wraps his arms around my back and pulls me against him. It's with such force I might have to rethink the scrawny comment. I'm not a small guy, but I grunt as our bodies slam together.

Our mouths meet, and his lips are surprisingly soft. He tastes like weed, but apparently, I like that. A lot. My body responds in a way I'm not really expecting. The flutter in my gut was one thing. The embarrassing hard-on is a whole other ball game.

Levi pushes his tongue inside my mouth, and I welcome it.

I'm out of my element, I have no idea what I'm doing, but he has it under control.

He can probably feel my heart trying to beat its way out of my chest, not to mention the hard dick between us.

I've made out with girls before. Hooked up. Even had sex with a couple of them. But this …

It's different.

Good different? Bad different? I don't know yet.

It's more *intense.*

I let Levi grip my hips and move me toward his bed. When the back of my knees hit the side, we both fall, Levi landing on top of me. I want to try to inch up the bed so my legs aren't hanging off the edge, but the voice inside my head tells me if I interrupt this, he's going to stop.

And I really don't want him to stop.

Levi breaks us apart and rests one elbow next to my head. He pulls his bottom lip between his teeth, and I wait impatiently for a question to fall from his mouth, but it doesn't come. Instead, he hesitantly reaches for the fly on my jeans, the silent question coming out in actions instead of words.

I nod, and he slowly fumbles the zipper down.

"H-h-have you ever done this before?" I stutter.

He shakes his head.

"Let me help." I undo my fly, and then he does his own.

I'm not sure what the protocol is here, and it's obvious neither is he. We're both breathing heavily, staring at each other, and the only thing I have in my head is *"Don't look at his dick. Don't look at his dick."* Only, the more I think it, the more I want to glance down at it.

So instead, I cup Levi's head and lean up to touch my lips to his again. He kisses me back, pressing our bodies together, and with our flies open and only the material of our boxers between us, I can feel every inch of his dick against mine.

My hips lift off the bed reflexively, and when Levi groans into my mouth, I get the impression that was a reflex too.

The hesitance strips away on both our parts. I writhe beneath him, loving the sensation on my cock, only heightened by Levi starting to move on top of me, meeting each grind of my hips.

He has me pinned underneath him, and I have the need to run my fingers through his shaggy hair and grip tight just so I can hold on.

Levi moves on top of me, getting frantic now, and while we continue to kiss, our lips have a hard time staying together. He must give up on trying at all because next thing I know, his mouth latches onto my neck, and he sucks hard.

I claw at his back and moan. Without warning, warmth fills my underwear, and I'm hit with an intense wave that steals my breath.

Levi thrusts two more times and stills above me, lifting his head and exposing his long neck. I release his hair and trail my fingers down over his throat.

He lets out a loud breath and then rolls off me, slumping beside me on his bed and throwing his arm over his eyes. "Well, this isn't awkward at all."

I want to ask if he means making each other come in general or the messes in our underwear, but I get the feeling I might not like the answer.

Levi stands and moves to a chest of drawers, pulling out a pair of underwear and throwing them at me. They hit me in my chest. "Uh ... for, umm ..." He points to the wet patch on my boxers.

"Uh, right." I stand and drop my jeans and underwear. I've grown up in locker rooms, so all of my teammates have seen me naked countless times, but this is different.

Even though Levi turns his back to me, I feel exposed.

I feel ... *confused.*

The Calvin Klein boxer briefs he threw at me fit snugly against my skin. I'm used to boxers where my junk doesn't think it's being suffocated to death.

That's when I notice Levi tucking himself away and doing up his fly without changing first.

Oh, shit. "Did you not ... like ... umm ... you know?" My cheeks heat. He's right. This is awkward.

He turns to me with that same flirty smile from earlier. "I did. But I think I got more on your boxers than mine."

"Oh. Okay. Umm, cool."

"And I mean, it was fun, but ..." Levi glances away, and the rejection stings like a bitch, but I shrug it off.

"Not your thing. I get it. It's not like we'll see each other again or anything. I'm guessing you're going to an East Coast school."

"Boston."

"Ah. Harvard." I pronounce it *Hahvid* like a Bostonian.

"Yep."

The awkwardness kicks in again, and I realize I'm still standing here, in *his* underwear, and I haven't put my jeans back on yet.

If I do it now, will it be more or less awkward than waiting for him to leave?

I grab them off the bed and pull them up my legs, but before I can get my fly done back up, the door to the room flies open, and both of us jump a mile.

My brother stands there with a mix of shock and gloating on his face. "Uh, here you are."

"Here I am." I zip up my pants.

"We need to go. Curfew."

Right. Shit.

I glance at Levi. "Good luck in college."

"Kick ass at sports."

I leave with Brady, ignoring the knowing looks he throws

my way while I say goodbye to the guys from the football team and for the entire walk to the elevators outside Levi's apartment.

As soon as the doors close, Brady turns to me. "You smell like weed, by the way. Dads are gonna be pissed."

"Switch shirts with me."

"With pleasure." Ah, my baby bro. Always there for me. Plus, any excuse for him to get our dads' attention. I'm the older child, the one who inherited Marcus Talon's talent. Brady is good, and he could totally make it to the NFL if he tried harder, but he has absolutely no aspirations to play pro football.

I think getting caught with weed might actually help him in that area. Can't play football if you're kicked off the team for banned substances.

We change shirts, his way too big on me and mine way too tight on him, but it works. Our dads will probably be asleep when we get home anyway. Hopefully.

But then Brady does the staring thing again. "Something you'd like to share?"

Nope.

It's obvious he knows something happened, but I don't want to make it a big deal. It wasn't a big deal to Levi, so I won't turn it into this big existential crisis. So even though the words taste bitter on my tongue, I recycle what Levi said back there. "It was fun, but it wasn't my thing."

Brady jumps up and down, shaking the whole damn elevator. "Can I please be the one to tell our dads you were the first to pop their 'sex with a dude' cherry?"

That's the last thing I need. "Fuck no. It was nothing."

And I'm going to tell myself that forever and ever.

CHAPTER TWO

NO MATTER how many times I'm recognized in San Luco by random people, it still amazes me when strangers tell me, "Great game last weekend." I wave and smile like I always do, knowing that this shit is only going to get worse after the draft.

I have one more year left of my college-playing days, and unlike the freak-out I had when graduation was looming over me in high school, the last three years playing for FU have conditioned me to be ready. I'm confident—maybe sometimes too confident—and I can't wait to sign with an NFL team.

Technically, I could've been drafted this past April, but my dads advised against it. It's not that they think I won't make it or I'm not good enough. They just wanted me to be as prepared as I could when I run out onto that professional field. It's not only me who's been planning for this my whole life.

And as the clock ticks down on my college career, the more excited I get about it.

Coming to Franklin U was the best decision Brady and I ever made. The campus is amazing, the beach is right across the street, the football facilities are state-of-the-art, and the team is treated like kings.

Literally.

The FU Kings are the best damn football team on the western seaboard, and we've played in two out of three championship games since I became first-string quarterback. We even managed to take home the title in one of them.

It's safe to say my life is right on track.

I cross the street to enter Shenanigans, a bar that is always filled with college kids, and head straight for the table where my brother is sitting with his best friend, Felix.

As I walk by Tyson Langley, I purposefully bump into him. He's a lacrosse player, and our school is notorious for our friendly rivalry between the sports. It's all fun and games, though, and as he flips me the bird, I pretend to catch it and put it in my pocket.

Then I grab a stool and park my ass next to my brother.

"You're late," Brady says.

"I had to say hello to all my adoring fans."

Brady rolls his eyes at me.

"Hey, when you're my agent, you're going to have to do something about my security. Hire me some bodyguards." I'm only half-joking. Brady's studying sports management, and he's planning to go to law school so he can be like our uncle. Brady will take over from Uncle Damon one day, and he'll be my agent. I haven't officially signed anything yet because the NCAA would kick me out faster than you can say "career over," but it's a given my uncle is going to represent me while Brady builds up his client list.

Felix laughs at my dramatics.

I point at him but talk to Brady. "At least someone finds me funny."

"It's because he wants to get into your pants," Brady says.

"Excuse me. I *used* to want to get into his pants. I'm a taken man now."

"Shame." I wink at him jokingly.

A curl from Felix's copper locks falls in his face. "How is this fair? I get a boyfriend, and *now* your brother flirts with me?"

"He's fucking with you," Brady says. "Like I already told you many times, he tried dick in high school, and he didn't like it."

And yet, four years later, he's still bringing it up. It's the only time I let myself think about Levi Vanderbilt.

"I may have popped that cherry first, but Brady here is the one who turned out to be full-blown homo." I snicker. "Get it? Full-blown?"

"You're still not funny," Brady says.

"Whatever. I'm fucking hilarious. Now, where's my drink?"

"You were late, so I drank it." Brady shrugs. "What are you gonna do about it?"

"I have no brother," I mutter as I get up to go to the bar.

I order a beer, and the bartender doesn't even scan my wrist for a band because Casey knows me. We hooked up on my twenty-first last year. And a couple more times after that. But there was no bad blood when it stopped.

Everyone on campus knows my priority is football, my future is football, but to make that happen, I don't have the time to focus on a relationship.

I have one rule when it comes to hookups: jersey chasers

are a no-go zone. They're the ones who are trying to lock down an NFL-bound player before they're famous. My go-to hookups are with girls who have their own focused goals. Casey is premed, and between studying and tending bar, she wasn't interested in anything more either. It meant getting together was infrequent, but I'd rather have dry spells than lead people on. I'm not that guy.

Casey hands over my beer, and I take out my wallet to pay, but she waves me off. "I'm in a generous mood."

"You just want me to leave a big tip."

"That too. I'm trying to save for med school, dude."

I lean in and kiss her cheek while sliding a tenner over to her. "For you."

"You're the best."

"I—" There's movement behind her, on the other side of the bar. I catch sight of a familiar face. I think.

He turns and moves through the crowd too quickly for me to be sure, but I keep staring, trying to see past the mass of bodies to see if it was actually him or I was imagining it.

"You what?" Casey asks.

It can't have been who I thought it was. I shake it off and train my gaze back to her. "I don't know."

She waves her hand in front of my face. "Are you having a stroke? Been sacked one too many times and have a head injury? Need me to check your vitals?"

I bat her hand away. "I thought I saw someone, that's all."

She looks over her shoulder. "Who?"

"Nobody. It doesn't matter. Thanks for this." I lift my beer and stalk away, but my mind is still on … *him*.

Nah, he couldn't be here. It's because Brady mentioned him, and this guy had the same color hair but not the same style. It wasn't shaggy around his ears but short and neat. I just ... those gray eyes.

Nope. Nope. Nope.

I'm not going there again.

The summer after he graduated was a confusing time for me. I didn't know if I was running from my hookup with a guy because it was a guy or because of the rejection from Levi.

It wasn't so much that I was worried I was bad at gay sex, though that factored in there for a while. Then I overanalyzed the sex I've had with girls and if they didn't like it as much as I did, and yeah, I went down that torturous rabbit hole until I read every article I possibly could about being good in bed. And okay, watched porn. A lot of porn. Turns out porn isn't so helpful in the "getting better at sex" category, but it's funner than reading about sex.

I reluctantly came to the conclusion that hooking up with Levi was a touchy spot for me because I thought I had a connection with him, which ... he obviously didn't return. That's the thing I got hung up on.

I decided then and there to let it go, but every time Brady mentions my one gay hookup, I'm hit with a seed of doubt again.

My brother doesn't realize he's doing it. I tell Brady everything, but this ... this is something I don't want to talk to anyone about. Not because I'm ashamed of it—it's not a secret I hooked up with a guy in high school—but because, well, if I told my brother or my dads what happened, they'd probably encourage me to explore my *feelings* and join Grindr to experiment, when everyone knows the healthiest way to deal with confusion and uncertainty is to squash it deep down and pretend it doesn't exist.

I make it back to our table, but Felix is gone, and only my brother remains. "Did I scare off your friend?"

"He went to play with his boyfriend." Brady nods toward the bar. "That still going on with you two?"

"Nope. We're just friends now." I sip my beer and lick my lips, but my gaze still roams the room, trying to find someone I'm convinced my mind manifested on its own.

"She still looks at you like she wants to jump your bones. Or your boner, at least."

"Does she?" I turn my head to look back at Casey, but she's busy working.

"You don't need the distraction. Especially this season. If you want to be the number one draft pick, you have to think with your head and not your dick."

"Hey, that rhymes. It sounds like a Dr. Seuss lesson."

"So, say it with me. If you want to be the number one draft pick ..."

I sigh. "Think with my head and not my dick. Got it."

"Good boy."

"You're going to be the most condescending agent ever, aren't you?"

"Only to my favorite clients." He winks at me.

"Maybe Uncle Damon *shouldn't* teach you everything he knows."

But honestly, I wouldn't have anyone else representing me. My brother's got my back.

I down the rest of my drink in one large gulp. "I'm going to get another one. You want anything?"

"Don't you have an early practice in the morning?"

I slump back down. Guess I'm done drinking for the night.

Yeah, my brother has my back, and he's going to be a great agent. Even when I don't like him for it.

We have a new center on the team this year, and yeah, he's all right, but I've never had a connection with any of the centers I've had since my brother. With Brady, I didn't have to think. We were fluid.

Johnson's making me work for it, and the last thing a quarterback wants is to be worried about fucking up the snap, let alone think about the play on top of that.

Coach has been training us hard since the beginning of the year. College football season is grueling, starting the last week of August and going all the way through to January if we make it to postseason. Which we will. But it means that by the time we get to October and we've already got midterms coming out of our ears, the team's morale is on the exhausted side.

It's really only the beginning, but the number of times Coach has us run plays, we've practiced more scrimmages than we'll perform during the entire season of actual games.

When we run an easy counterplay for the tenth time and we still can't get it right, I just about throw my helmet.

"What was that?" I yell to my teammates. I'm one of the captains and the quarterback. Their fuckups aren't only theirs but mine too, and I need this year to be perfect, damn it. "I'm not the only one NFL-bound here, am I? Because I can tell you now, none of us are gonna make the cut if we don't get our shit together."

"Relax, Cap," Green says. "We've only lost one game so

far this season. One in five. You should be thankful all our
screwups are happening during practice."

Ugh. He's right.

One in five. One in five.

I take a deep breath and calm down. Not completely, but
I'm brought back from the edge of losing it.

I might be more ready than I was this time four years ago
when my future was staring me right in the face, and I'm more
excited than ever for it, but that doesn't mean the pressure has
gotten any better. If anything, it's only gotten worse. Not only
pressure from my school and the team but my dads as well.

We've been on this train of thought since before I can
remember. I don't ever recall choosing football. When you're
football royalty, you don't choose the game. It chooses you.

Coach Nass blows his whistle and calls us in. "We're done
for the day. Hit the showers."

"We can get it," I say.

"Peyton, there is such a thing as overpreparing. If you keep
pushing your guys, they're going to forget how to football
altogether."

My lips twitch. "Did you just use football as a verb, sir?"

"You bet your ass I did. Now listen to me and hit the showers." Coach grins.

He made it to the big time and has lived and breathed football for his whole life. He might have only officially played
one season in the NFL, but he'd been on a few practice squads
—one of them being the Warriors. That's the team my dads
played for in Chicago. The team where they won their Super
Bowl together. The entire reason Dad didn't put up too much
of a fight over Brady and me going to this school was Coach
Nass.

If he says I'm pushing too hard, I'm pushing too hard.

"Okay, let's go," I relent.

The team heads for the showers, but I hang back, taking my time. I'm in no rush to shower and get to classes. I am in a rush to fill my veins with caffeine, though, so there's that. I pick up the pace, and by the time the rest of the team is showered and dressed, I've caught up and head out with Green.

He's a big, brawny guy on the outside but a softie on the inside. He slaps my shoulder. "You over your diva tantrum yet? The great and powerful spawn of Marcus Talon—"

"Shut up." I shove him.

He doesn't even stumble. It's like hitting a brick wall.

"Aww, pet." He pats my head. "Is someone a wittle sad?"

"Not sad. Just ..." Stressed, exhausted, anxious ... take your pick. "Annoyed that we're not connecting on the field like I'm used to."

We walk together across campus, and I don't know where he needs to be, but there's a Bean Necessities coffee cart up ahead with my name on it.

Before I can jump in line, Green wraps his beefy hand around my upper arm and pulls me to a stop. "Listen. You're way too hard on yourself, and I know you're going to argue with me that you have to be because of who you are and blah, blah, blah, but trust me when I say you're going to be no use to us if you burn out and decide to quit football and join the priesthood."

"Priesthood? Really?"

"I went with the most absurd thing I could think of." He punches my shoulder. "Self-care, brother. Learn it, and just do it."

He walks off, and I call after him, "I don't think that's what Nike meant when they came up with that slogan!"

The response I get is double middle fingers.

"Nice. Real nice!" I yell out.

I turn so I can join the coffee line, but I'm too busy watching Green's retreating back to see where I'm going.

And of course, that's when I smack right into someone else. Who's carrying coffee. Which we're both now wearing.

The hot liquid soaks my shirt, and I wrench my eyes closed and screw up my face, like not being able to see the disaster will make it disappear.

It does not.

"Shit, sorry. I wasn't expecting you to turn, and—"

We lock eyes, and my breath falters.

"Levi?"

He steps back and shakes off the spilled coffee that's on his hand. "Well, I guess the cat's out of the bag. I had hoped it would happen in a less dramatic way, but what are you gonna do?"

I blink. And then blink again. Turns out I wasn't imagining him at the bar. "What ... are you doing here?"

He rubs the back of his neck. His naked neck. No shaggy hair. Everything else about him still looks the same, except for his meticulously styled hair. I hate it. He looks ... like a Vanderbilt. All put together and snooty.

"So, funny story," he starts. Then pauses. "I always wanted to go to school by the beach ..."

And then it dawns on me.

He goes here.

To Franklin.

Levi fucking Vanderbilt.

CHAPTER THREE

levi

THIS IS the moment I've wanted to happen for four years and the very moment I've been trying to avoid for the last six weeks since I transferred here. To the very university Peyton Miller is reigning king of football and has been for the last three years.

His bright blue eyes are the same, and he's filled out with more muscle than in high school. He even has the ability to have permanent five-o'clock shadow now. I know this because this isn't the first time I've set eyes on him since I arrived in California.

I wanted this moment to be perfect, even though I knew it wouldn't be. I had pictured something less messy than scalding hot coffee down the front of me, though.

"You go here? Since when?" Peyton asks.

"The start of the semester. I managed to convince my father to let me go to law school in California, seeing as I want to take the bar here. Plus, I told you in high school I wanted to be a king. Now we both are. Franklin University Kings, right? Go sports!" My joke doesn't land.

"You ... moved? To California. Permanently."

I try to suppress a smile. "Yes. Lawyer. Me. Want to be."

That's not the entire truth, but I'm not going to go into all that family expectation shit the first time I'm face-to-face with Peyton since he became my sexual awakening.

Peyton stumbles back a couple of steps. "Sorry. I-I have to get to class."

"Wait ..."

He pauses.

And now I don't know what to say. *I'm sorry for the awkwardness after we hooked up four years ago? I might have decided to come to your school so I could see you again?* That doesn't sound stalkery at all.

It's not like I came here for him specifically. I just ... I wanted off that toxic corporate conveyer belt, churning out Vanderbilts and the next generation of the societal elite. And whenever I thought about running away from that life, I'd always picture that night with Peyton, our talk about colleges, and imagining how much calmer my life would be if I moved to the West Coast.

"Can I buy you a coffee first? Offer you a change of clothes at my apartment?" I trail my gaze over him. Uh, the spilled coffee, I mean. Yes. That's ... what I mean. "We should really stop ruining our clothes when we meet." Oops, was that out loud?

By the pink tinge on Peyton's cheeks, I'm going to go with yep.

I keep rambling. "You were getting in line for coffee, weren't you? And I mean, I need another one seeing as I'm wearing the first."

Peyton takes out his phone, looks down at his clothes, and

then glances toward the coffee cart. "Fuck it. I'll get Brady to take notes for me."

We get back in line, but the silence kills me. "You and Brady taking the same classes. Never would've guessed."

Peyton frowns, and I get the impression he thinks I meant that in a bad way. I didn't. A jealous way, maybe.

"Sorry. I know your brother and you are close. I just don't know what that's like, so it's weird to me that you want to be in each other's orbit all the time."

"We both grew up with the same pressures, so we're really the only ones who understand." He says this quietly, like he's ashamed of it, but what I wouldn't give for one of my siblings to understand. For a second, maybe have some empathy for me, but no. They're proud to belong in rich circles. Rich people marrying other rich people to make lots of rich little babies.

And I'm fine with that. I know I was born with a silver spoon in my mouth, and I could never claim to know what it's like without a billion doors being opened for me, but the thing with that world is if you don't meet their expectations, you're *nothing*.

We move closer in the line.

"So, what coffee will you have?" My tone is airy and light, but in a forced kind of way and not at all calm and collected like the night we hooked up.

It's hard to believe the guy with so much game back then grew up to be a bumbling idiot.

Peyton looks hesitant, like he wants to fight having me buy him a coffee, and I can't say that I blame him. If all of his socials have anything to say, it's not like he bats for my team. He's always posting photos of him and his teammates with girls, and I've tried to search for homoerotic subtext in the photos with any guy other than his brother, but even I know that's grasping at straws.

And last night, when I caught sight of Peyton at Shenanigans, kissing the bartender, it all but confirmed my suspicion.

While I lied through my teeth about our hookup only being fun but not earth-shattering, it seems Peyton didn't have the same revelation I did: I'm gay AF.

"I haven't decided yet, but I need to make this quick. My place is just off campus, and I'd like to change before my next class starts in an hour."

Disappointment that shouldn't belong here punches me in the gut. "Sure." I hope my tone can pass for nonchalant, but I doubt it.

"You're welcome to come back with me." He eyes me, and every inch his gaze touches burns like fire. "You could probably fit my clothes now you're not so scrawny."

Damn. As easy as that, the tension leaves my shoulders. "I wasn't scrawny in high school either, you dick."

"You were scrawny, but you've definitely … uh … filled out." He eyes me again but is trying to be subtler this time.

The totally wrong thing to say here is he can fill me out anytime because that wouldn't go down well. I'd go down well. On him. But no. Straight boy is straight.

If the universe loved me at all, he'd be bi, but that's wishful thinking on my part.

We get to the front of the line, and I order another latte—or in this fucked-up Franklin U system, a "study juice"—and point to Peyton. "And whatever he wants."

"I'll get the same, but with two pumps of caramel."

"Is that allowed on your team diet?" I ask while I tap my card to pay.

"Who are you, my brother?"

"Eww, fucking hope not."

Peyton tenses.

Oh. Right. No mentioning the thing that was fun but not really but totally mind-blowing and the thing that changed the direction of my life. Not mentioning it. At all.

When I don't elaborate, Peyton relaxes.

"Besides. I was at practice at 6:00 a.m. I need to survive the full day of classes somehow."

"With a side of caffeine for your sugar?"

"Yep. It's the only way I can make it drinkable."

We're given our order, and I let Peyton lead us.

We drink our coffees in silence because after all these years, there are no words.

"So, you've been on campus this long and I haven't seen you?" he asks.

Oh, look at that, my throat is dry, and I need more coffee. I sip slowly and try to think of a reasonable excuse for that.

"It's a big school."

"I saw you last night at Shenanigans, didn't I?"

I play dumb. "Oh, were you there?"

"I was. And you were right across from where I was standing." Yeah, he's not letting me get away with that.

"Okay, fine. I saw you there with your girlfriend, and I didn't want to interrupt."

Peyton laughs. "Not my girlfriend."

Hope blooms in my gut … And then he keeps speaking.

"I don't have time for relationships."

"Ah. Player on and off the field, huh?"

He scoffs. "Hardly. I'm too focused on my career to mess with anyone's emotions."

Except mine. Which he's unwittingly doing. Gah, I want to ask him straight up if he's into dudes, but then I have to remind myself that Peyton Miller is not the reason I'm in California.

He's *not.*

And I'll prove it by being honest with him. "I knew we'd run into each other eventually, and I did see you last night, but …" I bite my lip. "I kind of chickened out of talking to you."

"Oh, so you went with spilling hot coffee on me instead. I have to say, a simple hello would have worked."

"I wanted to make it memorable," I quip.

"First-degree burns are memorable, I guess."

My heart beats wildly, but I try to play off my nerves with a casual tone. "I thought you'd think I'm some stalker or that I'm here for you, which I'm not. I just … I didn't want you to think that I'm some football groupie."

"*You*? Mr. It Was Fun but I'm Not into Guys was worried I'd think you moved all this way for another awkward hookup? Contrary to popular belief, I'm not *that* conceited."

I want to correct him. I want to apologize for letting him think that he didn't mean anything. Hell, that he meant less than nothing. But I can't find the words. Just like I haven't had the courage to reach out to him. "But you are conceited?"

"Duh. Don't you know who I am? I'm football royalty, bitch."

"What was that thing about not being *too* conceited again?"

"It's a hard balance, but somehow I manage it."

"I bet you do," I murmur.

"What's that supposed to mean?"

"Nothing. You're just so … put together and nothing like

the scared guy I found clinging to the railing of my rooftop balcony. Contemplating jumping before I swooped in and saved his life."

Peyton chuckles. "Is that the story you tell everyone else? 'I saved Peyton Miller's life. You're welcome, football.'"

"Well, no, but now I will. Especially with you about to hit it big time. The draft is this year, isn't it?"

"April. But yeah. This is my last year here at Franklin."

We cross the quad toward the east entrance to the school, the opposite direction to my place. My apartment is on the beach side. The school is surrounded by different kinds of student housing and off-campus leasing, so every time I've ducked my head while walking home in case Peyton was nearby was probably pointless.

When we reach the road, Peyton turns left and then right into a long, hilly street, moving farther away from the beach.

"I would've thought your dads would rent you a condo on the beach out here."

Peyton smiles. "We had a choice of a fancy condo on the beach or a house a few blocks away. We chose the house."

"What? Why? You could've lived where the beach is *right there*." My apartment block is on the beach, and the sound of the ocean has lulled me to sleep every night. It's been amazing. Definitely better than waking up to freezing cold with snow in October and the smell of pretension in the air.

"Why do you think? Parties. Duh."

"Of course. What was I thinking?"

"I guess *Hahvid* took all the fun out of you."

You can say that again.

Peyton purses his lips. "What I still don't understand, though, is why you'd go to somewhere like Harvard for your undergrad but come to Franklin U for law school. I didn't think our law program was a top school."

"It's ... not," I admit.

"And your dad, *the* Lord Farquaad Vanderbilt—"

"The what?"

"Oh, that's what everyone used to call your dad in high school."

"They did?"

Peyton looks away. "Okay, that's what my *parents* would call him."

I laugh hard. "Holy shit. Your dads are cool."

"They'd always complain how your dad would storm into PTA meetings and be like"—He puts on an exaggerated deep voice—"'I donated a building here twelve years ago. Why don't I get a say on how much of the funding goes to the football team? We're in Illinois. Who plays football in Illinois?'"

"Wow. Great impression of my dad. It was really ... uh, uncanny."

"Needless to say, my usually laidback, Super Bowl-winning parents didn't like that. They always said your dad thought he was owed more because of your last name."

"I wish I could say things have changed, but they haven't."

"We're here." Peyton walks up the short drive to an elevated beige-and-white clapboard home.

"Are these steps really safe with all those parties you throw?" I follow him up to a terrace and then more steps to the front door.

"We really should have thought of that, but we were kind of set on the view." He nods behind me, and when I turn, there's blue in the distance. "This way, we get the beach and the parties."

"And all the girls?" I ask, and no, I'm not very subtle.

Peyton doesn't answer. Damn him. He opens the door and gestures for me to go first.

It definitely looks like two college guys live here. There are pizza boxes on the coffee table, shoes strewn around the room, red Solo cups everywhere, and it smells like dude.

Not that I'm opposed to the scent of sweat and ball sac. In the right moments, that stench can be sexy. In this moment? The only thing keeping me in this room is Peyton's insanely ripped body and his vivid blue eyes.

Plus, the memory of his face when he came.

"My room's this way. I'll get you a change of clothes."

He leads me to the room that sits over the garage, and it has that amazing view out the window. "How much did you have to fight your brother for this room?"

"Not at all. His room at the other end of the house is bigger."

"Bigger than this?" It's almost the size of my living room slash dining room. "Damn. Can I move in too?"

Peyton tenses again, just like he did when I dared to mention the night we hooked up.

Yep. He thinks I'm a stalker.

"That was a joke, by the way."

"I know." Peyton moves to a drawer, putting his backpack on the ground and his coffee on the dresser. A T-shirt is thrown my way, and then he opens another drawer and grabs me a pair of jeans.

"Thanks for these." I hold them up and drop my laptop bag.

"No problem."

We stare at each other, neither of us moving. Hell, I'm not

sure either of us is breathing.

What we did that night four years ago was so impulsive, and even though we'd known of each other for years before that, my graduation party was the first night I'd been drawn to him. Or to anyone, really.

I'd tried with girls, I really had, but I could never connect. Not like I did with Peyton.

The air between us had the same tension that's filling this very room—the same crackle of energy. I want to know if he feels it too, but I'm too chickenshit to ask.

He clears his throat. "Uh, you can use my bathroom to change. And I can hold your coffee while you do."

I hand it over. "Thanks. Again."

"No sweat."

I cross the room and close the bathroom door behind me, leaning back against it as I look up at the ceiling and silently mutter to myself to hurry up and get dressed and then get out of here.

I don't know why I thought this reunion would be anything but awkward. It's not like we're long-lost friends. It's not like our one night together wasn't awkward as fuck. I should've expected this.

I want to tell Peyton what I'm really doing here, but I can't. I need to keep up my ruse in case it somehow gets back to my dad that I'm not where I'm supposed to be. Peyton's dads and my dad are all public figures back in Chicago. They run in the same circles. The only difference between them is when the Talon-Millers throw a fundraiser for charity, it's because they actually care. When my father does it, it's because it's a tax write-off.

My shirt smells gross as I whip it off, and its fate has been sealed by the stain left behind. Death by coffee. It's not the worst way to go.

My pants go next, and then I pull on Peyton's jeans. They're a bit loose but shouldn't fall off me. When I pull the purple FU Kings football shirt over my head, I still can't believe I go to a school that has so much school pride none of the students care about wearing merch with *fukings* on it. And they're all in on the joke by pretending they miss it completely.

Either Peyton is a slow dresser, or he's purposefully trying to kill me because when I open the door, he's standing there, back to me, shirtless and only wearing low-hanging sweats.

He has those hot as fuck dimples at the base of his spine, and I want to lick them.

When I force my gaze away from his ass, I find him watching me over his shoulder. Oops. Busted.

Moving on. "I should go and let you get to class."

Peyton folds his arms and leans against his chest of drawers, narrowing his gaze at me. "Okay, what's your deal?"

"My deal?"

"I wasn't going to ask, but none of this makes sense."

"What doesn't?"

"You being here."

"You ... invited me here."

He'd have to know I'm being intentionally stupid. "Not my house, dumbass. FU."

"Fuck you too, asshole."

Peyton looks like he's trying to hold back an actual laugh.

"And on that note ..." I pick up my bag off the ground and shove my ruined clothes in there next to my laptop. "I'm gonna go."

Peyton steps into my space. All six foot one of football player. He's only an inch taller than me, but I still feel towered over. "Are you?"

"Yup."

"You know, refusing to answer why you're here makes me think it's a big deal, and then I want to know more. It'll be easier to tell me and get it over with."

I adjust my shoulder strap. "It's nothing. I got sick of all the East Coast crap, and I remember being jealous of you for coming to Franklin. When it came to choosing grad schools, I guess yours sounded like the complete opposite to the Harvard pressure."

He rubs his chin. "Real nice. Come to Franklin U. We're the opposite of Harvard because we're all dumb."

"That's not what I meant."

"Sure, it isn't. Well, now that you've insulted me, you should feel guilty enough to tell me what I want to know."

I swallow hard. "What do you want to know?"

He leans in, and he smells like coffee and fresh bodywash. My cock responds, and he's not even touching me. Peyton's standing so close that my growing cock brushes over his groin, and he looks down between us. He unleashes a smile so wide I begin to worry he's going to mock me for getting turned on.

Then all at once, he steps back, the spell is broken, but his smile remains. "Never mind. I think I got my answer."

I snap out of a lust-infused trance. "Huh?"

The sound of the front door opening echoes down the hall-way, followed by Brady's voice. "Bro, you home?"

"Okay, that really is my cue to go." I can't get out of here fast enough.

CHAPTER FOUR

peyton

IF LEVI WASN'T into guys—or at least, me—his dick wouldn't have filled out my jeans the way it did. His breath wouldn't have hitched, and his eyes wouldn't have begged me to kiss him.

It's that I loved every second of it that causes a problem. I don't have time to go through a sexual identity thing right now. Sure, that little voice in the back of my head has been telling me for the last four years that I'm bisexual, but I need to focus on football. Not my dick. And definitely not with the drama of coming out. The media is on my ass already about what draft position I'll get and whether or not I'll live up to my dad's legacy. Adding "Hey, I'm also queer, along with my bi dads and my gay brother" to the mix will be a shitshow.

Professional sports are different now, that's for sure. It's not like it was when my dads came out to the world. But at the same time, it hasn't changed *that* much. The queer community has been waiting and waiting for the day where no one has to come out, but the reality is, while there are more out players now than there ever was, they're still in the minority.

It's still a media minefield when someone else comes out.

I don't need that this year.

Brady knocks on my door and then points his thumb behind him. "Was that Levi Vanderbilt from back home?"

"Yep. He, uh, goes here now."

Brady looks like he's trying not to smile.

I sigh. "Go ahead and say it. We all know you and our dads are more obsessed with my one hookup in high school than I was." I never confided in my family about the whole liking my first and only experience with dick. I kept up the no big deal charade for so long that I almost believed it myself.

And then I saw *him* again.

He throws up his hands. "I'm not going to say anything."

"I don't believe that for a second."

"But I am going to do this." He starts dancing and singing, "Peyton's got a boyfriend."

"Real mature, Bray."

"Eww, don't Bray me, *Pey*."

I laugh. "Ah, but you forget, I don't mind my nickname … *Bray*."

"Do you think our dads wanted us to be twins? Pey and Bray? What kind of fucked-up Mother Goose, kids with rhyming names, is that shit?"

"I think they did it literally to piss you off. When you were born, they stood over you and said, 'Let's fuck this kid up by giving him a cutesy nickname.'"

"Now that you mention it, them naming us after famous football players who came before them is off brand for those two. I'm surprised they didn't actually name us Shane Miller 2.0 and Marcus Talon 5000."

"Why does Dad get the 5000?"

"Because he's the most awesome one. Duh. Just ask him." My brother points his thumb behind him again, and I freeze.

"What do you mean?"

"Oh, that's why I left class early. You know, the class you didn't go to because you were too busy being in your room with Levi Vanderbilt? They texted me to meet them outside class. They're here. In our living room. I tell ya, though, I'm so glad the lecture halls don't have windows like Montgomery Prep did. Remember when they'd turn up and press themselves against the side of our classroom, pulling faces?"

I wave my hand. "Whoa, whoa, whoa, rewind. You're saying they're here. In our living room. Where Levi just—"

"Left? Or … tried to?" He cups his ear. "I think I can hear them talking."

"Motherfucker." I charge past him.

His words fade as I practically run, but I still hear him say, "Today is so much fun."

To my horror, when I rush into the living room, Levi's standing there, his gaze ping-ponging around the room while my dads ask him relentless question after question without letting Levi get a word in.

"Levi, aren't you late for your next class?" I approach them where they're standing near the entryway and push Levi toward the door.

"Come on," Dad says, "everyone can cut class every now and then." Then his blue eyes that match mine stare me down. "Right, Pey? I was just telling Levi here that he looks good in your clothes."

I'd argue how they know they're mine, but considering Levi's wearing a FU football shirt, I can't really pull that off. "We had an accident."

"Accidental no clothes ... situation?" Pop asks.

I close my eyes and chant to myself. *They're my parents. They gave me life. They're embarrassing as fuck, but I love them.*

"A coffee accident," I clarify. "Apparently, I think coffee looks better on clothes than it tastes."

"It was my fault," Levi says. "I wasn't watching where I was going."

And even though we're telling the complete truth, my dads both look like they don't believe us. Their gazes flit between us, as if trying to read something deeper.

Dad turns to Levi. "We didn't even know you transferred to FU. Your dad never mentioned it."

"Oh. Umm. Yeah." Levi rubs the back of his neck. "Uh, law school. Going to take the bar in California."

"And you chose FU law." Dad's sentence sounds like a question, but I don't think it is. More like an accusation. Like *"Why FU when its law program is definitely not Vanderbilt-worthy?"* Or *"And your father let you do that?"*

"I should go." Levi turns to me. "Thanks for the clothes. I'll return them to you ... uh, another time." It's as if I can read his mind: *when your dads aren't visiting.*

Levi beelines it to the door, and my dads wave and give very enthusiastic "Nice seeing you" and "I'm sure we'll see you around."

Once the door is shut behind Levi, I let out a breath. "You had to be embarrassing, didn't you?"

Brady points at them. "Have you met our dads?"

We move into the living room, and Brady and I sit on the couch while our dads share a single armchair, Dad sitting in

Pop's lap. Because, you know, PDA and parental affection add to the torture of them being here.

But no one says anything. They all just keep staring at me.

I throw up my hands. "What? None of you have been friends with someone you had an awkward hookup with four years ago?"

"No," they all say in unison.

"Well, I must be a more mature human than all of you."

And now they're laughing.

Fucking hell.

"What are you guys doing here anyway?" I ask, hoping to change the subject.

"We can't come see our sons because we love them?" Dad asks.

"You can, but there's usually a reason you pop in unannounced other than you like to catch us in embarrassing situations so you can mock us about it. You know, you're lucky I'm going to play in the NFL and earn the big bucks. I'm going to need it to pay for therapy."

Brady snorts.

"We came to see your game," Dad says.

"It's on Saturday. It's only Monday."

"And to check up on you," Pop says.

"And ..." I roll my hand in a gesture for them to get to the point.

"And we came to celebrate Canadian Thanksgiving with you." Dad smiles.

"We're not Canadian. Plus, that was last week."

Dad and Pop share a glance that's full of guilt, and then Pop says, "Well, we're not going to be in the US for the American one, so ..."

"Ah," Brady says. "They've come because they feel horrible about abandoning us on Thanksgiving."

"We can cancel our trip," Pop says.

Dad's gaze flicks to Pop's, and Jesus H. Christ, do I look like that when I'm pouting? I hope not.

"Go and enjoy Thanksgiving," I say.

Dad is, of course, the first to take us up on that. "If you're sure." He nudges Pop. "They're sure."

"We can throw our own Thanksgiving here. Invite all the losers whose parents also hate them."

Dad doesn't fall for the guilt trip, but Pop looks genuinely sorry.

"Seriously. It's okay. Brady's just being a brat. Something new and different for him."

Brady shoves me, so I shove him back. Then we're suddenly in an all-out wrestle, and the only thing I can hear is Pop muttering something about it being a miracle we haven't killed each other in the last four years while they left us unsupervised.

I'd argue that they've left us plenty of times before that without supervision, but I'm too busy trying to get out of Brady's headlock.

I hate that my little brother is stronger than me, but he gets that from Pop. He slams me into the carpet, and my back hits the floor with a thud.

"Watch his throwing arm," Dad yells at Brady, but that doesn't stop him.

"Okay, okay. I tap out," I say.

When my brother climbs off me and we stand, Brady looks smug, and I'm tempted to push him back down, but that will only result in him taking me down with him.

"If you two are done, are either of you planning to go to class today?" Dad asks.

"You came and got me from class!" Brady yells.

"Hmm, true. We really are bad influences."

"You are," Pop says. "I said we could wait for them here. You're the one who insisted."

"Not that it mattered. Pey wasn't even in class, and who knows what we would've walked in to find had we come straight here."

"We spilled coffee," I exclaim.

"Mmhmm. Your pop and I 'spill coffee' all the time."

I screw up my face. "You know what? I am going to class. I might even ask if there's night classes I can take up for the next ... how long are you guys staying?"

"We fly out Sunday morning," Pop says.

"Okay, I'm making plans for the next six nights."

"You know where you could stay?" Dad is so setting a trap.

"Ha, ha, I could stay at Levi's because we share clothes and were naked and had one hookup. You guys are soooo funny."

Dad shakes his head. "I was going to say you could sleep at the stadium seeing as you have a 5:00 a.m. practice tomorrow, but hey, if you want to take it another direction—"

I give up. I try to leave, but I have to say, storming out of the house has a lot more impact if you don't have to turn right back around. I only get two feet out the door when I realize I don't have my laptop. And when I make my way back through the house, my entire family snickers. "I need my backpack," I mumble.

With our dads staying for the week and no way to contact Levi without creeping him on social media, I've resorted to walking the long way home past the law department each day.

No dice.

Not that I would know what to say if I did run into him. You'd think I could come up with an excuse as to why I was across campus, nowhere near any of my classes or the football facilities, but the plan was to wing it. I'd accidentally run into him once before, but it was proving to be more difficult than expected. Apparently, coincidences have to happen by coincidence and not be forced. Who knew?

When Friday comes and I haven't seen Levi on campus, I begin to wonder if I ran into him at all. If my family hadn't seen him, I'd worry I was hallucinating.

We have a light practice for the home game tomorrow, which consists of running drills on the field and no scrimmages.

Coach Nass has me throwing to each of my receivers, and every time we complete a pass, the last week of torturous practices fades away, and my confidence for tomorrow night's game builds.

We've got this.

But then, as I'm about to throw another pass, a loud "Woot" and cheering comes from the stands. My throw is off center, and even though some of the best guys in college football are on my team, not even Jerry Rice would be able to complete this pass.

I turn and glare at my dads, who are grinning from ear to ear.

I'm starting to think what I said to Brady might be right. Our dads had us just so they could fuck with us.

That's not even the worst part. Nope. As they move toward me, I realize someone's behind them. Levi.

Sure, I try to find him all week and fail. My dads come to a practice and bring him with them?

I turn to Coach, who releases me so I can go over to them —something no other parents could get away with at this school, but no one else is *the* Marcus Talon and *the* Shane Miller.

I take my helmet off and run over to the barrier where they're standing. "Blink twice if they kidnapped you," I say to Levi.

His gray eyes look almost blue in the fading light, and they shine in amusement.

"What are you guys doing here?"

"Why do our children keep asking us that?" Dad asks. "We came to see our boys to make sure they're doing well, and all we get is *Why are you here? Why are you going through my things? Stop butting into my life!* I'm beginning to suspect our kids are hiding something from us."

"Yes, and it would have nothing to do with you two getting a high from embarrassing us. Exhibit A." I gesture to Levi.

"Oh, Levi here?" Dad wraps his arm around Levi's shoulders. "We saw him on our way over here. Asked if he wanted to join us."

Levi looks at the ground. "Asked, steered me in this direction. Same thing, right?"

Typical.

"You Chicardigans—" Dad says, but Pop corrects him.

"Chicagoans."

"Agree to disagree. But you should stick together."

"Yes. Because SoCal is known for being uptight and rougher than Englewood. Not to mention the weather is so much harsher too. It got below seventy today. I thought we were going to die."

"Are you done with practice yet?" Dad asks. "We're all going to get dinner."

My gaze narrows. "Who is *all*?"

"You, me, your pop, Levi." Dad's tone is so casual, it's easy to miss the manipulative glee behind it.

I seriously can't wait for Sunday when their flight leaves. "I can't leave practice. Maybe another time. Sorry."

With perfect timing, Coach Nass yells, "That's it for today. Make sure you stretch and cool down properly. We don't want anything to be tight on the field tomorrow."

"The only thing tight on the field when we played—"

I cut Dad off. "Do not say something about Pop's ass. That kind of shit is not what your son wants to hear."

"How did Peyton grow up to be such a prude?" Dad asks Pop.

"It must be the mostly straight thing," Pop says.

I rub my temples and look at Levi. "Seriously, all you have to do is blink twice, and I'll have them arrested. *Please*."

Levi laughs again. Like he thinks I'm joking.

"If I agree to dinner, will you promise to be civilized human beings and quit it with the embarrassment? Just for one night."

Dad and Pop glance at each other, as if having a silent conversation, and then Dad nods at me. "Deal."

"I'll meet you out front of the stadium in ten."

I turn on my heel and head for the locker rooms, nerves swarming in my gut.

This is what I wanted all week—to see Levi. Now's my chance to take it, but with it happening in front of my dads, my nerves are tenfold.

Because they could say anything, and there's no way to stop them.

I shouldn't have told them about the hookup in high school or, at least, not told them who because that borders on outing someone, but at the same time, they're my parents, they're queer, and I knew they would never, ever say anything to anyone else.

Growing up in the open household that I did, I knew if I hadn't told them, then Brady would have. Or he would've at least heavily hinted and teased me about it, so I cut him off at the knees.

But the story has always been that it was no big deal, it was okay but awkward, and I had no desire to go there with another guy.

I thought they'd believed me, but with the way they're acting, I'm guessing they didn't.

I'm dreading this dinner. I don't know if Levi is out, how he identifies, or even if he's queer at all.

I was all cocky about his dick growing hard in my proximity, but that could mean nothing. Just like our hookup that made him come all over me meant nothing to him back then.

I don't want my dads to pressure him into a corner about his orientation. Not that I think they would—on purpose—but I sometimes think they can't remember what it was like to be closeted. They've always been so open. Sometimes too open. It's like they forget not everyone is like that.

If he is queer, I would put money on Levi not being out to his family. Especially his dad.

When I hit the locker room, I get wide-eyed stares from some of the freshmen, but the other guys don't pay me attention anymore. This happens when five-time Super Bowl winner Marcus Talon shows his face. Everyone realizes I'm not only his kid in theory, but he's real, and he's here. They all no doubt want an autograph.

And this is where people's true colors show. As if on cue, Addison Knight, a freshman offensive tackle who has been nothing but nice to me this whole time, commits the ultimate sin. "Do we get to meet them in person?"

My heart gives its usual squeeze when that doubt clouds my brain. Every interaction Knight and I have had runs through my mind—from him telling me he chose Franklin so he could joke that he's both a Knight and a king. Was that true? Or was it that he knew his quarterback would be a direct contact to the NFL world? When he came to a party at our house and asked if my parents were around, was it because he wanted to know how hard he could party or because he was only there to try to meet them?

This is what happens every time, and the entire team learned quickly that if they treat me like some kind of celebrity or kiss my ass because they want a meet and greet with my dads, it's the quickest way to get on my bad side. Maybe I need a designated representative to give a seminar at the beginning of every year. *Rule number one of FU football: Don't talk about the quarterback's famous dads. That's it. That's the only rule.*

Green tells Knight to "Be cool."

And I've found my representative. I love that guy.

So, as I try to shower and get dressed before everybody else so we can get away quickly without my dads being mobbed by my new teammates, I put on a brave face and ignore the mix of dread and excitement simmering under my veins over going to dinner with Levi. And my dads.

Together.

When I reach outside, they don't look like they're torturing Levi too bad. They're all smiling and chatting, but then Levi's eyes meet mine, and his wide smile falls to a cheeky little smirk.

I approach them and close my eyes. "They're talking about all the embarrassing stuff I did as a child, aren't they?"

"Apparently, your uncles call you and Brady 'Destruction One and Two'?"

"Oh, for fuck's sake," I mutter.

Tonight is going to be torture.

Kill me now.

CHAPTER FIVE

levi

PEYTON'S TEAMMATES file out of the stadium behind him, so Peyton lowers his voice.

"You guys promised to be normal human beings." Peyton sounds so defeated, and I have to say, it's all kinds of adorable.

Talon and Miller, as they've insisted I call them, are hilarious, but I can tell they're making Peyton uncomfortable.

I try to give him a reassuring smile, but then his dads make me laugh again.

Miller throws his arm around Peyton's shoulders and says, "I don't remember promising anything? You'll have to remind me. You know your dad and I are getting senile in our old, old, old age."

"Speak for yourself," Talon says. "I remember everything. Including promising to embarrass the fuck out of Peyton in front of his high school *friend*."

Peyton visibly cringes at the emphasis his dad puts on *friend*, and if I didn't know for sure before, I do now. What happened between Peyton and me at my graduation party is common knowledge in this family.

High school me would be freaking out about them telling my dad, but this me, I have nothing to hide from my family anymore. Well, that's not entirely true. I don't have anything to hide from them in regards to my sexuality.

Peyton telling his parents what happened kind of gives me hope that it meant something to him too, but everything else points to Peyton only being into girls. Though, Miller's comment about Pey being mostly straight keeps my hope alive.

Some of Peyton's teammates start filing out of the stadium, and Peyton pushes his dads toward the west entrance to the school. "Let's go get that dinner and get this over with."

Talon turns to me. "Our son loves us. I promise."

"Not right now, I don't."

We walk the couple of blocks away from college central to a restaurant I haven't been to yet since moving here. It looks fancy and expensive, and it's right on the beach, but as we get to the host to be seated, Talon slaps his forehead.

"Shit. We forgot we told Brady we'd have dinner with him tonight, didn't we?"

Miller also pulls the most ridiculous, over-the-top look, as if he's just remembering something. "We did. See, Pey? We are old and senile."

Talon steps up to the host and whips out his credit card. "Hi, I made a reservation for four this morning under Talon, but it's going to have to be changed to two. Let these kids get whatever they want and put it on this."

The host either recognizes Peyton's dads or is getting excited over the no-limit credit card because he immediately leads Peyton and me to a table by the window.

Talon and Miller give Peyton thumbs-up as they walk by outside, only cementing it even more that they know about us.

And now they're setting us up on a date. It's not the way I would have gone about it, but I can't say I'm upset by it. Peyton obviously doesn't agree with me.

He drops his head to the tablecloth. "I'm so sorry about them."

"I … I actually think they're kind of great."

His head snaps up. "You what?"

I shrug. "If I had to choose between those kinds of parents who obviously love you and mine who are cold, distant, and have expectations, I'd choose yours every time."

"Oh, you think they don't have expectations for me? If I don't become the next Tom Brady or Marcus Talon, they'll—"

"They'll still love you. They still love Brady, and he's not even playing football anymore."

Peyton frowns.

"They mentioned that fact in passing. Though, I already figured, seeing as he's not playing for FU."

"They made a joke about him being a traitor to the greatest sport in history, didn't they?"

"How did you know?"

"They really need to get new material." Peyton licks his lips. "And about all their comments, you know …" He can't find the words, but I know what he's going to say.

"I'm guessing they know what happened between us in high school."

"They do, but I promise they won't say anything to your family or—"

"My family knows I'm gay."

Peyton's eyebrows shoot up. "Y-you are? And … they do?"

And here it comes. The other conversation I knew I was going to have when coming face-to-face with Peyton again. I take a deep breath. "I knew by coming to this school, there was a good chance I was going to run into you and we'd have to have this conversation, but I've tried to think of the right words to say and still don't have them right."

"The ones saying 'Hey, Peyton. I know we hooked up a billion years ago and I said it was nothing, but I lied. You are the best, most awkward sex I've ever had, and I want to tie you up in my basement so I can have my way with you whenever I want.'"

The sound that comes out of me is half a whoosh of relief and half a small laugh. "Yes. All of those things, obviously."

"It's cool. I had more fun than I let on too. I told my dads and Brady that it wasn't a big deal, but it kinda was."

My heart is in my throat as I try to build up the courage to choke out, "So you're—"

Our waiter comes over to our table to pour us water and ask if we want to start with drinks.

I want to yell, *Not now!* But Peyton doesn't hesitate to order.

"A bottle of your most expensive champagne. Please." He turns to me. "And you'll have?"

I can't work out if he's being serious or not, and sure, it's just a bottle of champagne, but the way he ordered it reminds me of everyone back in my old circles. The ones who'd order the most expensive thing on the menu simply because they could. The ones who'd crash their Mercedes and then beg their families for a Beemer instead. I left the East Coast and that life for a reason.

My face must tell him so because he leans across the table and whispers, "I have a game tomorrow, so I can't actually drink it, but my dads are paying, remember? This is payback."

Okay, now that I can get on board with. Parental torture is my forte. "In that case, I'll have the same."

Peyton leans back in his seat. "Food-wise, we'll have one of everything on the menu."

The waiter glances between us. "This isn't another college prank, is it? You're not going to order all this stuff and then ditch?"

They must get that a lot here.

"Not at all. My father left his credit card at the front desk if you want to check."

"Not a problem, sir. The menu is quite extensive. Would you like the—"

"Just bring out everything as it's made. Don't worry about what order it's in."

"Very well. Enjoy your meals."

"Will your dads be mad?" I ask when the server leaves.

"Nah. All I'll have to do is go home and say, 'I'm totally bisexual now!' All will be forgiven."

My throat is dry, and I reach for my water to take a sip. On the way to putting the glass to my mouth, I quickly ask, "Are you?"

"Bisexual?" Peyton asks.

I nod as I swallow the cold water, but my mouth is still too dry.

"In theory."

"In ... theory ..."

Peyton smiles, and I notice it's the one thing he has that he doesn't get from his dad. When Talon smiles, it's playful and goofy. When Peyton smiles, it's with a confident eye glimmer that convinces me he knows all the answers and has his shit together.

Peyton goes to say something when our waiter comes back over with drinks. Does this guy have a coming out radar? *Ope, someone's about to admit they like dick! Better put a stop to it.*

He takes forever to pop the cork and pour us a glass each, and I'm this close to telling him to go away. I need Peyton to elaborate.

He doesn't.

Instead, he takes a sip of his champagne and screws up his face. "I was going to allow myself one glass of this, but honestly, it tastes gross."

"So uncultured," I joke. I sip mine and almost hate that I love the taste. Expensive wine. Expensive food. The tastes of growing up wealthy, while delicious, always makes the sense of entitlement churn in my gut.

"Very uncultured," he agrees, and I know that shouldn't shoot jealousy through me, but it does.

The Talon-Millers do wealthy the right way. I don't even know if that makes sense, but after spending very little time with them, I already know they're down-to-earth. They have personalities bigger than Mars, but it has nothing to do with the millions they're worth.

Their image isn't their money.

They're everything my family hates and everything I want to have.

"But anyway, you were saying?" Let's get back to the important part.

"What was I saying?"

Gah. He's killing me here.

"Something about you being bi. In theory." I take another sip.

"Ah yes. Well, you know, there's only ever been this one guy. One hookup."

The Dom Pérignon gets caught in my throat, and as I cough, it comes out of my nose.

Peyton laughs while passing me a cloth napkin. "So uncultured."

I wipe my face. "Sorry. I wasn't expecting that. After our hookup, I told myself it was nothing, went to college and tried to date girls, but it took until the end of freshman year for me to admit I was gay."

Peyton turns the stem of the flute in his hand, twirling the champagne he's clearly not going to drink. "I told myself it was nothing too. Like you said that night, it was a bit of fun but not for you."

"I'm pretty sure I didn't say that. *You* said that, and I didn't disagree with you. I was too busy freaking out about finding that missing piece of myself that I still wasn't ready to admit that I'd found."

He huffs and leans forward. "And here I was thinking I was so bad at gay sex that I never wanted to try again for fear of embarrassment."

"I scared you off that much, huh?"

"Being dismissed after having sex with someone kinda does that to a guy."

Hello, guilt. "Fuck. I'm sorry—"

Peyton holds up his hand. "It's all good. Though it's nice to know it was because you were freaking out, not because of anything I did or didn't do. And I'm sure if I met a guy who gave me butterflies the way you did that night, I would've gotten over my inexperience and gone for it. But it never happened again. Not yet anyway."

"Ah. That's why you're bi *in theory*."

His blue eyes meet mine. "It's not really in theory, though. I know I am. It's just … sometimes downplaying it makes it easier to say out loud. I haven't told anyone, though I think my dads knew I was lying when I said our hookup didn't mean anything."

"Yeah, with the way they set us up, it's obvious they think we both want it to happen again." I'm on board with that, but I don't think Peyton is.

Something happens to his face. It's not a wince, but it's close.

"Oh, that wasn't an invitation. I'm just pointing out that's what they think. I guess now if you're over your performance anxiety of being with a guy, you'll want to spread yourself around the entire queer population at FU."

Peyton shakes his head. "I'm not that type of guy. I rarely hook up."

"That's not what I heard."

He pulls back. "What did you hear?"

"That you don't do serious. Casual only." And that was as heartbreaking as thinking he was straight.

"Ah. Well, yeah, that is true. I have to focus on football. Relationships and marriage can come after I've won my first Super Bowl."

That part of me that has been in denial about moving here because of the feeling Peyton gave me four years ago can finally admit that it wasn't only freedom I was chasing.

It was Peyton himself.

Because hearing that he's straight would be one thing. Hearing that he's bi but still unavailable? It might be the most heartbreaking thing yet.

Nothing is ever going to happen between us because I've already done the casual thing. I've done the exploring, the secret meet-ups, the whole closeted dance. That's all I could ever be to Pey because he hasn't finished with that yet. He hasn't even started.

Coming to FU wasn't a mistake—this is the life path I want to take—but I can no longer deny that Peyton was a factor in it.

He was a big one, and denying it for so long in hopes I'd believe it has done nothing to dim the disappointment as I come to terms that something with Peyton is not on the table.

Multiple servers arrive with an array of dishes, but I've suddenly lost my appetite.

CHAPTER SIX

THE FOOD ARRIVES, and I dig in, trying to tell myself to only taste everything. Puking in the middle of my game tomorrow for all of ESPN to see is not my idea of a good time. But when I look over at Levi, he's not eating at all.

"Can't choose where to start?" I say around a mouthful of fried scampi.

"Something like that." He reaches for the brown paste that has no right to be called food with how it looks.

I watch as he spreads it on a cracker and lifts it to his mouth. "Is that as gross as it looks?" I ask.

He holds it out for me. "You should try it."

"I'll pass. I like my food not to look like it's already been digested."

He laughs. "Just as well. It's pâté."

"What is pâté?"

Levi grins. "Liver."

"Why would anyone want to eat that?"

"Because it's delicious."

"I guess you think caviar is delicious too." I shudder.

"That's actually one thing I do find gross."

"Oh, good. One thing we have in common, then."

Levi takes another bite of *liver*, and I have to say, I was contemplating kissing him tonight to see if it still has the same effect on me as it did four years ago, but now … no, thank you. All I'll be able to think about is liver breath.

He swallows his bite. "You'd think for two people brought up in the same city, in the same school, we'd have more in common than hating caviar."

I sip some water because the champagne really is gross. "True. There's the pressure we've both faced from our influential families. Sure, it's been two very different types of influence, but the pressure's there all the same. Until that night … until you told me about the expectations that were put on you, I thought Brady was the only one who understood what it was like to be me."

"Hooray for childhood trauma."

I laugh but then wince. "Do you ever feel guilty when you complain about your childhood? Yeah, my parents are annoying, but I grew up with everything, so I *shouldn't* complain."

Levi looks down at his plate. "I do in some ways and don't at the same time. It's hard to put in words, but sometimes on my way home from school, you know, driven by our family chauffeur, whenever we'd drive by the public school, I wished I was a normal kid and not a Vanderbilt."

"Ouch. Okay, I can say with absolutely no uncertainty that I've never wanted to trade my family—"

"Just have them arrested for kidnapping?"

"Exactly. So, yeah, you win that one." I cock my head. "Or is it technically losing?"

Levi leans back in his chair and drinks his expensive champagne. "It is what it is."

Learning that he hates his money and his name doesn't change my perception of him. He still has that air of confidence that you get from growing up with the privilege we both had.

"How did you convince your dad to come to California for law school? Isn't all your family businesses and money in Chicago or New York?"

"After the gay thing, he loosened the leash a bit. Not a lot, but some. I can create my own future. So long as it's law. Across the other side of the country works well because all those rumors about one of the Vanderbilts being gay are bound by California law to stay in California. True story. Learned it in today's law class."

My heart twinges for him. "Oh, so when you said they knew—"

"Doesn't mean they like it. I mean, they didn't cut me off or kick me out or stop paying my tuition or anything, but suddenly, my father was willing to let me go to grad school here. Couldn't drop out of Harvard, of course. Had to keep my 'extracurricular activities' to myself and not embarrass him, and now if it does ever get back to his circle of elite-class friends, they'll all say, 'Oh, the move to California makes sense now.' But ... could've been worse."

Our waiters bring out some more dishes, and our small table is suddenly full.

I turn to one of them. "Is it possible to get everything else in a couple of to-go boxes?"

"We thought that might happen, sir. It's not a problem."

"Thank you."

"Is that going to be your food for the week?" Levi asks.

"Nah. I know exactly where to take it."

When we're done stuffing our faces with as much food as I can get away with without repercussions tomorrow and Levi looks like he's going to throw up, there are so many leftovers, we each have four boxes of food to carry back to campus. Levi didn't hesitate to help me deliver them to some very starving college students.

"Where exactly are we talking these?"

"Liberty Court."

"What's that?"

"On-campus share houses. We'll take this to the Stormer house. They're, uh, known to get the munchies a lot, if you know what I'm saying."

Levi tries not to smile. "Yeah. I might be familiar with that."

My stomach flips the way it did back in high school and fills with warmth, the memory of him sucking on a joint and then sharing the smoke with me flooding my memory.

I almost trip over my feet.

Levi manages to balance his four boxes in one hand while saving me from going ass over tit with the other. "Aren't you a football player? Shouldn't you have a bit more balance?"

"You'd think."

"You all good?" Levi's hand is warm on my skin, and I'm tempted to say no so he'll keep touching me.

"Yup," I croak.

"So, Stormer house, you say? Noted."

"There are also dispensaries on every other corner in San Diego."

"Also noted." He side-eyes me. "Though, I have to say I don't really turn to weed as much as I used to."

"Aww, too good for it, Mr. *Hahvid*?"

"Pfft. It was everywhere on campus, but it no longer carried out its purpose."

"Getting high?"

"Getting my father's attention. In fact, working out I was gay made me never want to draw his attention to me again."

I have no idea what to say to that. When I hooked up with Levi that night, being scared of the outcome—questioning my sexuality, coming out if I had to—never even crossed my mind.

Sure, the career thing made me pause, but if my dads could do it a billion years ago, I could do it too. I never worried about what my family would say or do if they found out. Other than mercilessly embarrass me about it by throwing some ridiculous over-the-top penis party or some shit.

Which, thankfully, they didn't do, but only because I lied and said the hookup meant nothing and I was still straight.

When Brady came out, however, our dads took him to a strip club. I wasn't there, but he said it was one of the most mortifying experiences of his life. I didn't need to know any more than that.

"You don't need to feel sorry for me," Levi says.

"I don't. Well, I kinda do, but only because I can't imagine what that was like for you. My dads paved the way for so many queer kids, especially ones in sports, that parents not accepting their gay child still confuses me. I know it happens, logically, but it's still a shock every time I hear about it."

"I think I'm making it sound worse than it really is. If anything, I'm thankful for the distance it brought between me and the Vanderbilt pressure. My brother and sister have always thrived on it, so they can have it."

"Yet, you're still here, at law school, because your dad told you what to study."

Levi's mouth opens. Then closes. "Uh, about that ..." His gaze drifts to the street we're approaching, where cars line the road and music pumps from the Mundell house. There are a couple of people hanging out on the footpath, red Solo cups in hand. This is a typical Friday night on Liberty.

Levi looks in awe.

"Ain't nothing like a Liberty party. Other than one at the football house. Of course."

"Football house?"

"Mine and Brady's place. Duh."

"Duh," he mimics. "How dare I not know that?"

"You've been at this school for how many weeks now and you haven't heard of our epic parties?"

"Hey, I spent my first three weeks here trying not to run into you. I wasn't going to ask questions about you and give away that I moved here for you."

I stop dead in my tracks. "You what?"

He swears under his breath. "I don't mean for you. I mean ..." Levi blows out a loud breath. "Like I said the other day, that night, the way you talked about California, it sounded like everything I wanted and exactly what I wasn't allowed. I came here because of what you represented, not ... because of you specifically."

He looks like he's about to shit a brick, and I can't help smiling.

His eyes are wide, and his babble is adorable. "I didn't

move here for you. Like, to be with you. I want us to be friends."

That's when my face drops and my gut hollows out, but I try not to let it show. "Just friends?"

He nods.

Damn.

There's a beat of silence where I'm tempted to say how disappointing that is, but I decide to let it go. It's not like I can offer him much more anyway.

"We should get these to the house." I adjust the heavy takeout boxes in my arms a bit higher and lead the way.

We reach the steps of Stormer house and knock, but the noise from the other houses is either too loud or everyone inside is too high to realize the sound isn't coming from their imaginations.

I knock again, louder this time and continuously until I hear movement inside—someone running down the stairs. Or falling. One or the other.

The door flies open, and a guy with long, blond hair stands there with a confused furrow in his brow but a casual smile on his lips. I recognize him as a friend of a friend of a friend type thing, and I think his name is Chris.

"Delivery."

That just makes him more confused.

"We had all these leftovers, and I figured you and your roommates wouldn't let them go to waste. You know, in case any of you got … hungry. I'd normally take it to the guys on the team or the DIKs, but you're closer than the frat house, and we have a huge game tomorrow. Coach would kill me."

His smile widens. "Sweet. Come in." We follow him into

the dim living room, where there are guys playing video games and there's a dude in the corner nursing a bong.

The place smells like stale weed, but where I screw up my nose at it, Levi breathes it in.

"Mm, nostalgia," he hums, and I laugh.

"Free food," Chris calls out as we put the boxes on the coffee table.

That gets everyone's attention, and they come flooding from all directions.

"You should've yelled that at the front door instead of knocking," Levi says.

"Probably." I turn to the guys. "We'll leave you to it."

They all mumble thank-yous around bites of food, and we give them a wave as we take off.

When we close the door behind us, Levi asks, "Where to now? Got any more good deeds you need doing?"

"The only good deed I have left is going home to bed so I can actually focus on the ball tomorrow."

"Fair enough."

I have to be reading into it, but I swear there's disappointment in his tone. "I can walk you home first, though."

"You don't have to."

"I know I don't have to. But I want to. That's what friends are for." The word *friend* tastes bitter on my tongue.

"Right."

The entire walk to Levi's, I make sure to keep my hands in my jeans pockets at all times. Otherwise, I run the risk of pushing him against the nearest surface, kissing the fuck out of him, and then asking again if he only wants to be *friends*. If I did that, I'd be playing with fire because I know deep down I shouldn't pursue anything with Levi. Or anyone.

I have one focus. Football, football, and more football.

"This is me," he says and pauses on the stoop of his apartment building. His lips part to say something else, and I swear he's going to ask me if I want to come up, but my phone interrupts us.

"Sorry. Just gotta ..." I step back and see Dad's name on my screen. "Uh-oh. I'm in trouble. This should be fun." I hit Answer and don't even get out a hello before I'm being yelled at.

"You spent over two thousand dollars on dinner?"

"Good luck with that. Good night." Levi turns and disappears inside, and Dad's anger is suddenly gone.

"Oh, wait, was that him? Are you still with Levi?"

"Not anymore. I'm on my way home. You can yell at me in ten minutes. Unless I get abducted on the walk home. Which is possible. I swear I saw a UFO go by before. Maybe I can flag them down."

"I promise I won't yell. Again. No need to call upon the aliens to save you. See you soon."

We end the call, but I still don't really want to go back to the house. Not because of getting in trouble—I was expecting that—but because they're going to want details, and I'm not ready to share. Mainly because Levi is confusing as fuck.

He says he moved here for me and then says he wants to be friends. Usually, I'm the one throwing around the word *friends*. It's a reminder to me and whoever I'm with that things are only casual, but the way Levi said it, it came out with more ... permanence than that. His message was clear. We're going to be friends, only friends, and I will never see his dick.

I didn't expect to be hit with disappointment. The only other time I've experienced that gross emotion is after losing a game. Disappointment when it comes to people? Both Brady and I have desensitized ourselves to those who only want to use us to get to our dads. It might have happened at one point, but this is the first time in years that someone has gotten under my skin this way. But I don't think the disappointment is directed at Levi. It's directed at … me.

Yet, I don't understand why.

I don't understand *him*.

Shit, at this point, I don't even understand myself.

When I get back to the house, I pause outside the steps leading up to the front door landing and take a deep breath. My parents can read me like a book, my brother even more so, and I don't want to give away anything from tonight.

They'll want to help. They'll want to meddle.

No, thank you.

I breeze through the door with a casual "Hey," and then I hold my breath.

"Have a good night?" Dad asks. He's sitting on the single armchair in our living room while Pop and Brady are on the couch. My brother is trying not to laugh, and that sight alone has me fighting the urge too.

"It was fun."

"Fun like we need to call your uncle and figure out a coming out strategy for your career?"

I throw my head back. "No. And you know I can't be seen talking to an agent. Especially this year. I need to wait until the season is over."

"He's your uncle. Not just an agent."

"He's technically not my uncle."

"Semantics," Dad says. "He changed your diapers and babysat you. He's as much your uncle as my brother is."

One thing I can be certain of with Dad is if we ever mention biology when it comes to family, he will block that line of talk faster than a raging linebacker.

"I get that," I relent. "But … I don't want to risk it. Especially when we all know I'm going to sign with him." We're getting off topic. "Besides. Levi and I are friends. There's no need for any coming out crap. I know you were probably all hoping for the big bi revelation here, but I'm not … he's not … we're not there yet."

And now I've already told them more than I said I was going to.

Dad stands. "Fair enough. Either way, you owe us two thousand dollars. Good night."

My eyes widen as I swing around to glance at Pop.

He stands too. "You know your dad. He'll forget about it in a few days."

"No, I won't!"

Pop follows after Dad. "Think of it as payback for putting poor Pey through that god-awful setup I was against from the beginning."

At least one of my parents understands me.

As soon as they're out of sight, Brady lets go of his laugh. I slump down next to him on the couch and let out a loud breath.

"Holy shit," Brady says while trying to catch his breath. "I thought Dad was going to have a coronary when he got the alert on his phone from his credit card company."

"He did always say we would be the death of him. I wouldn't have put it past him to do it purely for the epic guilt trip it would cause. But it totally serves him right. Seriously, they crossed all kinds of lines. I'm surprised Levi didn't run screaming for the hills."

Although, technically, he kinda did.

"So, what is the deal with you and Levi? I thought the emphatic *it meant nothing* was bullshit. Dads obviously thought so too."

That's what I'd like to know. "Levi's confusing."

"Confusing how? By making you question your sexuality or—"

I wave him off. "Nope. This little baby bi can't read gay signals."

"Aww, my big brother is all grown up and embracing his identity." He wipes away a fake tear. "So proud."

I shove him, but he holds strong. Of course he does, the wide fucker. "Don't you start. You're worse than Dads, but I'm trusting you to be gentle, seeing as you know how gay dudes think."

"Oh, you're so right. That's why I'm swimming in boyfriends and successful relationships. Oh, wait …"

"Whatever. You could have a relationship at the drop of a hat. Everyone you've ever dated has fallen head over heels for you. You're the one who always says you want something *more*, but you can't tell them what *more* is because you don't even know yourself. Then you break their little hearts."

"Right. And you think I can help you how? I don't even know what I want, let alone any other gay guys out there."

"What does it mean when a guy says he wants to be friends?"

Brady rubs his square jaw in thought. "Now, I can't be sure here, but my wild guess would be … that he wants to be friends."

"But …" Ugh. I lean forward and run my hands through my hair. "There was more to it than that. We were having fun, teasing each other, and then he said something about transferring to FU for me, but in the next breath said he just wants to be friends."

"Hmm. He really said that?"

"That he wants to be friends? Yes."

"No. That he moved here for you."

"Yep. Then he kind of freaked out and rambled something about freedom and wanting to be friends."

"Yeaaah, I've got nothing."

I sigh. "Thanks for all your help, brother."

"I'm not the gay messiah, and I'm only twenty. I don't know everything."

"Wait, you guys have got a messiah? What do bisexual people get?"

"Free bi-fi. It's like Wi-Fi but better."

"Score. And on that note, I'm going to go to bed and forget tonight ever happened."

"Good and healthy plan. Plus, you have a game you have to win tomorrow."

Right. Football.

The thing I should be focusing on. The only thing.

"You're right. Eye on the prize and all that crap. It's not only my future on the line but yours too. What if I don't make the draft? Who will be your client when you become an agent then?"

"Hey, I'm taking over from Uncle Damon one day. I will own all queer athletes."

I smile. "Yeah, you might want to reword that when you meet prospective clients in the future. I'm not sure we want to be owned by our agents."

He shrugs. "Some might be into that kind of thing."

"And I'm out. I can talk gay stuff with you, but when it comes to sex stuff ... no. Just ... no." I head for my bedroom, but when I get to the hallway, Pop's standing there in only his underwear. I almost jump out of my skin. Shit. "How much did you hear?"

He continues to stand there, his eyes soft in sympathy, and then the next thing I know, I'm wrapped up in one of his bear hugs.

"I'm guessing all of it," I say.

When he pulls back, all he says is, "Be patient with him. It'll all work out."

I find myself holding on just as tight as he is. "How do you know?" I whisper.

He lets out a small laugh. "You sound like your dad and me. Stick it out and be what he needs you to be for now. If that's a friend, be a friend."

It's not exactly the advice I would have liked, but it's what I needed to hear.

I can do that. I can focus on football and be Levi's friend.

It's squashing down the butterflies and the way my body reacts to him that I'll struggle with.

CHAPTER SEVEN

I CAME HERE *because of what you represented, not because of you specifically.*

Ugh. As the words play over in my head for the millionth time, I stab the canvas in front of me with my paintbrush, completely ruining my work in progress that I need for a midterm coming up. Which only reminds me of all the things I haven't told Peyton.

Instead of fixating on the stupid stuff I did say, I should focus on the things I didn't. Like "I'm not really here for law school, but no one back home knows that."

Fuck, I hope his dads didn't go back to Chicago and tell my father they saw me here. Though, if they all think I'm here studying law, then it's not like Dad should be suspicious of them seeing me. So maybe it's a good thing I held back that little tidbit.

If my father found out he's paying for an apartment on the beach and tuition for an undergraduate degree in art, I'd need to flee farther away from Illinois than California.

Hawaii, maybe. Australia to be safe.

But lying to Peyton didn't sit well with me, and then I blurted half-truths all over him, flip-flopping from "I moved here for you" to "I only want to be friends."

I'm the biggest idiot on the planet, and I'm around ninety percent sure Peyton thinks the same.

Nonchalance is not my forte, so instead of playing it cool, I spouted some philosophical shit about freedom to try to cover my tracks.

I think we ended the night on an okay note—that we'd be friends—but I haven't seen him since.

Hiding … what? Not me. Never.

In my defense, it's not like I've been actively trying to avoid him like I was when I first got to FU, but he hasn't sought me out either.

And okay, so maybe after the home game the night after we had dinner was a shitshow, and then last weekend, he had an away game that redeemed the team, but it's not like he doesn't have time during the week to come find me. You know, between classes and practice … working on being the next big thing in football and working out. Okay, so maybe he doesn't have time to find me, and even if he did, it's not like he's going to be looking for me around the art department.

Ergh. It's totally on me to make the first move and follow through on all my *friends* talk.

Because I do want to be *friends.* Special friends. Special naked friends.

I groan and stab at the canvas some more. "Idiot, idiot, idiot."

Maybe I can convince my professor that this abstract piece is inspired by the trauma of embarrassment.

Painting is not entirely my thing. I like it, and it's cathartic, but my stuff isn't very good. I came here for sculpting, but an undergrad degree means I have to take an intro to all art mediums.

"Who pissed in your breakfast?" Remy says behind me, making me jump and swipe a blob of paint across the canvas. Remy's a junior, so we don't have any classes together, but the studio is open to art students when they need it. We seem to have similar free time on our schedules because our paths have crossed a few times.

He's kind of broody, and I was drawn to him immediately in a friend sense. I don't know how queer people tend to gravitate toward each other so naturally, but it happens.

"I suck." I gesture to my blobby, stabby painting.

He comes over to examine my work and runs a hand through his shoulder-length hair. "Yeah, that's not getting you an A."

"No shit." And just for fun, I stab at it some more.

"I'm tempted to ask what's up, but that might result in you actually telling me, and then I'd have to be nice and pat you on the shoulder and say, 'There, there,' while praying for a natural disaster to come and kill me."

And this is the only friend I've made so far since moving to San Luco. Well, other than Peyton. But can I really call us friends when neither of us is putting in any effort? If I do put in effort, will he think I'm a psycho? If I don't, will he think I'm playing mind games with him?

"Why are people?" I ask.

"Why are people what?"

"People."

There's a pause before Remy asks, "Are you high?"

"I wish." I put down my paintbrush and turn on my stool to face him. "There's this guy."

A smile spreads across his face. "Ah. Isn't there always?"

"We knew each other back in Chicago, but I use that term loosely. We hooked up. Once. After I graduated high school. But then I went to Harvard, and he came here, but now—"

Remy says, "Stalker," in between coughing.

"Exactly. I'm scared he's going to think I Felicity'd him, and I didn't ... entirely."

"What the fuck is Felicitying someone, and why does it sound kinky?"

"It's an old-school TV show. Back when my sister got mono in high school, she binged all these nineties teen shows and would talk incessantly about them. I know way too much about *Dawson's Creek* and *Buffy*. *Felicity* is about this chick who has one conversation with a guy at graduation and decides to go to the same college because she's low-key obsessed with him."

"Oh, so you did Felicity him, then."

I'm suddenly regretting using Felicity as a verb. "But I didn't. I mean, not really. And when I told him as much, I kind of convinced him I only want to be friends even though I want more."

Remy tentatively steps forward and pats my shoulder. "There ... umm, there."

I swat his hand away. "Fuck off."

He laughs and steps back. "Seriously, though. I get it. I'm kind of in a similar situation with a guy I grew up with. Just ... without all the stalking."

"I'm not stalking him."

"Sorry. Without all the *Felicitying*. And how's being his friend working out for you?"

"It's not. I haven't seen him since."

Remy rubs his clean-shaven chin. "In my dating experience, telling someone you want to be friends and then ghosting them actually means 'I never want to see you again.'"

He has a point.

I stand. "Okay, that settles it. You're coming with me to the football game tonight."

"Wait, how did I get brought into this?"

"Because, sadly, you're my only friend at this school so far, and if I go to the game alone, he really will think I Felicity'd him."

"Which you did," he mutters under his breath.

"No, I didn't. Ugh. Maybe I should go by myself."

"What makes you think he'll be at the game?"

I press my lips together because I can't exactly tell Remy who Peyton is without outing him. "Let's just say he'll be *on* the field." There are a lot of players on a football team, aren't there? That doesn't give it away?

"You're not talking about Cobey Green, are you? Because I hate to be the one to tell you, he's taken."

There's another queer guy on the team? Interesting.

"Not him, and, uh, I kind of don't want to tell you who he is because I found out that he hasn't exactly gone the dude route again since high school, so technically, he's closeted. And I don't want to—"

Remy holds up his hand. "Got it. You don't want to out him. But if I have to endure football, you have to at least let me try to guess who it is while I'm there."

I chuckle. "As long as it means I don't have to sit in the

stands by myself, you can try, but I'm not going to let you know if you figure it out."

"Deal."

Remy taps away on his phone while the game is played, and if it weren't for the fact I can't take my gaze off Peyton out there, I'd probably be doing the same.

He's so sexy in his purple jersey and tight gold pants. Tight, tight pants.

"Football makes no sense." I said what I said.

I got into Harvard, for fuck's sake, but all these guys do is face each other, attack, and if they're lucky, they advance a few yards. Then they do it all over again until they decide to give up and hand the ball to the other team. I'm sure there are rules about when they have to hand it over, but I've got no idea.

Remy ignores me and instead asks, "Where are you from again?"

"Chicag— Wait, why?"

"Ah. That makes it easier." He taps away on his phone again.

"That's cheating."

"There's a reason I don't play sports. I like to cheat."

"Fine. Look it up." I'm totally bluffing. "But don't come whining to me when the thrill of figuring it out isn't as good as what it would be if you used your powers of deduction."

"Yeah, that reverse psychology crap doesn't work on me."

Damn it.

A lump forms in my throat because if he googles Peyton, he's going to instantly know, but while I sit, anxiously waiting for that shoe to drop, Peyton gets a pass off, way downfield, and everyone in our section of FU fans gets on their feet. I do too because I can't see shit, and I don't really know what's happening, but Remy stays seated.

The guy in purple chasing after the ball in the air is running and running, but I don't think he's going to make it. He has two titans gaining on him, who are so fucking huge, they have no right to be college-aged.

I almost can't look at it, but I'm glad I manage to keep my eyes open.

Peyton's teammate catches the ball seamlessly, and jets must light under his ass because the two guys on his tail fall back, even though they're running as fast as they were before.

Franklin U crosses the … finish line? That's probably not what it's called, but whatever.

"Touchdown!" people around me scream.

Oh. Right. Touchdown. All the points. Go football.

In saying that, though, the vibe as the crowd erupts is somewhat intoxicating. The team celebrates with hugs and backslaps before they all head back to the team bench.

When the crowd sits back down, I land next to Remy, who finally looks up from his phone.

"What did I miss?"

"We scored a goal."

Remy smiles. "Even I know it's called a touchdown."

"Are those two words not interchangeable?" Maybe I should have gone to more football games in high school.

Remy shakes his head. "I'd like to see you tell a hockey player to score a touchdown on the ice."

"Fair point." I playfully nudge him with my shoulder. "But we're not here for the football anyway."

"I'm starting to think we're not here for funsies either." He puts his phone away. "I can't find anything on your guy."

Even though I find that next to impossible, I don't question it. Surely it's not that hard to search the guys on the team and where they came from. Though with … I lose count of the number of players on the bench when I get to thirty, so it would be a timely process.

"Shame. Need a new tactic, then." I regret the words as soon as I say them because from then on, instead of watching the game, Remy watches *me*.

Peyton's not on the field because Franklin doesn't have possession of the ball, so I'm not too worried. Yet. I am scared about what will happen when Peyton's back out there again because as much as I can force myself to look at the other players, I know where my gaze will inevitably end up.

Which is why, when the ball changes possession again and Peyton runs onto the field, I reach over and cup Remy's cheek and push it so he's watching the field and not me.

The stadium is busy but not crowded, and we're only four rows from the front, but in this moment, I swear Peyton's gaze finds mine.

My stomach flips at the thought of him noticing me, but maybe I'm wrong. Because he turns to his teammates, and they huddle together before breaking into their line.

"How long is left?" Remy complains.

"The timer at the beginning said fifteen minutes, but it took over half an hour for it to wind down. So … an eternity?"

"You owe me a drink after this."

I was hoping to wait around after the game to accidentally

run into Peyton on purpose, but as that sentence flits through my mind, I realize I'm being too much of a Felicity again, so I turn to Remy. "Why don't we go get it now?"

"You've given up on trying to make sense of football, huh?"

"Yep."

"Thank fuck. Let's go."

CHAPTER EIGHT

I SHOULD BE BEAMING as the team heads for the locker room after an epic win tonight, but I'm not. Because after two weeks of wondering if Levi even went to this school anymore, I see him in the stands. On a date.

I was lucky enough to shake it off because when it comes to football, I have to focus, but that doesn't mean the way I caught them looking at each other, with Levi's hand cupping the other dude's face, didn't play on a loop in the back of my mind.

A team is only as good as their quarterback. The only way we score is if I'm on my game. I'm just glad we were already on the board when I spotted Levi, or I could have crumbled under the pressure of not having Levi or a goddamn touchdown tonight.

"Celebration at Shenanigans," Mercer calls out.

Not that he needed to. It's team tradition. When we win, we celebrate there. When we lose, we commiserate.

Either way, we're going drinking tonight because come Monday morning, we're back in training for next week's game.

It sometimes feels like I'm on a never-ending conveyor belt. Football game, weekend parties, classes and practice, football game.

Sometimes, the routine makes me energized. It's familiar and keeps me in focus. But other times, like tonight, it makes me edgy.

The buzz of the win simmers under my skin, but it's mixed with flashes of Levi and that other guy.

I need to break the cycle tonight. I need something more than football and school. I need to hook up.

But I also need to stick to my rules. The bar will be filled with jersey chasers, and it would be so easy to take one of them home with me, but it's risky.

No matter how many times I tell them I can't have a relationship because of football, they think I'm being melodramatic or that maybe once I get them into bed, I'll change my mind.

I don't care if you know every move in the *Kama Sutra*, if you ignore my hard lines, I'm not going to fall for you.

This is why I'm careful when hooking up. It's why I haven't been with anyone all year. What I had with Casey was perfect because she was the same way. Maybe she'll be working at Shenanigans tonight and we can fall into old patterns. It technically breaks one of my self-imposed rules about no backsliding, but I'm desperate.

I don't want to stop and ask myself why seeing Levi with someone else has made me react this way when I'm not a jealous person, because if I do that, I might have to face the reality that the boy from high school still has a hold over me.

He has ever since the night he graduated.

After everyone showers and changes, we all agree to meet

at the bar whenever we can get there. Some guys are going right there, but I want to go home first and dump my bag and get changed out of the "business casual" rule Franklin forces on its athletes.

It used to be that if we won a game, we were allowed to go home in sweats.

But when Coach Nass took over, he changed that rule. We must dress the part and always look respectable on game days. I don't really understand it, but I'm used to it. I've been forced to do it since I started playing.

Brady meets me outside the players' exit, and we walk home together, but he senses something's up.

"I would've thought you'd be jumping up and down and screaming like a banshee."

"I do not scream like a banshee."

"All I mean is if you play like you did tonight when you're in the NFL, you'll be my easiest client. Your arm will be insured for millions of dollars."

"It was a good game." Okay, even I can hear the flatness in my tone.

"Okay, what is up with you?"

"Nothing. I'm just in one of those moods where it's the same shit, different day."

"Ah. One of *those* moods. You'll be fun Peyton tonight, then. As your future agent, might I suggest you refrain from drinking when you're in emo mode? It'll only bring you down more. Want to stay in?"

"You know the team will be expecting me. It's tradition."

"One night isn't going to make them send out a search party. They're probably already so drunk they won't even notice if you don't show up."

"You severely underestimate my popularity, little brother."

Brady grins. "It's why I'll make a great agent. I'm not going to make your ego bigger than it already is."

"What if my ego needs a boost?"

"Since when does Peyton Miller ever need an ego boost?"

"Since Levi said he only wants to be friends and then turned up to my game on a fucking date." And there it is. The real reason why this Levi situation is really getting to me. Him blowing me off … hurts.

"Ooh, yeah, ego smashed," Brady says. "Have you spoken to him recently?"

"Not at all. He said he wants to be friends and then basically ghosted me. Although it's not like we're on each other's socials or have each other's number."

"You haven't gone to see him?"

"I don't know his apartment number, and even I know it's creepy to hang outside the entrance to his building waiting for him to come home. I've taken the long way to classes by walking past the law department, but that strategy hasn't worked yet."

"I have a really good and novel idea. It's really easy. Are you listening?"

I already know whatever comes out of my brother's mouth next will be the obvious choice.

"You could add him as a friend on socials. Follow him. Uh, *online*. I don't recommend you actually follow him because yes, that would be creepy. But maybe you should swallow your damn inflated pride because of all the attention you've gotten from everyone during the entire course of your life and put in some effort for once." He mock gasps. "What's that like? Having to actually work for something."

"Fuck off. You know I—"

"*Besides* football. Face it, Pey, you've never had to try to make friends. Sure, some of them proved to be users, but you still never had to work for it. Maybe Levi is on a date because he asked to be friends and then you sulked for two weeks like a little bitch."

"Are you going to call me a little bitch when I'm paying you twenty percent of my millions and millions of dollars?"

He shrugs. "If you're acting like one. Yes."

"Then I hope for my sake Uncle Damon doesn't retire for another twenty years, and you'll never become my agent. I think I'll be ready for retirement around forty-two."

"Nope. You have to beat Tom Brady's record for most Super Bowl wins and the record for the oldest quarterback to still be playing—whoever that is now. Dad depends on you to defend his honor."

"I still can't believe he named you after someone he didn't like." Then again, that's Dad for you.

"Please. He did it so that when we both became hotshot football players in the NFL, the most famous Brady would be me. Not Tom."

"That ... actually checks out."

"Of course it does. It's why he was so disappointed when I quit playing. His evil plan that was decades in the making had gone to waste."

"At least I'll still be the most famous Peyton."

"Exactly. Peyton Manning who?"

We make it back to our apartment, and as soon as I'm dressed again, we head back out. We live close, Shenanigans being down the hill from our house and on the beach, so it's a five-minute walk.

Five minutes where Brady won't stop asking me questions about Levi.

"So what are you going to do about Levi?" Brady asks.

"Put in the effort to be his ... *friend*." I wince.

"Even if you want to jump him."

"I don't want to jump him." Okay, maybe I do, but also ... sex with a dude. It's been a while since I even thought about it, let alone contemplated the logistics.

Rutting against Levi when we were eighteen was one thing. That was instinctual. More than that? I wouldn't really know where to start.

"Sure, you don't. Because no one ever thinks about jumping the dude who gave them their sexual awakening. Never happens." We reach the bar, and Brady holds the door for me.

"Thought about it, sure, but it's not like I can act on it." I glance around the crowded bar, looking for my teammates.

"Because of public perception?" Brady asks over the noise. "You know it's not going to be a huge deal to come out."

"It's not just that. Levi is a complication that I don't need when the draft is in six months."

"A complication you don't need, sure. But he is a complication you want."

"Stop getting in my head. Levi is off-limits. Levi is—"

"Here," Brady says.

My gaze snaps in every direction. "What?"

"He's here." He points behind me.

When I turn, Levi's gray eyes meet mine across the room. His smile fades.

The dude he's with has his back to me, but when he looks over his shoulder at what Levi's staring at, the side of his mouth turns up, and I can't be sure because I don't hear it, but I swear his mouth moves and says, "No way."

My brother snaps his fingers in front of my face. "Play it cool. Geez. I know you have game when it comes to women, but I'm getting the impression your charm doesn't extend to men."

"What do you mean?"

"You're basically eye fucking a guy who's on a date with someone else. No class, bro. Come buy me a drink so it looks like you don't care who he's with."

"You should buy me a drink. You said it yourself, I'm all emo."

Brady slaps my shoulder. "You may as well get used to paying for everything for me. You'll be paying my wage one day, and growing up the way we did, I have become accustomed to a certain standard of living."

"You're such a jackass when you want to be."

"Spoiler alert: I always want to be a jackass. Especially to my little brother." He tries to give me a noogie, but I step away.

"You're *my* little brother."

"Yes, but I'm twice your size. So really, who's the little one?"

"Just hurry up and get my drink." I shove him. "I owe Dads like thousands of dollars."

Brady bursts out laughing. "That's right. Ah, when being a smartass backfires. Good times."

"It was still worth it." Especially because I got to spend time with Levi. Who I won't look at again. Nope.

Not happening.

I turn to find his eyes still locked on me.

Fuck.

One of us is going to have to make the move. I don't want it to be me.

But it's going to be.

Right after a drink.

Once the guys from my team catch sight of me, I no longer have to worry about buying my own drinks, and before I know it, I've downed enough alcohol to have the courage to go approach Levi.

"I'm going to do it." I put my empty glass down and try to get off my stool, but my brother's hand wraps around my bicep.

"Where do you think you're going?"

"To talk to Levi."

"Dude. Brothers don't let other brothers drink and pick a fight."

"I'm not going to pick a fight. Levi and I said we'd be friends. So I'm going to be *friendly*. I'm not even drunk." Well, I'm not *that* drunk.

I have a good buzz going, though.

"Your funeral. And you will die of embarrassment. Ooh, can I record it on my phone and put it up on the school site for everyone to see? That would be amazing."

I put my hand on his head and then shove. Hard.

"Fucker," he calls out as I leave him with my teammates.

He gets along with them really well. He comes to weight training sessions because Coach fawns over our family and lets us get away with pretty much anything, so Brady's practically one of the team. Plus, Brady gets along with everyone. He's one of those people who can adapt his personality to those around him. With the team, he's another dude bro. With his best friend, Felix, he's more laid-back and thoughtful. With me, he's both supportive and an asshole, so I guess I'm the lucky one who gets the best of both worlds.

As I walk toward Levi's table, I take a breath and tell myself I'm doing the right thing. I'm being the bigger person.

But when I reach them and both Levi and his date just stare at me, I lose my voice and want to shrivel up and die in a black hole.

"Peyton, this is Remy. Remy, Peyton."

"No shit," Remy says. "I think everyone on campus knows who Peyton Miller is. I hate sports, and I still know that."

"Uh … nice to meet you." Hey, look at that. I talked. Go me.

Silence falls between us, and I'm so glad I decided to be the bigger person. This is working out great. So great.

Remy takes out his phone. "Oh, a text message. I need to be somewhere … not here." He turns to Levi. "I'll see you in the studio."

Levi winces, and I watch Remy leave, confused by what he meant.

"Studio?" I ask and take Remy's seat.

Levi blinks at me.

"Oh, I'm sorry. Did I scare him off? *Oops*."

"Was that your plan all along? To make things so awkward, my friend had an actual excuse to finally ditch me after complaining all night about being dragged to your game?"

It's my turn to stare blankly. "What?"

"I had no one to go to the game with, so I kind of forced him into it."

"Friend. Not ... date."

Levi smiles, like my obvious jealousy is a prize he's won. "Not date."

Even though that fills me with relief, it doesn't make any sense. "You looked cozy in the stands."

Levi doesn't even flinch. If anything, he's more entertained. "Now, granted, I don't know much about football, but I'm certain the quarterback should be focusing on the field, not the people in the crowd."

Yes. A joke. I can work with that. "Oops, I've been doing it wrong this whole time."

The weird tension breaks with a laugh, and that Vanderbilt confidence I know Levi for is shining through more than ever.

"Remy came with me with the intent to make me balls up and see you again, but then all the football was too much for him to handle, so we came here," Levi explains.

"You were at the game ... to see me?"

"I figured if we are actually going to be friends that maybe we should converse at some point."

"Is that what friends do?"

Levi sips his beer. "Well, that and hook up. You know, it's how you cement a friendship, I'm finding."

My gaze narrows, and I swivel my head toward the door and then back to Levi. "*All* friendships?"

He leans forward, resting his elbows on the table. "Nope. Just one in my case."

I mirror him, bringing us close together. So close I can see every tiny speck of silver in his gray eyes even in the dim lighting of the bar. "But that hookup was so long ago. What's the protocol on getting *re*acquainted with friends?"

"Hmm." His tongue darts out to wet his lips. "That might be a case-by-case situation."

"How so?" I ask.

"Where one friend is at in terms of … let's say *openness*. And where the other is in terms of being okay with the first answer."

"I have no idea what that means or which one I am. I think it was you who told me in high school us football players are supposed to be dumb. I need it spelled out for me."

"If I go home with you tonight, will either one of us wake up with regrets tomorrow?"

"I never regret sex."

"Even when it was with me? Even if going there again means there really is no mistaking it for curiosity like I tried to convince myself it was four years ago?"

Ah. He thinks I'm going to have some big gay panic, because unlike him, I didn't test out my bisexuality more than our one tryst.

I reach across the table and cover his hand with my own. "Levi—"

Some drunk dude bumps into me and wraps his arm around my shoulder. He smells like cheap beer as he yells right next to my ear, "Peyton Miller! You had a great game tonight."

I lean away from him, letting my hand slip from Levi's. "Thanks, man."

He claps my shoulder and stumbles away.

"I can't believe that actually happens to you. Do you even know that guy?" Levi asks.

"Nope. Want to get out of here so we're not interrupted again?"

The hesitance in Levi's eyes makes me pause.

"Unless you don't want to." God, please want to.

"That's not the issue. At all."

"I promise I won't gay panic all over you."

That does the trick. The wariness in his gaze disappears as he stands. "Then let's go back to your place."

Levi goes to step by me, but I stand too and hold out my hand to block his chest.

"Let's go to yours instead. Brady won't interrupt us there."

And the hesitance is back. "O ... Okay."

We leave the bar, and I shoot Brady a text telling him I'm leaving, and he responds by sending me an eggplant emoji, so I can't help replying, "*That's what you are.*"

We're mature like that.

As we walk along the beach path toward Levi's apartment, he's silent. I want to ask him what he's hesitant about, but I'm also not sure if I want the actual answer.

"Are you still worried about me freaking out?" I ask. "Because it won't happen."

His features still stay pinched.

"Mainly because I'm bi, so I can't have *gay* panic." I do the whole drum ba-dum-tss sound, and that doesn't seem to ease his mind either.

I stop walking, and Levi pauses but doesn't turn around.

"Do you not want to do this?" I ask. "I'm getting a whole lot of mixed signals here. You moved here for me, you want to be friends, you want to go home with me ... Oh. Are you, like ... Do you have a fancy, genius boyfriend back at *Hahvid*?

Will this be cheating or something? Because I'm not cool with that."

He faces me. "It's not about you. Well, it's not entirely about you." Levi steps closer. "Yes, I'm worried you might regret sleeping with me tomorrow—and that maybe it will ruin any chance we have of being actual friends. I don't have many of those out here yet. Just you and Remy, and I haven't even spoken to you for two weeks."

It's my turn to take a step closer. "I promise. I'm good at separating feelings from sex."

"That's the other thing I'm hesitant about, though." He averts his gaze. "I'm not. So while I want this—I really, really want it—I'm worried that my lines will blur."

If anyone had said this to me at the beginning of the school year, I would've run for the hills. Levi is different, but I can't pinpoint why. Maybe because he comes from my old life. Before I had rules for having sex with people. Before I hit my limit with jersey chasers or friends who use me.

But the thought of Levi being scared of falling for me? It sounds like a challenge. One I fully want to take on. If it weren't for football, my entire future riding on this year, I'd be clubbing him over the back of the head and dragging him to my den.

"I get it," I say. "And if you only want to be friends, we can do that too. There's no pressure here. We can go back to your place and hang out. Watch TV."

"Well, that's the other thing ..."

"What other thing?"

"Maybe instead of telling you, I should show you."

I put my hands up. "Hey, whoa, I just agreed not to have

sex with you, and now you want to show me your dick? There you go with all the mixed signals again."

"It's not my dick." Levi grabs my wrist and drags me the rest of the way to his apartment.

The building is only a four-level walk-up, and I'm surprised when we only get to the second floor. With Levi Vanderbilt's money, I expected a penthouse. If this place even has a penthouse.

It's an older-style condo, but it all makes sense when he opens the door. Wide beach views, hardwood floors, a kitchen that belongs in a five-bedroom apartment instead of a one-bedroom apartment ... Now, this is Vanderbilt-worthy.

But as we move in farther, I stop in my tracks.

There are plastic sheets hanging on two walls behind his couch, kind of where I assume the dining table is supposed to go, but he doesn't have one.

"I've figured out what you need to tell me, and if it's that you brought me here to murder me, you should know my dads will never stop looking for you. They will hire big bad guys with guns to hunt you down."

Levi bursts out laughing. "That's assuming they could even find me."

I stumble back a few steps, and Levi shakes his head.

"You're so dramatic. Follow me."

"To your kill corner? No."

"Oh, for fuck's sake. It's sculpting equipment."

"Like to sculpt your victim's faces after you take them off?"

"As in my art project. For art school. Because ... Because I lied."

Art school?

Levi runs his hand through his hair, shaking out some of the neatly placed strands. The ends remind me of the shaggy, longish hair he had in high school—the big fuck-you he'd send to his dad by looking disheveled. "My father thinks I'm in law school, but I'm not. I came here for art. For a new life. One that's not Vanderbilt expectation and pressure."

I find myself happy for him. "That's amazing."

"It is?"

"Scary. But amazing. You don't think he's going to find out, though?"

"That's why I kept up the lie, even with you." He lowers his voice and mutters, "Especially with you."

"Why me?"

"Because in a roundabout way, hooking up with you at graduation gave me the courage to go for what I truly want. Growing up, art was the only subject at school that felt like an escape. I even convinced my father to let me take some classes outside of school because 'it would look good to have extracurriculars on my college applications.' He reminded me that I would get into Harvard without it because of who he is, but I made him proud by wanting to do it on merit and on my own. It was all bullshit. I just wanted to get covered in clay and express myself in a way I hadn't been able to verbally. Art is everything to me, and I don't know if I'll be able to make a living out of it yet or not. I don't know if I'm any good. But I'd like to try. Because it represents new life and new opportunities. And it reminds me to go for what I want. Just like I did that night on the roof with you. You're the reason I'm here doing the thing I love and choosing my own life."

My chest warms. "That's what you meant by you moved here because of me."

He nods.

"It's not because you're obsessed with me and want to have all my babies."

Levi laughs. "At the risk of dinting your ego, no. Though I wouldn't mind you trying to get me pregnant. You've never been with a guy before, so, you know, maybe you're not aware it doesn't work the same way as it does with girls."

"I am a dumb football player after all."

"Sure. Dumb. Is that why when I transferred to this school, I saw you'd made the dean's list three years in a row?"

I step closer to him and put my finger to my lips. "Shh. Don't tell anyone my secret."

"That you're a smart jock?"

"A smart, *bisexual* jock. I'm a true unicorn."

"I want to say something about wanting to play with your horn, but you know, make it funny."

"But you can't come up with something because you're too busy thinking about my … horn?"

"Exactly. Insert joke about horny unicorns here." Levi's gray eyes meet mine, and something weird happens in my chest.

It's all fluttery and nervous but warm too. Like the feeling I get with my family. Or when I visit Chicago. It's like that choked-up emotion I get on the field when we win a game. It's like … home.

Levi's mouth opens, but before he can say anything, I can't hold back any longer.

I close the gap between us and cover his lips with mine, swallowing the small gasp that leaves him and then wrapping my arms around his back as he melts into me.

And all I can think is he's exactly where he belongs.

CHAPTER NINE

DAMN. It's graduation night all over again. Only this time, Peyton's the confident one, kissing me first instead of the other way around.

Thinking back to that night, I was so confident in the way I carried myself. I was calm on the outside when I was a bundle of trembling nerves on the inside. I guess the weed helped cover it. Plus, I'd been drinking. It numbed me enough to be able to fake it on the outside.

I'm supposed to be older now. The one who has had more experience than Peyton. But I think my spirit has been worn down so much over the last four years that the confident Vanderbilt I was raised to be has been taken over by the insecure artist I am deep down.

The one who doesn't know if his art is even any good.

The one who questions if throwing away my socialite life to sculpt clay or wood or any other material I could bend to my will was a smart move.

But this, right here, in Peyton's arms, with his mouth on mine, I don't have to fight either side of me. The rich, privileged kid or the artistic soul searching for an outlet. I get to be a normal college student, making out with the guy he likes, with no pressure.

I thought hooking up with Peyton might have been a mistake because I'm a relationship kind of guy. I'm a feelings kind of guy. But I can't deny the freedom of this not meaning anything.

Back in high school, we were both fumbling idiots, but now, Peyton's lips are confident. His mouth is overpowering. He licks and tastes, and while it's easy to get lost in him, to melt under his touch, his exploration of my mouth doesn't match up with the stiff way his arms are embracing me.

He has one hand behind my head, holding me to him, and the other on my back, but where my hands wander over his chest and down his abs, his are still. Like he's scared to move them.

And as much as I'm enjoying kissing Peyton again, I need to make sure he's comfortable with this.

I force myself to pull back from his mesmerizing mouth to take a breath and ask a question I might not want the answer to. Because if it means having to stop, I'll do it, obviously, but I really don't want to fucking stop.

"Having second thoughts?" I rasp.

He shakes his head. "I … I'm kinda realizing the dynamic has changed since high school. You're very experienced, and I'm not. Not with guys."

That I can work with. "I'll make this really easy on you, then." I step back and strip out of my shirt and then unbutton my pants. "You can touch me anywhere. Do anything you want. Ask me to do anything you want."

"Anything?" There's a gleam in his eye that turns me on something fierce.

"I have very few limits, but if you hit one, I'll let you know." I drop my jeans to the floor, taking them off along with my shoes and socks, but I hesitate with my boxer briefs.

The last time we did this, it's not like either of us got a good look at each other's cock. But as Peyton's heat-filled gaze roams over me, I decide to take the leap. If a dick is going to scare him off, it's probably better to happen while he's looking at me like that.

I dip my fingers into my waistband and gently tug, loving the look on Peyton's face as he watches. When my dick springs free, he audibly gulps, and I take that as a sign to keep going.

They fall to my ankles. I step out of them and reach for my hard cock.

"Got any ideas of what you might want to do yet?" I stroke myself, swiping the bead of precum off the tip of my dick with my thumb.

"A few, but I'm happy to let you take the lead on this one."

"Same deal applies, though. If I do something you don't like—"

"I'll tell you."

"Good." I grab Peyton's hand and drag him through to my bedroom. It's pitch-black in here because I keep my blinds permanently closed. The large window only overlooks the parking lot, and the bright streetlights always keep me awake.

I gently push Peyton down on my bed. He's still fully clothed, so I tell him to undress while I get supplies.

The sound of him shuffling around to scramble out of his

clothes follows me to the bathroom, where I close the door and turn on the light.

I need a silent pep talk in the mirror to get me to open the drawer where I keep some extra lube and condoms. I could've gone for my stash in my bedside table, but I need the break to get under control.

Peyton Miller, the idealized image of the guy I hooked up with in high school, is currently on my bed. Naked. The man who has shaped my life in ways he couldn't even know from just one night of awkward teenage sex.

Now I want to give him as good an experience as he gave me back then. I want to awaken him from the inside out and draw all of those unexplored feelings to the surface.

What it's like to be with a man.

What it's like to taste a man.

I want to give it all to him, every opportunity.

But it's a lot of pressure, and it would be difficult to take if I fail at enlightening him. Logically, I know it would be because he's settling a curiosity, and maybe he's not as bisexual as he thought, but I don't want him to be disappointed by this experience or walk away even more confused.

I can do this.

I had sex with countless guys in Boston—making up for lost time and all that. I know how to go out there and push every button Peyton has.

And if this does all go to shit, at least I will have this. A do-over with the guy who gave me my own awakening.

So far, I'm doing a great job of making it less awkward. We're both naked but in separate rooms.

I don't think this is what people mean when they say they're into edging.

Okay, enough overthinking. I'm doing this.

I grab the supplies, even if I'm not sure we'll need them. This might not go that far. Then again, it might. So to prevent me from doing more analyzing that I don't need to, I take them both.

When I open the door, Peyton is sitting on the edge of the bed, completely naked, leaning back on his hands and putting his insanely fit body on display.

The light from the bathroom creates shadows and hard lines on each and every one of his muscles.

When my gaze meets his eyes, he smiles hesitantly.

"You going to stand there all night? I was beginning to think you got lost in there."

"I was just …" I almost say preparing myself, but in this context, that will give the wrong impression.

"Second thoughts?"

"No. I know I want to do this, but it's a lot of pressure. To make it good for you."

Relief washes over his face. "And here I am worried about *you* enjoying this. I'm like a virgin again."

"That's oddly reassuring."

"Can you please come over here and touch me?" The pleading is what gets me.

I give in immediately. "Well, I did promise you could ask for anything you want." I move to stand in front of him, keeping the bathroom light on so I can see every inch of his naked skin and commit it to memory.

"I want to touch you too," Peyton murmurs.

I run my fingers through his short blond hair. "Touch me anywhere you want."

He starts off slow and hesitant, trailing his fingers over my pec. I'm nowhere as defined in the muscle department, but he doesn't seem to mind.

He moves his hand lower, across my abs, and then the softest brush against the head of my dick sends electricity shooting down my spine.

Peyton's pink tongue darts out to wet his lips. He's so close his breath hits my cock, and I swear he's going to lean in and put his mouth on me, but then he glances up through thick lashes, more hesitance in his eyes, and I decide to take things into my own hands.

He did say he wanted me to take the lead. It's something I like doing, but in this instance, I'm worried about going too fast for him. Too far.

I could drop to my knees and show him what to do, or I could guide him and encourage him. It's a tough call because I want to do both those things, but the thought of not getting his lips on me keeps me standing.

I still have hold of his hair, so I grip tighter. "Do you want a taste?" I use my free hand to stroke myself.

Peyton glances at my cock and nods.

I step closer and rub the head over his lips. "Lick the tip."

Tension leaves him, his shoulders relaxing as he leans forward. It's as if he was waiting for direction or permission because now that he has it, he doesn't hold back.

Peyton licks over my slit and then closes his mouth around the head and sucks.

"Holy fuck, Pey." I throw my head back.

He pulls off. "Is that a good holy fuck or an 'ouch, don't bite my dick off' kind of holy fuck? It was hard to tell if that was pleasure or pain."

I chuckle. "Good kind. I promise. Don't overthink it. Just do what you like being done to you."

"Show me what you like first."

"Show you?"

"On me." His voice is barely above a whisper.

I smile and drop to my knees between Peyton's legs. "A blowjob's a blowjob, and I will like anything you do, but if you want ideas …" I run my hands up his thighs and love how they tense under my fingertips. "I like it when hands get involved too."

I cup his balls with one hand while stroking the base of his dick with the other. Peyton's breath becomes stilted, and when I lower my head, taking him in my mouth, he stops breathing completely.

His cock is heavy in my mouth, his taste salty and heady, but I'm too busy focusing on his reactions to enjoy it.

There's nothing sexier than the noises a man makes while I'm going down on him, and Peyton doesn't disappoint. The only thing I'm self-conscious of is if I moan in return, it might pull him back to reality. That he's being blown by a guy.

I glance up at him, and all those negative thoughts float away when we lock eyes. He's watching what I'm doing to him, his gaze laser-focused on me. He's definitely not imagining I'm someone else, let alone pretending I'm a girl.

I've always been wary of hooking up with bicurious guys because of that. There's a difference between a bi guy who knows who he is and a newbie trying dick because of curiosity. And maybe that's a double standard because the last time I was with Peyton, we were both that inexperienced guy, and I did to him exactly what I'm scared of Peyton doing to me: I pretended our experience didn't mean anything.

And that has the ability to cut deep.

Peyton didn't even hook up with another guy because of it.

I want to make it all up to him now, give him the experiences he's been holding out on because of something stupid eighteen-year-old me did, and as I lower my head again and let out that moan I've been trying to keep in, his thighs tense, and he shudders.

With that insecurity out of the way, I'm able to give him my whole focus.

I stroke him while I bob my head and play with his balls with my other hand, squeezing and releasing.

He quivers and squirms like he's trying not to thrust upward into my mouth, and I set myself the goal of driving him to the point where he can't help himself.

I get my wish when my pinkie finger slips behind his sac and presses against his hole. Peyton's hips jackknife off the bed, but I'm prepared for when his cock touches the back of my throat. I leave my finger where it is, slowly teasing his rim with no intention of taking it further than that.

This is enough. He's exactly where I want him. He grips my hair tight and moves in and out of my mouth without any help from me.

Each time he thrusts inside, Peyton tries to cover a grunt, and it comes out as a strained cry. I love it.

The taste of sticky precum hits my tongue, and I drink it eagerly.

"Levi," Peyton breathes. He sounds desperate and like he's clinging to the edge. "If you don't … Fuck. I'm gonna … unless you move away. Nrgh."

I try not to laugh around his dick. I pull off slowly but with a hard suck. Peyton shudders again. And when my mouth leaves him, my hand takes over for it because I'm not going to let him come down from this until he's unleashing in my mouth.

"Did you want something?" I ask.

He nods. Then shakes his head.

"Great direction there, Pey. Very clear and succinct."

Peyton throws his head back, looking up at the roof before meeting my gaze again. "Only a Vanderbilt would use the word *succinct* during a blowjob."

Reminding me of my last name is not the sexiest thing in the world, but Peyton's flushed skin, his rapid breathing, and the way he looks like he could fall apart at any moment outweighs the family minefield.

As if unable to hold himself up anymore, he falls backward on the bed, his legs still hanging off the end.

"You want my mouth or my hand when you come?" I ask.

His abs contract, so I take the opportunity to lean forward and lick along the hard lines between his six-pack.

"Fuck. I want both. All. Nothing. God, I want to come."

There he goes being succinct again.

"I want to taste you when you come. Is that okay?" I ask.

"Yes. Oh fuck, but it needs to be now."

I replace my hand with my mouth, and as soon as my lips close over the base of his cock, cum hits the back of my throat.

Peyton makes even more sinful noises when he comes than when he's simply turned on, and my own dick leaks at the sound.

I love it when my partners get vocal during sex. Not necessarily words, but when they can't hold back their sounds of lust and pleasure, it really does something for me. It drives me wild with need.

I have to touch myself so I can get relief. I keep sucking on Peyton's cock, drinking all of him in, while I take pleasure from my own hand, but when he's done coming and he leans back up on his elbows, I slowly pull off him while licking him clean.

His gaze drops to my hand. "Can I?"

It takes nearly all my strength to let go of my dick and stand. I was so close to release, and it was tempting, so tempting to let myself go, but I'd rather have Peyton's lips on me. Or his hand. I'm really not picky.

"What do you want to do?" I ask.

"I want to make you come. And I know I was supposed to be paying attention, but it's possible my brain turned to mush almost as soon as I had your mouth on me."

I laugh. "How did you make the dean's list again?"

"Refrained from having sex while studying. Helped me retain information better."

"I'm willing to take a makeup quiz whenever you want, but I can take it into my own hands this time." I step closer to him. "If you let me use your mouth."

"And if I choke?"

"I won't let you. I'll go easy on you since it's your first time."

He still looks nervous, but as if shaking off his nerves, he gives me a confident smile and says, "Bring it."

I press the head of my dick against his lips, and he opens for me, but instead of moving in and out of him, I stop when I'm about a third of the way in and stroke myself. The warmth of his mouth wraps around me and settles in my gut. My balls tingle, and it's not going to take long for me to shoot my load.

Peyton tries to take me deeper into his mouth, but I hold his head back.

"I'll likely punch you in the face if you get too close to my fist, and you wouldn't have a good excuse for how you got the missing teeth. You play football, not hockey."

And okay, lesson learned when Peyton pulls that irresistible mouth away from my cock so he can laugh and choke at the same time.

"Sorry. No making jokes while my dick is in your mouth. Got it."

He closes his hand over mine on my cock. "Let me take over?"

I love how his confidence has gone from hesitant to faking it to right now where he has a look of determination on his face. He's going to make me come, and no way will I hold him back from going for it.

I remove my hand and give Peyton free rein. He mimics what I was doing, jerking me while his mouth works the tip. With each stroke, he gains more confidence, slowly taking more of me between his lips, until he's moving his mouth and hand in sync.

When he looks up at me, I nod, encouraging him to keep going.

"That feels so good."

That only makes him go faster.

Between his rough calluses and the wet slurps as he sucks on my cock, I have to force myself to hold back from sliding deep inside his mouth. I promised I wouldn't, but holy hell, I'm getting desperate.

And then he hits me where I'm weak. Peyton moans around me, the vibrations on my dick too much for me to handle, and I don't even get the chance to warn him as I come inside his mouth.

I have to grip onto his shoulders so I don't fall, and he manages to keep pace even while swallowing the first load he's ever taken.

He slows along with my breathing until I pull out of his mouth, and he looks up at me with these bright blue eyes that beg for praise.

There's some of my cum on the side of his mouth, so I lean down and kiss it away.

"That was so hot," I murmur against his mouth.

"So hot," he agrees, but in the next second, he wraps his arms around my back and pulls me down onto the bed.

He rolls us so I'm on my back, pinned underneath him, and I have to say, there are worse things than being stuck under Peyton Miller.

"Can I kiss you?" he asks.

"I'd be disappointed if you didn't."

He leans in and touches his lips to mine. It's so soft it takes me off guard because I was expecting a full-on comedown make-out session.

This is a little too unnerving, though. It doesn't say casual at all.

And I can already tell that if we're going to do this—hook up a couple more times—it's going to be difficult for me to separate lust and real feelings.

To remind myself of what this is, I force his lips to part and lick my way inside. I take control of the kiss, but he matches me, keeping with my pace until I can feel him harden against my thigh.

I break my mouth from his. "Seriously? Again?"

"I take it your exploration of your sexual identity didn't include being with a football player?"

"How did you know?"

Peyton lowers his mouth to my ear. "Because you wouldn't be surprised by my stamina."

"Looking for round two already?"

"Mm, I don't think it would take me much like this." Peyton rotates his hips, dragging his cock along my skin. It's so hard already, and the fact he got so turned on by blowing me settles some of that insecurity that's trying to come back.

Peyton doesn't stop grinding against me, but he lowers his head next to mine, his breath in my ear. It's like the first night we hooked up, only he's the one on top this time. He sets the pace, and when he comes for the second time tonight, I feel it on my abs and stomach.

He slumps on top of me, out of breath and sweaty.

"Are you done now?" I ask.

"At least until morning."

"I don't know how I'm going to keep up with you." But I sure as fuck want to try.

Peyton rolls onto his back, and even if the urge to get up and clean myself off is strong, I don't want to leave his side yet.

Even though I know I should.

CHAPTER TEN

OKAY, my intention wasn't to sleep over because I rarely do that with anyone unless there are extenuating circumstances like we're drunk or getting home is an issue, but after two orgasms, there was no choice other than to pass the fuck out.

I wake when Levi's voice fills the room, but if he's talking to me, he's going to have to wait until I've at least had a sip of coffee.

I crack one eye open to see Levi sitting on the edge of his side of the bed. He has his boxers on but nothing else, and I almost reach over and kiss my way down his spine, but his words stop me.

"School's going fine, Dad."

Oh, shit. Mr. Vanderbilt himself.

I might leave Levi to it.

I slide out of bed as quietly as I can and put on my underwear from last night. Levi's apartment has wide windows in the living room, no curtains, and it faces the beach. The last thing I'd want to do is give beachgoers an eyeful of my dick.

It's definitely noteworthy, and they will all want it, but

naked pics leaked online is the last thing I want this close to the draft. Or ever, really. A scandal like that is almost as bad as coming out in the sporting industry, and here, it would be a double whammy.

I go searching for Levi's coffee machine, and it's hard to miss when it takes up a good chunk of the kitchen counter. The problem is we only have a Keurig at home, so a proper espresso machine is daunting.

There are two options here. I go interrupt his phone call by getting the rest of my clothes and going for a walk down the street to Bean Necessities, or I can figure this thing out.

Clothes seem like so much effort, though.

How hard can an espresso machine be to work out? Really. I've ordered a million coffees over the last four years to get me through midterms and exams. Hell, sometimes I've needed it just to stay awake in class. I've seen how they're made, so it will be easy to replicate.

First, they take this handle-looking thing and put ground coffee in it, but I can only find beans on the counter.

Levi's machine looks fancy enough to have a grinder in it, so I try that.

I pour some of the beans into the handle and then work out how to attach it to the machine. It's a little bumpy, but I get it in there. Sort of.

After I find mugs, I put them under the spout of the handle. Okay, now, which button to push ...

I want to make Levi a cup too, so I hit the button that has the two cups on it. It does nothing.

My gaze catches on the side of the machine where a button says "ON." That would probably help.

It makes a startling gurgling noise as it turns on, and I'm

assuming that's the grinder grinding the beans. When it's done making the noise, I hit the button for two cups again.

I am not prepared for the spray of water that comes out the side of the handle and lands all over the counter and the floor. None of it goes in the cups.

That can't be right.

Then the whole handle falls out of place, more water goes everywhere, and coffee beans explode all over the ground, ping-ponging off every surface on the way down, including one that hits me in the damn nipple.

"What the fuck?" I rub my chest while I frantically try to stop the machine from continuing to spew water everywhere, but I don't know what button to push.

I give up and unplug the whole thing.

When a slow clap starts behind me, I cringe.

I slowly turn, wincing at Levi's smirk. He's fully dressed now, and I'm standing in the middle of his apartment, drenched and practically naked.

Even if I don't feel it, I can pull the confident act out when I need it. "My dads always taught me that taking initiative is a good thing. And that even if I get it wrong, it's the thought that counts." Totally did all of this on purpose.

Levi rubs his chin. "Well, it depends on what your thought was. Was it to make a mess of my kitchen?"

"It was to make us both coffee."

"In that case, I suppose I can forgive you. I'll clean up and make the coffee. You ... can go find a pair of my underwear to change into." He gestures to the front of my boxer briefs, which are all wet.

"Ooh, is this like a frat thing? Whenever you hook up with

someone, you give them a pair of your underwear? I've heard of T-shirts."

"Maybe you need to stop making it a habit of ruining yours."

"That sounds less fun, though."

Levi lifts his hands, gesturing to the mess. "Which part of this is fun?"

"The part where you clean it up for me?" I give an over-the-top smile.

"Go get dressed."

"You're the best." On my way past, I drop a kiss on Levi's cheek, which seems to shock the hell out of him, so I give him a peck on the mouth too before moving toward his bedroom.

I find a pair of his boxer briefs in his top drawer, but now we're not in high school and I'm at my most physically fit, they're really tight on me. On the plus side, they make my cock look huge like I'm trying to smuggle an anaconda down there.

I'm tempted to go back into the kitchen like this to tempt Levi into another round before I should get back home.

Brady's probably already thinking about all the ways he could torment me about Levi, so I refrain from torturing both of us and put the rest of my clothes back on to go back out there.

The coffee machine whirs, and Levi moves about his kitchen effortlessly. I'm too busy watching him to notice when I get caught on a sheet in his kill corner.

It moves with my foot and falls to the ground, revealing a clay sculpture on a table.

"I told you it was your kill corner," I shriek when I take in the headless body. It's just a torso and arms. No legs or anything juicy below the hard V thing Brady's always saying is sexy on a guy. I don't understand the appeal of the V, but I do like how the abs are defined, the nipples hard, the shoulders are wide, and there's a prominent vein running down the right arm. "Hey, is this me? Wow, you like my body so much, you've molded it into clay so you have something to hug at night."

Levi appears with the two mugs of coffee and hands me one. "It's for class, Mr. Conceited. I know *the* Peyton Miller probably doesn't hear this much, but not everything is about you."

"Lies." I go to take a sip of my coffee when the pattern in the milk stops me. "Wow, you can draw like flowers and stuff in your coffee?" I take a sip but then splutter at the horrible bitter taste. "That's—"

Levi cocks an eyebrow at me.

"—uh, really good?" I take another sip and wince. "Really smooth."

"Sorry. I forgot you need your coffee sweeter than baby unicorn burps." He walks over to his kitchen counter again and brings back a sugar canister with a pour top. "Tell me when." He tips it, but it comes out slowly, and as it continues to pour, Levi's face contorts. "I really hope you never get diabetes in your life."

"Okay, I'm good. I think."

He hands me a spoon, and after stirring, I take a sip.

"Damn, now that's good coffee. How did you learn to do that?"

"Are we really sure yours can be classified as coffee?"

"It still has caffeine in it, so yes." I drink some more and hum.

"Our housekeeper taught me when I was bored back in high school." He shrugs. "I liked it. That was the beginning of my caffeine addiction."

"Did your parents send you to rehab for that?"

He laughs. "Fuck no. They encouraged it. Told me coffee is the key to getting through law school."

"The law school you're not actually going to," I point out.

"That's the one."

"What did your dad say this morning? Don't you ever get scared to answer his calls in case, you know, he somehow finds out?"

"Terrified. Every time I see his name on my screen, I hold my breath when I answer it."

"Here's an idea. You could always not answer it."

"I could, but then he might actually come out here to yell at me. It's better if it happens over the phone."

"So, I'm guessing your lack of lawyering isn't the reason he called this morning?"

"Nope." Levi lifts his mug to his lips, and I watch as he swallows, trying not to flash back to last night when he was swallowing me down. He breaks me out of that imagery. Thankfully. "He was asking ... well, no, Mom asked him to call to see if I was coming home for Thanksgiving in a few weeks. She probably figured he had more of a chance of getting me there than her begging and pleading with me."

"Brady and I aren't going home either. When our dads were here torturing us mercilessly, they told us they're going to be on vacation."

"Really?"

"Well, no. They said *out of the country*. But that's dad speak for vacation alone so they can still bone like they're twenty years old. Brady and I learned early on not to ask too many questions about our parents' lives. It somehow always devolved into conversations about sex. I tell you, it was borderline child abuse."

"Mm." Levi grunts.

"What?"

He shakes his head. "Nothing. I still can't get over how differently we were brought up, considering we're from the same world. My parents were never open about that stuff, which yes, I'm thankful for, but it also made it a weird time to navigate. Especially while trying to work out I'm gay. While your parents were talking about sex and not at all preparing you to use an espresso machine, mine were leaving us to be raised by nannies and housekeepers."

"True. It's actually astounding to me that you can make this good coffee on your own." I take another sip, and it's damn delicious. "This is even better than the stuff we can get from Bean Necessities."

"Yes, well, it helps if you grind the coffee beans first." Levi smiles.

"I thought your machine must be super fancy and did it itself."

"Uh-huh. And tell me, how did you make it onto the dean's list? Did you sleep with her?"

"Yep. You jealous?"

"Of you sleeping with a fifty-year-old woman? Nah. You can have her."

"Thanks for that image." I shudder. "And no. I'm smart when it comes to tests. Brady taught me in high school how to cram for an exam. Don't ask me to recite any of it now. Once the test is done, I forget all about it."

"That will be fun for you if football doesn't work out. How do you expect to get a job?"

I gasp. "You bite your tongue. Football is the only option for me."

"And ... you're okay with that?"

"Why wouldn't I be?"

"I dunno. The way you talk about the pressure and everything. I thought maybe that was one thing we had in common."

I turn to him and use my free arm to wrap around his back and pull him against me. "We do have that in common. The pressure can be crushing, but also? I kind of love it. People react to pressure in different ways. I thrive, but Brady rebels against it."

"Hooked up with the wrong brother then. Sounds like Brady and I have more in common."

"Are you hoping to make me jealous?"

"Would it work if I was?"

"Maybe if you were talking about anyone but my brother. Brady and I are tight. He knows you and I hooked up, so he wouldn't go there, and let's just say, you're not his type anyway."

"What's wrong with me?"

"You're shorter than him, skinnier than him, and you can read big words. Everything he hates in men."

Levi laughs. "Ah, he's into the type of guys who have more muscles than brains? I can relate."

"Hey."

"What makes you think I'm talking about you?"

"Wow. You're savage first thing in the morning."

"I only become nice once all of this is gone." He raises his cup.

"Okay, I'll wait until you're finished to ask you to spend Thanksgiving at my place, then."

"You want to spend Thanksgiving with me?"

"Don't get too excited. Brady and I have invited a lot of the guys who aren't going home for the break. We're going to cook a turkey and everything."

"Do you know how to cook?"

"Nope."

"Oh, I am so in. If for nothing else than to see if you handle a kitchen the same way you did my espresso machine."

I'm regretting inviting Levi over for Thanksgiving as Brady and I stare down at the still-raw turkey. At 4:00 p.m. We maybe, possibly, put it in the oven without turning it on and then got distracted watching football.

"At least everything else was store-bought and is ready to go," I say.

"Great. We'll have potato salad and pumpkin pie."

"Protein shakes?"

"We should've ordered in," Brady mutters. "I don't think we have enough food for everyone either. How many people did you end up inviting?"

"Not the entire sixty-man roster if that's what you're worried about."

"How many?" Brady asks, and I can already see him as my agent now. He has the disapproving glare down pat for when I fuck up a play or get in the tabloids for all the wrong reasons.

I pull on my ear. "About half of them? Plus Levi. Oh, and

Ty from the lacrosse team with his boyfriend, Brax. I think my friend Charlie was also going to bring his boyfriend, Liam. But that's it. I swear." Ish.

"Fucking hell." Brady makes his way over to the counter we keep all our liquor on and puts bottles and bottles of it on the dining room table. "Dinner is served."

"I really don't think people are going to mind that change of plans."

"What should we do with the turkey?" Brady asks.

"Cook it on super high and see if it cooks in time?"

"Happy Thanksgiving. Please come in and get salmonella poisoning."

"So ... that's a no?"

Our front door opens—the guys on the team know they're welcome here anytime and waltz right in—but when we make our way to the entrance, it's just Brady's bestie, Felix, and Felix's boyfriend ... I want to say Michael? Matthew? Close enough. He's the big cuddly teddy bear that eclipses Felix in size.

Felix lifts his nose into the air. "Why can't I smell turkey cooking?"

"So, funny story ..." I start.

Felix turns to his boyfriend. "I told you those burgers on the way here were a smart idea."

"You've already eaten?" I act offended. "We've slaved over a hot stove all day for you, and you eat before you get here?"

Brady shoves me. "Don't scare off Marshall"—Ha, I knew it started with an *M*—"with that shit. Felix has finally found a guy who likes him for who he is. Don't ruin it for him. He might never find another one."

Felix pouts. "There's an insult in there somewhere."

"Was I trying to be subtle?"

Felix flips off my brother.

Marshall hands over a plate to me. "I, uh, made pecan pie."

"Awesome. Thanks. Looks like it's pie and vodka for dinner."

Felix left the front door open when he walked in, so of course, perfect timing, Levi steps through as I say this.

He laughs. "I can see cooking went as well as making coffee did."

Not one to ever be a wallflower, Felix immediately asks, "Who are you?"

What am I supposed to say here? My date? A dude I hooked up with a couple of weeks ago, have randomly DM'd a couple of times since but haven't seen again because football and school are taking up all my time? The messages haven't been flirty or even mention what happened, but they've been friendly enough. He asked for recommendations on where to get good Chinese food. We asked how our classes are going. That kind of thing.

I wanted to ask to see him again but really couldn't.

Brady senses my hesitance and comes to my rescue. "That's Levi Vanderbilt. We went to high school together back in Chicago."

"He's in the law program," I add. Because my immediate reaction is to somehow save his cover story for being here even though no one asked for that information.

Levi gives me a smile and hands over a bottle of wine. "I knew I should've brought a plate of food instead, but I went against my gut instincts."

"Your gut instincts were right. I'll add it to the rest of our dinner." I turn and put it with the bottles of vodka, rum, whiskey, and tequila.

"Jesus," Levi says when he looks at the pile. "Do we have anything to line our stomachs first?"

"We have pie." I grin.

"Oh, we're so going to die."

"What happened to you in your old age?" I ask. "Oh, is it the *Hahvid* effect? It removes the partying part of your brain and replaces it with old-white-guy syndrome."

Levi playfully slaps me. "Quit it with that Harvard shit."

"Don't you remember all those epic parties back in high school?" I ask. "Sure, we never actually hung out at them, but you would drink like a fish."

"Exactly. I think my body rebels whenever it remembers."

I lick my lips because now my body is remembering what else his body can do.

"Why … why is this turning me on?" Felix blurts.

Thank you so much for making this awkward, I want to say but don't.

Marshall pulls Felix to his side. "Because you're a horndog."

"Right. That." Felix nods. "What is it with the straight-guy thing? They're so hot."

Levi and I speak at the same time but say very different things. "It's because they're unobtainable, and that's appealing," I say.

"I pass for straight? Haven't had that happen for a few years."

"Oh, sorry," Felix says. "I shouldn't have assumed." But then his face lights up. "Wait. You went to high school with them." He points to me and Brady. "You're gay. Did you and Brady ever—"

"Nope," I cut in. "Not going there."

Levi smiles over at me.

Felix gasps. "Are you the one who took Peyton's guy virginity? The one he claims made him realize he was super straight?"

Levi laughs. "Ouch, Pey. That cuts so deep."

Felix jumps up and down. "Oh my God, this is so much fun."

"And we're going to need to start drinking," I say. "Like, right now."

I grab Levi's wrist, take the wine he brought off the table, and lead him to the kitchen to our stash of red Solo cups.

"Football players are so classy," Levi says as I pour us drinks.

"Hey, I was going to start on the hard stuff, but as you put it, you need something to line your stomach first."

"Red wine wasn't on the list of options to do that."

"I meant we can drink this before eating pie." I take a huge gulp and cringe. "This tastes expensive."

"So, so, *so* classy," Levi deadpans.

"Let's go out back. We have a huge yard and couches and stuff."

"You don't want to hang with your brother and … whoever that little guy was?"

"That was Felix, and no. It's bad enough having to field all the jokes that Brady will use as ammunition. Both of them together is impossible."

"Okay, so Brady, Felix, and who was the big guy?"

"Marshall. Felix's boyfriend. But there's really no need to

try to memorize names. You'll want to give up when the team shows their faces."

"Just how many people are coming to this thing?"

I try to calculate a guess. "Maybe forty? Fifty?"

"Damn. Tonight is going to get messy, isn't it?"

I nudge him. "Happy Thanksgiving."

CHAPTER ELEVEN

IT'S BEEN a long time since I've been to this type of party. Sure, back in Boston, we'd drink and hang out, but it usually involved some type of study session beforehand and an early night because there was no such thing as a day off from Harvard. If you didn't have classes, you had study groups, assignments, or meetings with professors you can't be hungover for.

And I wasn't lying when I said it's been a while since I've drunk this much.

Peyton hasn't left my side on the couch in the backyard all night except to get us more drinks. Or pie. He appears to be alternating between drinks and pie, and fuck, he can eat a lot without feeling sick.

I'm slumped backward on the couch, leaning my head against the cushions, and I shudder. "Okay, don't think of the word 'sick.'"

Peyton stares at me over his shoulder. "Good tip. You feeling vomity? Need me to take you to the bathroom?"

There are deep laughs, but they sound far away. Or really close. I don't know.

People have been approaching Peyton all night, talking about football and basically kissing his ass.

"Eww, don't say ass."

"I didn't. I said vomity."

Reflux hits bad, and I get a taste of pie trying to come back up.

"Oh, shit. I didn't think you actually meant it." Peyton wraps his arms around me, and I swallow down the vomit. "Can you stand?"

"I can try."

"Love the confidence. Okay, ready?" Peyton helps me up, and I'm a little wobbly, but nothing major.

He keeps his arm around me the whole way to his bedroom and even while he kicks the door to his bathroom open.

"How are you not drunk?" I ask.

"All the pie. Plus, I am drunk. Just not as drunk as you."

"I don't think Hemingway was ever as drunk as I am right now."

"And here I was hoping we could fool around when everyone goes home."

"Drunk sex is fun."

"When you're this out of it, it's a felony." He closes the lid to the toilet and plonks me down.

The whole bathroom spins. "Fair enough. Am I moving, or is the wall?"

"You kinda look like it's hard to hold your head up."

"Oh, cool. Drinking gives me the cognitive function of a baby."

"And yet, you're using words like 'cognitive function' and not even slurring. You really are a Vanderbilt."

"Ergh. I don't want to be a Vanderbilt."

"Ah. You can take the boy out of the Vanderbilt, but you can't take the Vanderbilt out of the boy."

"That doesn't even make any sense." Does it?

Peyton gestures to me. "Exhibit A. Picking on my grammar while drunk off his tits."

He's right. I might hate the lifestyle I was brought up in, but there are certain things that are so ingrained in me that I can't help it.

"Do you think you're going to be sick?" Peyton asks softly.

"I don't think so."

"Okay. Let's get you to bed. You're in no shape to be walking home."

I don't even bother fighting him on it. He guides me to his bed and pulls back the covers for me to climb in.

Once he empties the trash under his desk and puts the empty container beside me, he tucks me in and kisses my forehead. But in a flash, he's gone, and I reach out for his hand.

"You're not staying with me?"

"I'm just going to kick everyone out, and then I'll be back."

"You don't need to tell them to leave for me."

Peyton smiles. "It's cute you think I'm doing it for you. I'm doing it because I want to spend my night with you, and I don't trust any of those bulldozer teammates of mine to not do damage to the house."

I smile back.

He wants to spend his night with me even though we're not going to hook up.

Peyton Miller is making it really hard not to fall for him.

It's only a few hours later when I wake to that familiar queasy feeling in my gut but an unfamiliar body next to mine.

I roll over to face him, relieved when I see Peyton's peaceful face and not some rando. Even better, I didn't sleep-walk into Brady's room and accidentally cuddle up next to him. I've been known to sleepwalk when drunk. Hasn't happened since high school, where I'd go to bed in my room and wake up in the guest bed or asleep on the couch in the stuffy library, where my dad kept all his law books. But with how drunk I got, it was a real possibility tonight.

I need some painkillers. My head pounds already, and it's still dark out. When I fish out my phone from my pocket, I see it's only 3:00 a.m.

I unceremoniously roll out of bed and almost fall flat on my face. I'm not drunk anymore, but I definitely think I'm dehydrated. I stumble into Peyton's bathroom, checking the cabinet and drawers for Tylenol or anything equivalent. There's nothing.

Maybe they keep it in the kitchen. Or the second bathroom, which I know is in this house somewhere. I just don't know where.

Whenever I needed to go last night, I'd use Peyton's because he said all of his friends know that his bedroom is off-limits, and if anyone is caught fucking in there, they have to buy Peyton new bedding. Mattress and all.

When I get to the hallway, low murmurs come from somewhere, so people must still be here, even though Peyton said he was going to kick everyone out.

My eyes are bleary as I move down the hall into the living room on my way through to the kitchen, but when they come into focus, I have to wonder if I'm sleepwalking after all and having a really weird dream.

Peyton's brother, Brady, is sitting sideways on the couch, shirtless, making out with some guy, but what throws me off guard is the second guy behind him, sucking on Brady's neck and rubbing his hands all over Brady's chest and down, down—

I should not be watching this.

Though I can see now what Peyton means about Brady liking bigger guys. They both look like they could snap Brady in half, and Brady is not small.

I turn to go into their kitchen, but in my still half-asleep state, I miss the entryway and clip my shoulder on the frame. "Ah, fuck."

I grab hold of my arm and turn. Brady and his company break apart really fast.

"Don't mind me. Just looking for some painkillers for my hangover." I can't get into the kitchen fast enough, but their voices travel after me.

"I thought you said your brother sleeps through anything."

Brady huffs. "That's not my brother. That's someone I thought went home already. Go to my room. I'll be there in a minute."

I pretend I can't hear them and search the drawers in the kitchen, but Brady's presence is domineering as he enters the room.

He steps up right behind me and opens a cabinet above my head. "Everything you need is up here."

I refuse to look at him, and I'm pretty sure my cheeks are red with how hot they are. "Thank you."

I experimented a lot in college, but when I say that, I mean with, like, toys and sex positions. Not multiple partners. At once.

It's not a huge deal to me. You know, you do you. Love is love. Sex is sex. It's all … whatever. Not my business. It's more that I interrupted them and now I can't look Brady in the eye without blushing that makes me want to hide. I'm usually a lot cooler than this.

"So, they're, umm—" Brady starts, but I cut him off and force myself to face him.

"All good. I didn't see anything."

Brady smiles. "Now, we both know that isn't true, but I just wanted to ask if you maybe wouldn't mention this to Peyton?"

"You want me to lie?"

"Is it really lying if we pretend this didn't happen? You're drunk. You're seeing things."

I nod. "I can pretend, sure. If Peyton asks, which he won't because he's sound asleep, I'll say you helped me find ibuprofen for my head. But can I ask why Peyton doesn't know?"

"Why my brother doesn't know I'm hooking up with two random dudes?"

I hang my head. "Oh. When you put it like that …?"

He moves to the sink to fill a cup of water for me and bring it back. "Thanks. Now, take these and go back to bed. With any luck, you still have so much alcohol coursing through your system you actually will forget when you wake up in a few hours."

I hold up two tablets and throw them back. "Here's hoping."

"Goodnight."

Right. Bed. "Night."

We both take off in opposite directions, vowing to never speak of this again.

When I get back to bed and climb in next to Peyton, he stirs but doesn't wake. That is until I maybe, sorta, accidentally on purpose cuddle up to him.

"Levi?" he rasps, but he hasn't opened his eyes.

I want to ask who else would it be, but I might not like that answer. "Just went to find some painkillers."

He tries to sit up. "I'll go for you."

I pull him back down. "It's okay. Brady was still up. He got them for me."

Peyton settles back and opens his arms for me. He still hasn't even cracked an eye open. "That's good. Did you end up being sick?"

"Nope."

"Awesome. I can do this, then." He brings his lips down on mine.

He tastes like stale alcohol, and I'm sure I don't taste any better, but neither of us cares.

Peyton's only in his boxers, but I'm still fully dressed, thanks to falling asleep almost as soon as my head hit the pillow earlier. I want to rectify the clothing situation, but my hands are too busy roaming all over his hard chest to take a break and strip out of my clothes.

As if reading my mind, Peyton reaches for the button on

my jeans. It's a struggle as he gets the fly down, and I try to help him by wriggling out of them.

His mouth leaves mine. "Fuck it." He sits up, fully awake now, and maneuvers himself between my legs.

My jeans are gone a second later and then my underwear.

While he takes off his own, I ditch my shirt and watch as his cock springs free. I want him in my mouth again. I want him inside me. But I don't know what Peyton wants.

My gaze meets his, where he's starting down at me, watching me take him all in.

"What do you want to do?" I whisper.

"As much as I love all the ideas running through your head while you look at me—"

"You a mind reader now?"

"Nope, but you look like you want to devour me whole, and as tempting as that is to do again, it's the middle of the night, I'm tired but so fucking horny, and this is purely about getting off."

I touch my chest. "Be still, my beating heart. You really know how to put the romance in coming."

"Who needs romance when you can have orgasms?"

"Now, that's something I can't argue with."

Peyton smiles. "Cool. Because there is something I want to try."

"Yeah?"

"I saw this thing in porn where—"

"And now I'm scared."

"Is this so scary?" He grips my cock and gives me a stroke.

"No. Not scary at all. Keep going."

"I plan to." He lowers himself on top of me, still with his

hand wrapped around my dick, but then his cock slides into his fist, against mine.

His other hand rests next to my head, his fingers scrunched tight into my pillow. It allows him to hold himself up while he rotates his hips, dragging his cock along mine. He looks down between us and watches us moving together.

"It's even hotter in person," he mumbles. "Feels better than just my hand too."

We're both leaking precum, making it smoother for him to thrust against me, but I get stuck on his words.

"You've jerked off to gay porn?"

He slows his pace, and I immediately regret asking. "What, like you haven't?"

I run my hand down his back and grip his ass, pushing him into me so he'll move faster. "Not what I mean."

"Oh, you mean because I'm only a baby bi that my porn preferences would still be hetero?"

I'm about to argue when he lowers his head next to my ear.

"What if I told you I started watching gay porn and getting myself off while thinking about you? Imagining we were the ones in the clip doing hot, gay things together ..."

I throw back my head. "Pey ... Fuck. I want that. I want all of it."

"Another time. I want to come and go back to sleep."

"Priorities."

"Sleep, sex, food, football. They're all my needs, and it depends on the time of day in which they're prioritized."

"Happy to help out, but you want to maybe step it up a notch? Less talking, more frotting." I impatiently lift my hips.

"You're the one who sidetracked me with all the porn talk."

"And yet, you're still not mov——"

Peyton shuts me up by kissing me hard. It's a smart strategy on his part because all words die, and the only sounds to pass my lips are the moans encouraging him to move faster on top of me.

He holds me close this time instead of watching what he's doing.

Peyton fucks into his fist, our cocks rubbing against one another, and it feels amazing. Goosebumps break out over my skin, my breath catches while my body chases that high. Peyton's soft groans drive me closer and closer to the edge, pushing that line between climbing and falling.

And when he breaks his mouth from mine and his hard breaths hit my skin, my body finally gives in to him and tenses. I come all over Peyton's hand and my own stomach. Moments later, Peyton joins me, adding his own cum to my stomach.

He kisses his way from my neck to my mouth, his lips becoming pliant as I kiss him back. His muscles loosen, his body going slack on top of me. I could go to sleep like this, with his weight on top of me and a satisfied smile on my face.

Peyton eventually rolls off me and onto his back, a sated sigh leaving his lips as he does. "Shower?"

"Can't be bothered. We can do that when we wake up. Until then, I'm using your shirt to clean up this mess." I wave my hand over my abs.

He reaches over the side of the bed and then throws a T-shirt at me. "At least it's not my underwear this time."

"True." I wipe myself down and then throw his shirt on the floor.

Peyton pulls me back against him and spoons me. "All in

all, it was a pretty great Thanksgiving. I'm thinking about making it a tradition."

"Next year, I'm not getting drunk, though."

Peyton's arms tense around me, and I realize my fuckup way too late.

Rule number one when sleeping with someone who doesn't do relationships: Don't mention being any part of their future. Ever.

CHAPTER TWELVE

I THROW my helmet in my cubby, frustrated to say the least. We might have gotten only a few days off for Thanksgiving, but it might as well have been an entire season with how that practice went.

The rest of the team wasn't the problem. It was all me. Sure, I was making passes and pulling off plays, but it was a fight to make it feel smooth and seamless. This is the year I need to make count, and while I'm glad that mess of a practice couldn't be seen by anyone outside the team, if I play that badly next week, there's a chance the whole team won't be selected to play in the semifinal next month.

With college hockey or most other sports, it's the teams with the highest scores that go to finals and playoff games. Football is more difficult to work out because only four teams are selected from the power five conferences. Teams used to be selected by computer, but it's now done by committee so they can take in extra factors other than only scores. They take in schedule, head-to-head final results, comparison of results against common opponents, past championships, and all this crazy in-depth criteria.

There are only three games left of my college football career—that's if we make it all the way—and then it's a three-month wait until the draft. Three months where I need to make sure I stay on top of my game even if my season's over.

Because football should be my only focus.

Football and not Levi Vanderbilt.

The worst part about what Levi said the other night—about him not drinking at Thanksgiving next year—is that I could actually picture it. Even if I'm going to be in the NFL and I don't even know which team or where yet, one thing *is* certain: it won't be here. Unless San Diego wants to take their team back from LA, my future is anywhere but San Luco.

Still knowing that, it was easy to imagine a repeat of Thanksgiving. Too easy. And that's what scares me.

Because up until Levi came back into my life, I had nothing on my mind but football. Now I'm torn.

I've worked way too hard for way too many years to get distracted this close to the end. I can't do it. Telling myself that, though, doesn't make the frustration disappear. If anything, it makes it worse. Because even though I know I can't get carried away with Levi, I want to.

"Whoa, what's with the violence against the thing that is supposed to save your head?" Green asks beside me.

"Nothing. Everything. It's the game this weekend, it's the playoff, the draft …" *My sex life* …

Green smacks my shoulder. "You're being way too hard on yourself. We've had a killer season. Sure, there have been some challenges, but we're here now. This is the end. No matter what happens during the next game, there's no way you're not getting drafted."

Deep down, I know this, and like I told Levi, I'm generally good under pressure, but *this* ... this might be too much pressure. As the draft closes in, so do the walls around me.

My dads have been talking about being the number one draft pick since before I even knew what the draft was, and if I had a dollar for every time someone called me the next Marcus Talon, I wouldn't even need to play football because I could live comfortably until I was dead.

For years, everyone in the football world has said how I'm going to smash all the records. I'm the next GOAT.

What if I fail?

What if I don't make it?

What if everyone puts all these expectations on my career that no one could live up to?

"Are you okay?" Green asks. "You look pale."

"All good." But now that he mentions it, I might need to sit down.

My mind fuzzes over, and my pads sit so heavily on my chest it's like I can't breathe. This has never happened before.

Green grabs my water bottle and shoves it in my face.

I'm not dehydrated, but I take it anyway because I'd rather the team think that I am instead of what I suspect this is.

I ... I think I'm having a panic attack.

The most annoying thing about it is I don't know what's causing it: football or Levi?

Football *and* Levi?

He shouldn't even be a factor in any of this at all, but because he said one thing about a hypothetical future Thanksgiving, my brain has zeroed in on it and obsessed over how flippant the comment was ... or wasn't.

And this is exactly why I haven't let myself get mixed up with annoying, distracting problems like serious relationships in the past.

Usually when emotions and feelings start to take hold, I end the casual hookups and go back to being friends. It has been easy because I've seen the warning signs of them creeping up on me.

Like the urge to text just to see how they are instead of with purpose.

Hanging out without the expectation of it leading to sex.

Taking them to a party and not looking at anyone else but them.

I've already done all of that with Levi, yet I didn't notice it, and now that I have, I can't believe I missed it. All the signs have been right there, but I couldn't see them. Maybe I could blame it on knowing Levi back in high school, of our one-time hookup back then, or maybe deep down, I've seen my actions for what they are but have refused to acknowledge them because Levi's different than all the other hookups I've had.

I don't think it has anything to with him being a different gender than I'm used to or that it's all new and exciting. I think it's because I know, without having to say anything, that he understands me.

We understand each other. We're totally different in that I'm sporty and he's artsy. We're both confident in different ways, we were raised in different environments, yet deep down, we're exactly the same. We both know what it's like to have intense pressure pushing down on us. We both know what it's like to grow up privileged, to have the world handed to us on a silver platter. Others on the outside see that and think we're spoiled brats, getting anything and everything we want, but Levi and I both understand it's not that easy. Those privileges come with strings. Especially for him.

And because of that, we have a bond I hadn't planned on making with anyone at this stage of my life.

Even now, when I know I need to cool it for a while and refrain from seeing Levi, all I want to do is walk out of this locker room and text him. I want to go see him.

And even though I know I shouldn't, as soon as the room stops spinning and I shower and change from practice, contacting Levi is the first thing I do.

Me: *Fun fact. I might not be so immune to the effects of pressure after all. Turns out I am not invincible? What the fuck is up with that? I want a refund on my superpowers.*

Levi: *I want to make a joke here about asking for a refund on your face while you're at it, but I'm guessing you're looking for sympathy here not insults. Are you okay?*

I laugh and text back: *My face? Puhleeze, I should send more money to whoever graced me with such an amazing bone structure and jawline.*

Levi: *Your dad? You're Marcus Talon Junior.*

I wince and reply: *That's the problem. My season is about to finish, all my dreams are about to come true. Everything I've worked for. Everything I am. Everything my dads raised me to be is now.* I hit Send but I'm not done. I quickly follow up with: *What if I fuck it all up?*

Levi: *Do you want a supportive message like 'You won't fuck it up because you're awesome' or would you like me to offer to blow you so you don't have to think about it for a while?*

Me: *Where are you?*

Levi: *My place.*

Me: *I'll be there in ten.*

It takes only seven minutes to reach Levi's house, and as soon as he opens the door, I forget my manners and don't even say hi before advancing on him.

I can't help it. He looks adorable in an apron covered in paint and clay, his hair messy like it used to be in high school. He even has a smear of clay on his forehead.

I push my way inside and drop my bag, immediately pressing him against the wall with my hips pinning him in place. My mouth is on his a second later.

But he doesn't put his arms around me, and his lips are tentative. I force myself to pull back, but I keep my hips where they are, pressed against his, our cocks already hard between us. "Something wrong?"

He holds up his hands, which are a lovely shade of off-white from drying clay. "I was almost finished and about to wash up, but I think someone practically ran here."

"I did. And I don't care about your dirty hands. Kiss me."

"All right, but you can't ask me to do your laundry afterward."

"Deal."

Levi surges forward and fuses his mouth to mine. His arms wrap around me, and without warning, he pushes off the wall and spins us so I'm the one who's pinned. My back hits with a thud, but I don't care.

"Get your cock out for me," Levi murmurs against my mouth before breaking away. "I won't be able to use my hands this time because trust me, this stuff is a bitch to get off your skin. The last place you want it is anywhere … sensitive."

"Maybe we should revisit you getting washed up first."

Levi smiles. "Don't worry. I'm very good with only my mouth too."

"Can't wait to find out how good." I undo my pants.

I drop my jeans and underwear to my ankles and lift my T-shirt to tuck it under my chin.

Levi sinks to his knees, keeping his hands on his thighs over the top of the apron. And when he smirks up at me, looking so confident, I almost want to call a bluff.

Thank fuck I keep my mouth shut, though, because the second his lips wrap around my cock and he sucks all of me down to the back of his throat, I know this is going to be over with quickly.

Instead of bobbing his head and running his mouth all over me, he keeps my cock deep inside, only moving in small but powerful sucks. The suction and tightness around the head of my dick has me coming even sooner than I thought possible. It takes less time for me to come than it did for me to get my ass over here. I think even Levi is surprised by how fast it is because he has to pull back and take a breath.

The last of my cum dribbles out his mouth and down his chin before he uses a clean part of his apron to wipe it off.

"Damn." I slump against the wall.

Levi stands. "All better?"

"Yes and no. I'm anticipating jokes about having no stamina and being a little … premature."

"Nah. I think that just shows how much you needed that." Levi leans in and kisses my cheek. "It's also a compliment. I've still got skills."

"You should get an award for your skills. A parade even. Hero's medal of honor." Even to my own ears, my tone is flat.

"Then why don't you seem less stressed?"

I can't answer him. Not only because I don't want to, but because I actually don't know the answer.

The truth is the buzz in my veins is settling the anxiety clawing at the back of my mind, but at the same time, dread builds in my gut.

Which again makes me question what my real issue is: football or Levi?

All I know for sure is I'm not in the right mindset, and that needs to change. Preferably before this weekend.

Levi puts his hands on my shoulders, and I already know I'm going to hate to see what my shirt looks like after this. He must read my mind because he starts massaging my tired muscles and wipes his hands all over me. Then he looks at me so innocently, like I don't know what he's doing.

He shrugs. "I figured if the blowjob didn't help, maybe distracting you by being a brat might."

"How generous of you."

"You're welcome." He finally steps back, and I pull up my underwear and jeans. "You want to stay for a bit and talk about it?" Levi heads for the kitchen, washing his hands in the sink and taking his apron off.

I want to stay so fucking badly but not to talk about what's up with me. I want to stay because I want to hang out with him. I want to spend all my free time with him.

And I think I have my answer to my problem.

I can't spend any more time with Levi while I work toward the NFL. I already like him too much, and if we keep doing what we're doing, I'm going to fall ass over tit in love with him.

CHAPTER THIRTEEN

levi

I FROWN. "PEY?"

He hasn't moved since pulling up his jeans, and he's still hovering in the entryway to the apartment.

When he messaged, I wanted nothing more than to invite him over and talk him through whatever he's worried about, but considering I haven't even heard from him since the day after Thanksgiving when we awkwardly shuffled around each other wordlessly until I said I should get home and got the hell out of there, I figured he was looking for something more physical.

Now I'm thinking that was the wrong move because Peyton shakes his head and says, "Sorry. Umm, I'd love to stay and hang out, but this is a huge week coming up for me. Last game of the season and all."

"Oh, is it a home game?"

"It is."

I could drag Remy to another one. Maybe. But then I think about how the last one turned out and realize even bribery wouldn't work on Remy. Bribery might work on Brady, though. He'd already be at the game, and he does owe me one for keeping my mouth shut about his late-night visitors. Bribery, blackmail ... same thing, right?

The morning after our 3:00 a.m. run-in, I realized the guys he was with couldn't have been so random after all. The way Brady said it, he implied they were random guys who were at the party, but I distinctly remember them both being older and he told them to go to his room, and they immediately knew where it was.

So yeah, I could hold that knowledge over Brady's head if I wanted to.

Or I could put my big-boy panties on and go by myself. Though, that sounds a little sad.

Hopeless gay boy watches the star quarterback play football while everyone around them has no idea that they're hooking up. Yeah, that doesn't sound like fun.

"Does that mean after this weekend, the pressure will ease?" Maybe we can catch up then.

He shakes his head. "Not if we're selected to play in the playoff. Then we have a few weeks to train for that. So, I'm going to be busy for a while." Peyton averts his gaze, guilt written all over his face.

Yep. As I suspected, this was a flyby booty call. Not that I can blame him. I did lure him here with the offer of sex, so that's on me.

"Maybe we can catch up again after you win all of the football, then." My offer is empty because I don't want to be that guy. The one who waits around for breadcrumbs from the guy they like.

"Win *all of the football*?" he asks in amusement.

"Go Kings," I deadpan.

"Thanks for the support." Peyton picks up his bag off the ground.

"You're welcome. But for real, good luck. Uh, break a leg? I don't know what's good luck in these situations."

"Telling a football player to break a leg? Definitely not good luck."

"See, I'm learning things."

"I'm gonna ..." Peyton tilts his head toward the door.

"See you around."

He leaves, and I'm left with a sense of finality. My biggest fear of moving to California and going to FU has come true. I would have rather had Peyton as a friend than not at all, and even though it wasn't explicitly said, I know I'm not seeing him again.

At least, not until after football is done.

The realization football will never be done for Peyton hits me like a sucker punch to the gut.

While I don't think coming to SoCal was a mistake—I'm doing what I love here—crossing lines with the person who made me want to create my own path in life was.

That was definitely the blowoff.

I look back at the project I was working on before Peyton showed up and want to kick my own ass. It's another life art project that needs to express an emotion between two people. It needs to be obvious without a prompt, and I thought what I'd created represented love, but as I stare at the two hands intertwined, I have to laugh at myself because the message in my sculpture is clear: companionship.

Past me knew what was coming, even if it was on a subconscious level.

I'm an idiot. I take the rough sculpture and throw it in the trash.

Time to start again.

But when I check, I'm all out of clay. At least, I don't have enough for what I want to make. I'll need to stop by the art studio to grab more.

I go to my room to clean up, change out of my messy clothes, and wash up properly when I notice the dried clay on my forehead.

"Real fucking cute." I get a wet cloth to wipe it off. Peyton couldn't have told me it was there?

After making myself presentable, and with my keys and phone in hand, I head out. The sun is close to setting now, but the studio is open all hours for art students. There're allocated time slots you sign up for if you need to use the space, but I'm just going to get supplies.

When I reach campus, my name is yelled from somewhere close.

I lift my head to see Brady, his best friend, Felix, and Felix's boyfriend, Marshall, coming toward me. They're about the only names I remember from everyone I met at Peyton's Thanksgiving party. The others are a blur.

Felix is waving like a madman, Brady is avoiding eye contact, and Marshall has a warm smile on his face. When they get close, I go to say hi, but I'm not expecting Felix to hug me.

I stumble back. "Oh. Umm, hi."

"What are you up to?" Felix asks as he pulls back.

"Dropping by the ar—uh, law building. For a class thing."

"You have class? At this hour?" Felix looks puzzled.

"Ah, no. I need to pick up some notes a friend left me."

"You should come out with us when you're done. We're heading to Shenanigans for, well, shenanigans."

Brady still hasn't looked at me, and I can't blame him. He does, however, turn to Felix. "The man is busy. You don't pass law school without studying all the time."

Felix laughs. "That will be you next year."

Brady grunts. "Don't remind me."

"You're … doing the law program?" I ask. "Here?"

"Nah, he's moving to New York to start his big important job while he goes to law school there," Felix answers for him, and I try not to let my relieved breath come out too loudly.

Peyton knowing I'm not going to law school is one thing, but Brady? Then again, I'm holding on to a secret for him. It could be a tit-for-tat kind of situation if I wanted it to be.

Hopefully, it doesn't come to that.

"Come for a drink with us," Felix says again. "All study and no play is not good for your health."

I glance at Brady. He avoids eye contact.

At first, I think it's because of his three-way situation, but then a dreaded thought crosses my mind. Does he know what happened in my apartment literally half an hour ago? Did Peyton leave my place and immediately call his brother? They are close. Close enough to share that kind of thing with each other.

My need to know what he said outweighs my need for clay. "The notes can wait. They'll still be there for me tomorrow."

Brady's gaze narrows, and my paranoia picks up.

"Awesome," Felix says. "Let's go."

We leave campus and move as a group. Felix and Marshall are holding hands, which means Brady falls back in step with me.

"How are you doing?" I ask as casually as I can manage.

"All good here. How are *you*?"

The emphasis on that last word scares me. "Is there a reason I wouldn't be anything other than good also?"

"I dunno. You were pretty drunk the other night. Have you recovered? Do you … remember much?"

My internal panic settles somewhat. This *is* about his late-night visitors.

I try not to let my lips quirk as I say, "Yeah. I remember most of it."

"Most?"

"Well, yeah, I remember waking in the middle of the night and you getting me painkillers and water. That was sweet of you, by the way. Though I don't know what you were doing awake at three in the morning all by yourself."

Brady smiles, but then Felix turns, and he must be listening in.

"Oh, you mean how you walked in on Brady and his Navy SEALs half-naked and about to do the horizontal mambo?" He frowns. "Wait, in a three-way, are you all horizontal? At least one of you has to be upright. Or, I guess you could be on your sides, with—"

Brady shoves the back of Felix's head. "Shut it."

"Why? Everyone here knows."

"You told him, huh?" I ask.

"He doesn't keep secrets from me," Felix says proudly. "Only from his big brother. Which I still don't understand."

"Because it would kind of be coming out, right? I know Marcus Talon and Shane Miller are cool and open and every-thing, but saying 'I'm in a relationship with more than one person—'"

"It's not a relationship," Brady says. "It's nothing. That's why I haven't said anything. It's got nothing to do with … there being more than one of them."

I get the impression he was going to say something else but stopped himself.

"How are you going to survive in New York?" Felix asks. "I've heard it's a city of bottoms, and we all know you like to be thrown around."

"For fuck's sake, Felix. Stop talking." Brady runs a hand over his light brown hair. "Do I need to remind you who Levi's dating?"

And as much as I want to correct him, I'm too damn relieved that he still thinks Peyton and I are still fooling around. Technically, we are, but I know deep down that we're not. Just because Peyton hasn't said the words "You'll never see my dick again," that doesn't make them not true.

We make it to Shenanigans, and Marshall holds the door open for us all.

"What are we drinking? Brady's treat," Felix says.

"Is that so?" Brady asks.

"Hey, I bought you drinks last week."

"When there were only the two of us. How convenient."

"I'll get the drinks," I say. "What do you all want?"

They give me their drink orders, and Brady says he'll help me carry them over while Felix and Marshall go find us a table.

At the bar, the blonde girl I saw Peyton flirting with that one time approaches us with a warm smile toward Brady.

"You want your usual?" she asks.

"Yep. Two, thanks. Plus, a vodka and Sprite and a—" He turns to me.

"Whatever IPA you have on tap." It's still too soon since Thanksgiving to be drinking anything heavier.

Past me hates myself for drinking that much.

She makes our drinks and takes my credit card for payment, but when she hands it back, she only addresses Brady. "I haven't seen your brother around lately."

Brady sips his beer. "He's been really busy. You know, football."

"The season ends soon, doesn't it? Can you tell him I said hi? Midterms are kicking my ass. He'll know what I mean."

"Yeah, everyone in a thirty-foot radius knows what you mean." Oops, did that come out loud?

"I'll let him know." Brady grabs Felix's vodka and nods to me to follow him with Marshall's drink. When we're away from her, Brady leans in. "No need to be jealous of Casey. She and Peyton are just friends."

"Mm, friends with benefits. I'm sensing a theme with him." I don't mean it to sound so bitter because I knew what we were going in, but the idea that I had Peyton's cock in my mouth earlier today and he'll be inside her later or tomorrow …

"Peyton might not do serious relationships, but he doesn't fuck around on people he's seeing. I guarantee you, when I tell him Casey wants to fall into old patterns, he either won't call at all, or he will to let her down gently."

I wish I could believe him, but I don't. It's not a matter of gender or that I think she can give him something I can't, because I've never bought into the bullshit stigma that bisexual people can't make up their minds, but there is the fact that he's a college student, on the brink of the rest of his life, and we haven't established rules between us.

And after today, I'm anticipating being ghosted.

He has to focus on football, not exploring his bisexual side with his high school hookup.

He's free to do what he wants.

I just wish what he wanted was me.

Maybe I should have gotten something stronger than an IPA after all.

We get back to the table, where Felix and Marshall are leaning into each other and laughing. They're a cute couple.

Damn it.

Past me needs a serious slap in the damn face.

Felix rambles while we drink, and his bubbly personality is infectious, but after only one drink, Felix and Marshall make eyes at each other, and I already know what they're going to say before they say it.

Felix stands. "We're out."

"This is the real reason you invited Levi out, isn't it?" Brady asks. "Because you knew you'd be cutting out early to go have sex with your boyfriend."

Marshall's cheeks turn a tinge of pink, but Felix is shameless.

"Yep." He grabs his boyfriend's hand, and they both say their goodbyes as they leave.

Brady and I are both silent as soon as it happens. I sip my drink, and then he mirrors the action.

"And it's back to being awkward. That's fun," I say.

"I can't help it. You have the power to make my life hell."

"How?"

"You know things about me that only Felix knows. Well, and Marshall by association, but Marshall isn't part of my circle, so it's not a big deal."

The struggle in Brady's eyes is evident, and without thought, I put my hand on top of his to comfort him. He stares at our hands and then at me, but I need him to trust me when I say, "I wasn't lying when I said I won't tell your brother anything. Who you're with isn't my place to say. You'll come out to him when you're ready."

"He knows I'm gay, dude."

"Does he know you're poly?"

"I'm not." His tone is a little too defensive, and I'm guessing he's not comfortable with that label. Which is fine. Maybe he's not. Maybe the SEALs are college fun, and one day, he'll settle down with a singular man.

"Well, whatever or however you identify, it's not my place to say anything." I take my hand back. "But can I ask something? Feel free not to share with me, though."

"Sure."

"Why is it a big deal for your family to know? Your parents, I get, but Peyton? He loves you. I was there when you two grew up together, and while we might not have hung out, you two were thick as thieves. Always together."

"I keep telling myself I want to keep it from Pey because he'll tell our dads, but he won't if I ask him not to."

"I think you know why you won't tell him. Deep down, you know."

Brady blows out a quick breath. "I'm leaving."

I hold up my hands. "Okay, okay, we won't talk about it. You don't need to go."

He laughs. "I meant I'm leaving *them*. Kit and Prescott."

"The SEALs?"

"Yeah. I met them a few months ago, and we all agreed it was just fun whenever they're in town. But with graduation in

May and them being redeployed sometime in the next couple of weeks, it's going to be over. So there's no point telling Peyton when it's going to end soon anyway, and it's something he'll hold over my head as a joke."

I'm getting a better understanding now. He wants more, but he knows it's not an option, and can't I fucking relate to that.

"I'm not in law school," I blurt.

Brady's brow scrunches. "What?"

"I'm in the art program. Not law. I don't want to be a lawyer. I'm telling you this because if you're worried about me telling Peyton your secret, you can go straight to my father and tell him I'm using his tuition money for a pointless degree and I will never become a lawyer like he wants."

Brady pauses. "Damn. *No one* knows?"

"Your brother does, but I trust him."

"So you trust him with your secrets but not with where he puts his dick when you're not with him?"

"I didn't say that. Besides, he's allowed to stick his dick in whoever he wants. We're not … together. He made that clear from the beginning, and he made it even clearer when he came over this afternoon, got off, and then left." It's impossible to hide the bitterness in my tone.

It's easy for Brady to fill in the blanks: Peyton and I aren't together, but I want us to be.

Brady's back to being silent, but it's a different kind this time. Almost like it's in solidarity. "Fuck this. I'm buying us more drinks. We need them."

Can't say I disagree.

CHAPTER FOURTEEN

IT'S LATE when Brady comes through the front door. I'm in front of the TV, rewatching the team's last game and dissecting every flaw. It's borderline unhealthy.

Brady thinks so too because as he walks by me, he picks up the remote, turns the TV off, and then slaps the back of my head.

I look up at him. "What was that for?"

"You're an asshole."

"What did I do now?"

"You know what you did."

I stand to meet him, though he still towers over me. "I really, really don't. So why don't you fill me in?"

"I understand the type of pressure you're under. You know I do. Hell, I went through it at the high school level and hated it. I also know I'm one of the ones putting pressure on you to do great. To *be* great. But that doesn't mean you get to be an asshole to really sweet people."

"Whoa, who was I an asshole to?" And how did he know? *Please don't say Levi. Please don't say—*

"Levi."

Fuck.

"Uh-huh. There it is." Brady points to my face.

"There what is?"

"The Talon-Miller look of guilt. You look like our dads when you do that."

"How do you know I did anything?"

"I ran into him, and we went out for drinks."

"What? When? Why?"

Brady cocks his head. "You do remember I went to school with him back in Chicago too, don't you? We're friends now. We've bonded over how stupid Peyton Miller is."

"Wow. Really? Taking his side without hearing mine? What happened to brothers forever and all that shit?"

"Hos before bros ... brother." Brady grins.

"You don't even know what happened. I doubt Levi even knows. I ... I freaked out."

"Because Levi likes you, and you're scared he's going all jersey chaser on you? Yeah, you're not as subtle as you think. He got all that."

My heart sinks. "Is that what he thinks?"

"What do you expect? You went over there, got off, and then bailed. Poor form. He likes you, and you're using him."

"It's not him liking me that's the problem," I mumble. "And I'm not using him."

"Then what ..." Brady's entire face lights up. "You have feelings for him. Big, strong, scary *feelings*. This is the best early Christmas present ever."

"This isn't a good thing, Bray." I only use that nickname when he's in trouble.

"Yes, it is, *Pey*."

"No, it's not. Because it's already affecting my game. Instead of focusing on this weekend, my physical fitness, all I can think about is Levi and how much I want to be with him. Everything I've worked for is on the line."

"Ah. You always have been shitty at compartmentalizing."

"How am I supposed to separate the two?"

"Easy. When you're playing football, focus only on football. When you're with Levi, focus on Levi. It's not rocket science."

"Okay, and then what about classes? The draft? What happens when Chicago picks me and I move back home?"

"First, Chicago isn't going to choose you. You'll be snapped up long before they get a chance for their number one pick. Two, if that did happen, at least you'd see Levi again. You know his dad is going to march his ass home when he finds out he's not actually in law school out here. And three—"

"Levi told you that? Why?"

"Like I said, we're friends now. And I'm Team Levi. Find a way to pull your head out of your ass and make it right." Brady storms toward his bedroom.

He's right. I know he is.

But I don't know *how* to make it right.

Something has to give, and if it can't be football or classes, that only leaves Levi.

I have no idea what to do.

I take out my phone and stare at Levi's name and the messages we've sent back and forth since he first came back into my life. I'm not usually someone who texts a lot, and if I do, it's always for a purpose.

When I want to find a hookup, I send a simple: *WYD* to whoever I'm seeing at the time.

They're all one-word answers or acronyms. There's no asking how they are or talking about life in general.

It's been different with Levi from the start. He said he moved here for me, and I didn't freak out. He said it would be hard not to fall for me, and I was flattered. These things would normally make me run the other way and cool things off, but they only made me want to spend more time with Levi. But when I think about why he's different than past hookups I've had, I can't find any logical reasoning other than he's from my childhood, my old life, and he knows what it's like to grow up surrounded by the pressures that come with all of that.

Some might argue that him being a guy and all my other exploits being women might have something to do with it too, but it's not even a factor in my feelings toward him. If anything, his gender is more of a reason to back away because coming out this year only adds to the other bullshit the media will put me through leading up to the draft.

I need advice, and normally I'd turn to Brady, but seeing as he is firmly on Levi's side on this—though I don't know why; his future career is tied to mine, so he should be worried about me—there's only one other option. And I really, really, really don't want to go to them with this.

With a groan that starts at the back of my throat, I hit Call on Dad's number.

He answers almost immediately. "Before you start, you can't talk us out of coming to your game this weekend. We're already packing for our flight tomorrow morning, and your coach has invited us to be down there on the field during the game to keep up your team's morale."

"Jesus Christ, that's not embarrassing at all. But this isn't about that. I need … advice."

"What's up? Is it your arm? Have you been pushing too hard? What's going on with football?"

It figures he'd think it's about that.

"It's not about football. Well, not directly. It's about … Levi." I'm met with silence. "Dad?"

"Hang on, you need to be on speaker for this."

I could do with Pop's opinion on this too.

"Hey, Pey," Pop says at the same time Dad asks, "What's happened? When we were there, it seemed like you two would only be friends."

"Nothing's happened. Like, stuff has happened, but not, like advanced stuff or anything, and we're not together. Or dating."

"That has to be code for hand stuff," Dad says to Pop.

"What we've done doesn't matter. It's all the stupid *feelings* that come with it."

Dad sniffs. "Our little boy has his first feelings for another boy—"

"For once in your life, can you be serious? Please?"

"No," Dad says but follows it up with, "Ouch. Why'd you hit me?"

Thank you, Pop.

"I've never been this way with any of the girls I've been with, and you know my priority has always been football, and if it were any year but this one—"

"It is poor timing," Dad says. "When your dad and I were in college, we were nowhere near ready to deal with the feelings we had toward each other. It took us six more years to get there."

"Sure. '*We.*'" Pop scoffs.

"Okay, your pop never made me aware that we were falling in love. Better?"

"No. You say that like it was my job to point out how *you* felt about me."

I cut in. "As much as I love it when you two bicker between yourselves instead of, you know, parenting, I kind of need direction."

At the same time, I'm given two different answers.

Dad's response is the obvious one. "Focus on football, not dick."

While Pop's is something I should expect from him but don't. "Follow your heart."

"Well, that clarifies everything. Thank you so much for your help."

"Could it be anxiety over your future?" Pop asks.

"What do you mean?"

"Self-sabotage. All athletes go through it at one point. Maybe your infatuation with Levi is your brain's way of needing time off football to recharge."

"Are you saying my feelings for Levi aren't real?"

"No, but it's possible."

Dad sighs. "Listen, Pey." His tone has taken on a serious quality that I've only ever dreamed of hearing from him. Sure, he can be serious when it comes to football, but even then, he always has a playful and goofy side. He has always made sure football was fun for us and not shoved down our throats. He didn't only share his love of the sport with us, but he wanted Brady and me to love it as much as he does.

"One thing I learned from falling for your father is if you find the love of your life, the universe has a way of making sure you're together," Pop says. "Even if it takes six years for it to happen."

"Your focus right now needs to be football," Dad argues. "You're so close to the end and everything we've worked for. Like Pop says, if it takes six more years to be with Levi, then that's what it does. You might even forget all about Levi Vanderbilt once you're in the NFL."

"I've been telling myself that for weeks, but I still can't … I keep …" I grunt. "I can't get Levi out of my head. What kind of media shitstorm am I looking at if I have a boyfriend when I'm drafted?"

Silence. Again.

"We need to get Damon in on this call," Dad says.

"Don't do that. You know I can't use him as my agent yet."

"Well, it's talk to Damon now, wait until your season is over, or deal with this yourself. What do you want to do?"

I really have to think about that because I don't know. The season could be all over this weekend after our last regular season game. It'll definitely be over next month at the latest if we're chosen for the playoff. Then I can have all the talks in the world with Uncle Damon about my future because I'll be free of the NCAA clause that states players can't have representation while playing Division I football.

One month to focus solely on football.

After that? Maybe I should take Dad's advice and leave it up to the universe.

"I'll do the right thing," I mutter to my dads. And when we end the call, I do something I need to do, but it feels so wrong. I text Levi, each word I type making my stomach churn.

Is it okay if we cool it for a while? I really need to focus on football.

It's a cop-out, and I hate it, but there's no other option for me at this point in my career.

I don't know how I'm going to make it a month. It hasn't even been a week yet, and as we hit the field for our last game of the season, my gaze goes to the thousands of faces in the stands. Levi probably didn't come.

Not after the single-letter text I got in response to the one I sent him. "*K.*" It's not like I could've called him out on it either because what I did deserves that kind of response.

I've been strong by sticking to my resolve and what Dad said. Football has to be my only focus. It helps that Dad and Pop flew in and have been in my head all week about plays and working out. They basically haven't left my side, and I can't help wondering if they're babysitting me so I don't sneak out so I can have sex with the big distraction that is Levi Vanderbilt.

What is this, high school?

I'm not saying it's unwarranted, but still.

Brady brings Levi up almost every day any spare chance he gets when our dads aren't listening, but my brother doesn't get it. He doesn't understand how it's hard for me to stay away from Levi but even harder to chase after him.

Brady doesn't get attached to anyone he hooks up with, and he never had the drive or the passion for football. Playing anyway. He loves the game as much as the rest of our family, but he's never had that pull in two opposite directions, so he doesn't know what uncertainty is like. My brother has known what he has wanted to do with his life since freshman year of high school, and he has never met anyone who makes him question it all.

Not that I'm questioning football. I want football, and I want Levi, but we're in a hopeless situation where having one risks the other and vice versa.

As the team takes our spot on the sidelines, my gaze catches Brady. Not only him but the guy next to him as well. He brought Levi. To my last game.

I should be mad, or maybe I should worry about that throwing off my focus, but I'm not. Damn, Levi looks good. He hasn't styled his hair, and in the last few weeks, it's grown out and reminds me of how it used to be. I want to run my hands through it.

Pop's large hand grips my shoulder. "Is your head in the game?"

"Are you asking for you or dad? Depending on your response, it will affect my answer."

"For me."

"Then you should know that if it was, you wouldn't even need to be asking that."

Pop turns me toward him and puts his hands on my shoulders. "I will deny I ever said this, but if you want to walk out of here and not play this game, if the pressure is too much, say the word, and you and I can run away to Mexico. Dad will never find us to kick our asses."

I snort. "As much as I love that you would do that for me, it's not football that's getting me down. And it's not Levi. It's ..."

"It's that you want both but are under the impression it's not going to be possible?"

"Exactly."

"Here's the thing. There came a time in your dad's and my relationship where we had to choose between hiding our relationship or coming out, which in turn could have affected our careers. It almost felt like we needed to choose each other or football. We were stuck between hiding it or making the conscious choice to say, 'Hey, you're the person I want to be with, and if that comes with consequences, we can face them together.' Even if it means we lose our careers. Our money. We chose to make each other our number one priority while still going for the things we wanted. And we have a Super Bowl win to prove it."

"Two. Technically."

"Nah, I don't count that first one. I only played a couple of regular season games that year. But my point is, we did it. We put everything on the line and got everything we ever wanted."

"What are the chances of something like that happening twice? My biggest fear is either spending too much time with Levi to the point football suffers or focusing only on football like Dad wants and losing Levi because I'm not there for him enough."

"Those are both hypothetical situations, though."

"What do you mean?"

"You're acting like a relationship is the worst thing that could happen to your career. Sure, there will be some media scrutiny, but you're Marcus Talon's son—you were always going to be in the media spotlight, no matter who you date."

"That's true," I murmur.

"You're worried about the fallout of something that hasn't even happened yet. You're in your head, which means that if you get out on that field tonight and fuck up, it's not Levi's

fault. You possibly dating or not dating Levi isn't to blame.
The only person to blame is you because you're making this
into a bigger issue than it needs to be."

He's right. He's so right.

But acknowledging that doesn't make the unease go away.
Not completely anyway. Irrationality doesn't give a shit about
logic.

"Thanks, Pop."

"Your head in the game now?"

No, but if I keep reminding myself that it doesn't have to
be one or the other, I think I can be ready. "I ... I think so."

"Just remember that your whole future doesn't actually ride
on tonight's outcome. No matter what happens out there,
you're getting drafted. Your record stands on its own. The only
change it might make is you won't be the number one draft
pick, and that's not a bad thing. At all."

He's right about that too.

"It'll be less pressure," I say.

"Exactly. I know your dad has raised both you and Brady
to want to be the best. To strive to win. That's how your dad is
built. But I want you to remember, coming in second or third
isn't the same as losing. I didn't have the greatest offensive
tackle stats, but I still made my mark on the world of football,
and you can do it too. There's a spot for you in the NFL. All
you have to do is get out of your head and take it. That is, if
you still want it?"

I love that he's double-checking this is what I actually
want. Brady and I talk about how hard it is being the sons of
Marcus Talon and Shane Miller, but the truth is, if we turned
around and seriously told our parents we wanted to be
anything else—an artist like Levi, have a boring office job so

we could be 'normal' for once in our lives, or in Brady's case, a sports agent—we know we'd have the support of our dads.

It just so happens that I love football. "I do want it." But I also want Levi.

I look out at the stands again, directly where Levi is, and his eyes catch on mine. If I follow my heart like Pop says, it doesn't have one destination. It has two.

It's a harder path to follow, but I'm hoping committing to it will make it easier. There is no either-or for me.

Dad bounds over to Pop and me and slaps my shoulder. "Ready to get out there and show them what you've got?"

This time, I actually am. "Ready to get out there and win."

CHAPTER FIFTEEN

levi

THE WHOLE GAME, I go back and forth between worrying that Peyton will be mad that I came and enjoying watching him kick ass. Well, *he's* doing well. The actual game is close.

Me being here is exactly what Peyton asked me not to do. He wants to cool things, and here I am, cheering him on anyway. I'd like to say it's because I'm a bigger person and we can still be friends, but it's not. Brady dragged me here. Apparently, we're friends now? Or he likes to see his brother in awkward situations and lives for it. Yeah, it's probably the latter. I'm just collateral damage in that game.

Brady's had his head in his phone the whole time. In the brief moments he hasn't, he explains what's happening on the field so I can understand better. It still makes no sense to me, but there's something about the atmosphere of a game that gets me excited.

It's in the way the crowd's anticipation grows the closer to the end zone the team gets, the collective disappointment when it doesn't happen, or even better, when it spills over to a celebration as one of our guys crosses the line for a touchdown.

For the first time in my life, I might not understand football, but I do understand team mentality. It's not only the football team on that field; it's the entire school. If Peyton wins, we win, and that high carries over.

Though, at the moment, there's nothing but anxiety filling the stadium. Fresno State has evened the score, and now, time is running out.

Franklin U has possession of the ball, and they're slowly making their way down the field, but I have no idea if they're going to manage to score again.

My heartbeat thrums fast and hard. I've never been a competitive person before—I did debate club and all those other academic contests because my father made me, not because I enjoyed them—but in this moment, there's a growing need inside me to see victory.

Sure, it might be for Peyton's sake more than mine, but the adrenaline of it all is addictive.

Felix says something to Brady about watching the game instead of his phone, but I can't take my eyes off the field to join in on their conversation. His words do catch my attention, though.

"Peyton's not even on the field."

"Ah, look again." I point.

They're so close to the end zone now. One good throw from Peyton and they could score if one of his runners can get there. I don't know who is who or what position does what, but I'm getting the gist of what needs to be done.

Brady and Felix bicker back and forth, but I'm back to not paying them any attention. All my focus is on Peyton as he throws the ball the farthest I've ever seen him throw. One of his teammates is waiting for it in the end zone.

Everyone gets to their feet, watching as he catches it, and Franklin pulls ahead with only a couple of minutes left on the clock.

"Fuck yes!" Brady yells.

But when I look, he's staring at his phone again, not celebrating over the touchdown like the rest of us.

Felix looks over Brady's shoulder. "You have a three-way to get to, don't you?"

I try to hide my amusement, but a laugh slips out.

Then Brady's eyes are on me. "Can you cover for me with Pey?"

I'm hesitant, not only because I haven't seen Peyton since he blew me off, but because while I'm okay with keeping Brady's secret, I draw the line at flat out lying. When I tell him as much, Felix cuts in.

"You're going to have to tell your brother eventually."

"No, I won't. The guys are about to be deployed, so this is our last chance. Gotta go. If he asks, tell him I was here for the whole game, but once it was over, I left without explanation."

In the next second, he's gone, and the final buzzer sounds a couple of minutes later. Though it feels like another twenty. This whole stop-start nature of football is both exhilarating and annoying. When you think the game is going to end, the clock stops, and we have to wait.

"You okay on your own?" Felix asks, and it's sweet of him to care.

"I'm a big boy." Even if I'm shitting myself at having to be the one to break this silence Peyton's been throwing at me all week. Then again, it's not like I *have* to see him. Brady didn't specifically ask me to go tell Peyton anything. Just said if Peyton asks. If I don't see Peyton, then I don't have to lie to him.

Felix stands to leave, but then he sits right back down.

"What are you—"

"I have to watch this."

"Watch what?"

He nods toward the field, where the visiting team is filing out to go toward the locker rooms, but Peyton's team is still celebrating on the field and waving to the crowd. That's not what Felix is looking at, though.

Peyton is walking toward us. His helmet is off, his hair covered in sweat and plastered to his head. He looks so good in his purple-and-gold jersey, his tight gold pants showing off his powerful legs.

The last game I went to, they were wearing the same purple color, but when I saw a game on TV last year when I was contemplating coming here, they were wearing a white jersey with purple pants. There must be significance to the uniforms—like, they wear one for home games and the other for away or something, but it doesn't matter because Peyton looks mouthwatering in both.

Peyton picks up pace as he gets closer to the stands and jumps the barricade with his laser-focused gaze on me.

Oh shit, oh fuck, oh damn my stupid heart skipping a beat. My mouth is dry. I try to move, but my legs don't work, and I can't make myself stand as the clacking of his cleats on cement echoes in my ears.

He said he wants to cool it, and now he's charging up the steps to do what? Kick me out? Pull me out in front of everyone and embarrass me so I hate him and really will leave him alone?

Peyton climbs the steps and towers above me. He holds out his hand to help me up while wearing the sexiest smile I've ever seen on him. And that's saying something because Peyton Miller can be sexy by just breathing. His smile? It's damn breathtaking. And right now, it's trained on me.

I accept his help with a shaky hand, still unsure of what he's doing, and he pulls me up.

And then, in front of thousands of people and ESPN, he does the last thing I expect. Peyton leans in and presses his lips against mine.

I'm taken aback and almost stumble—*real fucking graceful, Levi*—but Peyton's there to hold me close to him. His strong arms close around me, and with his pads on, he's twice my size.

His gloved hand cups my cheek, and my lips part, letting his tongue slip inside my mouth, but when hollering and deafening screams fill the arena, I pull back.

My cheeks are warm, and I'm sure they're bright red.

"Meet me after I shower and change?" Peyton murmurs.

All I can do is nod, my entire body numb from shock.

It's all over as fast as it began, and Peyton bounds back down the steps of the stadium and back onto the field to follow his teammates down the tunnel to the locker rooms.

A loud sigh comes from Felix beside me. "Seriously, why does Peyton work this out for himself after I've become a taken man? When I think of all the sexperimentation I could've done with him the last couple of years—"

"It's nothing," I say without thinking. Though I don't know why. Because that? It was anything but meaningless.

The people surrounding us stare blankly at me, as if waiting for an explanation to come pouring out my mouth.

"Let's get out of here before we go viral."

Felix pats my shoulder. "Yeah, good luck with that. There were about a hundred phones pointed in your direction when it happened."

Well, fuck.

Peyton takes a long time to meet me by the players' entrance of the stadium, and with each passing moment I'm left waiting, the deeper the paranoia becomes.

I end up sending him a text to come to my house when he's free.

That ends up being worse because the pit of doubt in my gut only grows when minutes tick by one after the other with no word from him. I thought it was the thousands of eyes on me making me edgy, but it has nothing to do with that and everything to do with Peyton making a great big grand gesture and then possibly not following through.

But when there's a buzz at the door for him to be let up, I let out a loud breath of relief.

I hate that a guy can strip away my confidence little by little, but Peyton isn't just some random guy, and it's not his fault I'm like this. I've never been so invested in someone before, where the fear of rejection is so high. Especially because I know Peyton's in a tough position with his football career. I have no doubts that if his future agent or his parents tell him to end it with me, he will.

His dads were supportive last time they were here, but that was before everything was so … public.

I open the door and wait for Peyton to climb the steps to get to the second level. Then he's there, fresh from a shower, wearing a suit, and being way too casual about it. No one has the right to look that good and not flaunt it, but Peyton's not like that.

He might have an athlete's ego when it comes to football, make jokes about how awesome he is, but the way he carries himself is completely different.

He smiles wide when he sees me waiting and greets me with another off-guard kiss, as if he's finishing the one we shared earlier in front of everyone.

With no one to interrupt us this time, I don't want it to end. I grip his jacket lapels and pull him inside my apartment.

He doesn't have his gear bag that he usually carries with him, so he's free to move his hands all over me. They run down my back, grip my ass, then wander back up my body and tangle in my hair.

We stumble backward, blindly trying to find my bedroom as we both refuse to part. When my back hits the corner of the kitchen island, it becomes a safety hazard to keep going.

"Ow, fuck." I laugh.

"You okay?" Peyton's blue eyes are filled with the type of concern that makes my heart melt. It's genuine and patient.

"I will be if we can get to my bedroom without getting any more bruises."

Taking my hand, Peyton steps back and pulls me down the hall. "You know, I was kind of hoping you'd be naked by the time I got here."

"That would've been a bit presumptuous, don't you think?"

He shrugs. "Maybe, but I would've enjoyed it."

As soon as we're in the safety zone of my bedroom, Peyton turns on me and goes back to where we were, kissing, groping, and desperately holding on to one another like it's going to be all taken away at any moment.

There are things that need to be said. Questions I still have about what this is or what it could be. But I'm willing to hold them back and take this for what it is.

I want to take everything from him just in case it ends with him walking out again like last time.

This could be it. All that I get.

One kiss in front of cameras isn't a claim of forever. The whole thing could be easily explained away to save his career. The questions flitting through my head, wanting to know what exactly is happening with us and what's suddenly changed, are easily ignored because the need I have for his body is louder.

As heartbreaking as it would be for Peyton to take it all back, it will hurt even more to stop this and end things here.

"I want you inside me," I say against his lips.

"Why aren't we naked yet?"

"We need to fix that," I agree.

We pry apart, and I'm naked a lot quicker than Peyton. It helps I don't have to wrestle a tie, belt, tight suit pants, and socks and shoes. While he strips out of them, I go to my bedside table, where I have my usual stock of supplies on hand.

My cock is so achingly hard, I give it a taming stroke. Or, try to. Next thing I know, Peyton's crawling across the bed toward me and wrapping his arm around my waist from behind while his free hand lands on top of mine on my dick.

"Let me do that." He leans in and nips at my cheek and my neck.

I let him take over and regret it immediately because his hand feels so good. "Wait ... I—"

His hand stills. "What's wrong?"

"It's not going to take much to send me over the edge."

"Oh, thank God. I thought you were about to change your mind."

I shake my head. "Not possible at this point."

Without warning, Peyton pulls me down on the bed and rolls us so he can climb on top of me. His lips fuse to mine again.

I lost the supplies somewhere between falling and being pinned to the mattress, but I don't even care. Peyton surrounds me, and as I run my hand down his chest between us and over his amazing body, his abs tighten under my fingertips.

He kisses me hard and rough, his tongue dominating mine, and I can't help moaning into his mouth.

I keep trailing my fingers down until they brush the head of his cock, which is wet with precum. My stomach is sticky, and it turns me on like fucking crazy knowing that he's leaking for me. *On* me.

I want to taste him, but that will only sidetrack me from what I really want. No, what I *need*: Peyton filling me up, stretching me wide, and then taking me until there isn't any doubt who I belong to.

Blindly, I feel around the bed for wherever I dropped the lube without breaking from Peyton's mouth. My fingers wrap around the bottle, but the sound of the cap catches Peyton's attention.

He pulls up, but I hold him to me so he can't get far.

"I can do that," he whispers.

"You know how?" I half tease. Only half because it is a genuine question. I've been topped by guys before who thought too much lube would desensitize them, so they were telling me I was ready when I really, really wasn't.

"I'm assuming it can't be that different to getting a woman ready."

"I wouldn't know."

"Really? You never?"

"I hooked up with girls, sure. Kissing. Blowjob. Things like that. But I knew something wasn't … right. So I didn't even try to go all the way with one."

"How about you let me do my thing, and you can tell me if you need more from me?"

I had no idea that confidence in admitting not being sure about something could be so hot. That Peyton wants to make sure I'm okay and he's open to communication … Fuck, I fall for him a little more.

"Levi? I'm going to need an answer."

"Oh, right." I nod. "Yes. Do it."

"Remember to tell me if you need something else."

"I will."

Peyton moves down my body, kissing along my skin while he takes the lube from my hand. I raise my head and watch him as I lift my legs and put my feet flat on the bed.

I kind of expect him to go straight for the prepping part, but surprising me, he wraps his lips around the head of my cock when he presses the pad of his lubed finger against my hole.

The urge to watch is too much, but my neck hurts from

trying to keep my head up, so I lean up on my elbows for better viewing.

Peyton pushes his finger in, slowly at first, fighting against the pressure as I bear down on him. At the same time, he takes more of my cock inside his mouth.

His lips are wide, and I can imagine what it would feel like to lift my hips and slam in between them, making them stretch further. It takes all of my control to refrain from doing that.

We're on the bunny slopes, not a black diamond run.

I try to say something to encourage him, let him know how good he's doing, but all that comes out is a shuddery breath.

His lashes flicker as his gaze lifts to mine, his bright blue orbs filling with heat. My cheeks are flushed; I can feel the warmth from them, and when Peyton pushes his finger inside me deeper, my whole body breaks out in the same euphoric glow.

"Keep rubbing that spot." I throw my head back and enjoy the tingles running down my spine and into my balls.

My gut burns with want, my cock leaks with pleasure, and when Peyton hums around the taste, I almost come too soon. Way too soon.

I grip his hair tight and pull him away from my dick. "Need ... breather ..."

Without having to tell him, he adds a second finger, bringing back the sting in my ass and dimming the pleasure. He might not have done this before, but fuck, he knows what he's doing.

I lie back again, looking up at the ceiling while trying to concentrate on my breathing and letting him in more.

Peyton's stare burns into me, even though I can't actually see him. It's like he's touching me with his gaze. He's watching me for my reactions. "Out of all the possibilities of things I'd find sexy about hooking up with a guy, I didn't think sucking cock would be high on the list of things I love."

I huff. "Blowjobs are awesome. Giving or receiving. Maybe you should get back to it."

"You calmed down a bit?"

"Yep. Give me your mouth again." The anticipation of it is enough to send me back to spiraling close to the edge, but I breathe through it. Even when the pressure of his mouth tightens around me. Or when he bobs his head, sucking hard on the upstroke.

I'm not going to come.

Rotating my hips to try to move with him, I barely notice the fingers in my ass still stretching me. I'm taking them a lot easier now, and I'm close to being ready, but this feels just so. Damn. Good.

"I'm almost ready. Maybe one more finger?"

He lifts his head, and I complain with a whine. That must be enough instruction for him because he lowers his head again and does as I ask.

It's tight, but I'm so worked up, I take it and the sting. I continue to meet his moves with my hips, though they lose the timing, and we're no longer in sync. Peyton takes my erratic moves in stride, even when I accidently bump his nose with my groin.

I can't keep this up. The sensation is too much. It's going to have me coming down his throat instead of while he's inside me. And I want him inside me.

Screw it. "I'm ready."

The relief when he pulls off my cock is short-lived because he replaces it with his free hand. "Are you sure?"

"Yes."

He strokes me hard and slow, but I'm so close, all it does is draw me closer and closer.

"Shit. Yes." I can't breathe.

Peyton sits up between my legs, pulling them over his thick thighs. He lines up his cock, and it presses against my hole, but then I tense.

"Fuck. Condom. Where did they go?"

Peyton's eyes widen, and he pulls back, looking frantically for them on the bed. "Sorry. I totally spaced."

"It's okay, so did I." I hate to ruin the moment, but I don't want us to do anything either of us will regret once the heat of the moment passes.

"Ah. They fell on the floor." He leans over and picks them off the floor, tearing into one and rolling it down his thick cock. It's not a monster dick, but still big enough to make it feel like he's splitting me in two. That little moment of doubt I usually get at this stage seeps in.

I pass him the lube. "Use some more of that too."

"You want it to feel like a slip 'n' slide, huh?"

"Now there's an image, but yes, basically."

He stares down at me while stroking himself, spreading a liberal amount of lube over the condom. "Let's try this again."

This time, when his dick finds my entrance, I don't freeze up. I let him slide right inside me, and in this moment, he gives me everything I've thought about for four years.

Peyton Miller, California, becoming an artist … It's a life I never thought I could possibly chase, let alone have.

I hold on tight for the ride and refuse to let go. Because this isn't just sex.

It's everything I've ever wanted.

CHAPTER SIXTEEN

HOLY SHIT. When Brady said having sex with a dude is a lot better than any woman, I thought he only said it because he's gay. That's a given in his case. But I can't deny this is the best sex I've ever had, and I haven't even come yet.

Hell, I could not come at all and still think it was so damn amazing. It's not the action; it's not moving inside of Levi that makes it great. It's how present he is. How he stares up at me with lust in his eyes and his lips parted, like they're anticipating more.

I want to lean in and kiss him again, but as I slam inside him in the position I'm in—leaning up on my left elbow with my right hand planted firmly next to Levi's head—I can see every expression on his beautiful face.

Levi might be a Vanderbilt, but it's only in name. Right now, he looks like debauchery and sin wrapped up in a disheveled socialite. He has never been more attractive to me.

"Pey," he breathes.

I thrust inside him once more, and he cries out. "What do you need?" I ask.

"Your hand ... dick. Friction."

There's a joke about me making him lose the ability to speak properly, but I swallow it down for fear of ruining the mood. His skin is a pretty shade of pink, his eyes keep glazing over, and I want to give him anything and everything he wants.

I put my weight on the hand holding me up and reach for his cock with my other one.

"Yes. That," Levi hisses.

I stroke him, moving my hand in time with my hips, getting faster and faster with each pass.

Levi's fingers dig into my back, and I know he's close. His eyes roll back in his head, his body tenses, and then warmth fills my hand. He falls apart beneath me, grunting through his release.

My cock throbs as I keep going, making sure he gets everything he possibly can out of his orgasm. His ass is so tight, and I have to grip the comforter to stop my hand from slipping as I thrust harder and faster.

Levi doesn't let me go, just continues to hold on while I keep fucking him. He meets my every move with his hips. Takes all of me. And just when I think I could keep going all night, my orgasm slams into me harder than a defensive end sacking me.

My muscles turn to jelly and can barely hold me up as I empty into the condom.

Levi grabs the back of my head and pulls me down on top of him so my entire weight is against him and my head is buried in his shoulder.

Before I have to pull out of him, I rotate my hips slowly, drawing out every last ripple of pleasure I can.

Then we're both still.

Silent.

But the buzz in my veins is loud.

Levi taps my shoulder. "Peyton?"

"Mm?"

"Your phone's vibrating on the floor somewhere."

Shit. I guess it's not my veins buzzing after all.

Slowly, I pull away from Levi and climb off the bed, stumbling to the bathroom to get rid of the condom. Levi joins me a few seconds later and runs a face cloth under some water to wipe himself down.

He smiles sheepishly at me, and it's so fucking cute I can't help pulling him against me and kissing him softly.

"You should check your phone," he says when I pull back.

"I should." I don't want to, but I need to.

I haven't told Levi yet, and I really don't want to have to break the news to him, but my impromptu public kiss has already gone viral.

Once upon a time, coming out like this would be scandalous. Now, it's not shocking, but it is still news. I remember my parents saying one day in the future, no one will have to come out because it will be so widely accepted.

But today is not that day.

Not to mention the entire coaching staff losing their heads over pulling a stunt like that when I know we're supposed to be on our best behavior. Especially when media is involved. We have so many more rules than professional players that any little misstep can cause the team pain.

For instance, when someone scores a touchdown in the NFL, they might dance, spike the ball, or even leap into the stands to celebrate. Sure, they're fined if they cross the line into lewd behavior, but if we so much as do a shimmy or a fist pump, we're penalized fifteen yards on the next play.

Something as crazy as running up the stands to kiss a random boy ... yeah, I know why my phone is going off. I'm just too scared to answer it.

I lean in and kiss the top of Levi's hair before facing the music, but as soon as I put my underwear back on and pick up my phone to a million notifications, I'm filled with the urge to power it down because that's a whole bucket of nope.

The blowup does make me realize I need to talk to Levi about it, though, or he might leave this apartment in the morning and walk into an ambush of questions.

Levi walks out of the bathroom and moves to his dresser. "Who was it?"

"Who wasn't it?" I mutter.

He takes a fresh pair of underwear out and slips them on. "What does that mean?"

"I ... I think we need to talk."

"Is this because of the kiss? Has it blown up?"

I take a deep breath, but my words still come out in a rush. "It has, and as much as I wish I could say I regret it, I don't. But I will regret it if you're brought into the media circus it's bound to bring. It was really poor timing, but before the game, Pop said something that really resonated with me. That no matter what, no matter who I'm dating, the media spotlight will always be on me because of where I came from. Who my parents are. And when I made that final pass that won us the game, I wanted everything Pop said I could have if I chose it. I could have football and a relationship with a man. So I did a selfish thing that will impact you, and I really should have spoken to you first, and—"

Levi steps forward and cuts off my rambling with his mouth on mine. His lips are soft and reassuring, and when he pulls back, he's smiling. "That was a moment I will never, ever forget, and if you had asked me beforehand, the only thing holding me back would have been concern over how it would affect you."

My lips quirk on one side. "I'm going to hold you to that when the media are relentlessly trying to get you to talk to them."

He leaves the room and comes back with his phone. "Nothing yet."

"Let's enjoy the peace while we can."

"So, we're doing this? You and me? Is this dating or ..." His cheeks flush. "I know you said you don't do relationships, and you need to focus on football—"

"This is different."

"Why?"

I press my lips together, trying to find the right words. "Because you understand me. You don't see me as Marcus Talon's son or the next NFL superstar. You see the insecure boy who's under so much pressure to do well, and ... you take me away from all of it. From the beginning, even that night back in high school, you've been more than a way to relieve some stress. I want to be with you, and I've never felt that for anyone before." I close the gap between us again and lower my forehead to his and breathe him in. "In the same way art and California has been your escape, you're that for me."

"You were part of my freedom too," Levi admits. "The whole idyllic picture of moving away from the East Coast."

"You know this is going to get messy, don't you? Not only

because of the media, but the draft is in April. I graduate in May, and—"

Levi's arms wrap around my neck. "We don't need to think about next year yet. Let's enjoy this. While we still can."

I kiss the tip of his nose. "Can I stay tonight?"

"You don't have to get home to your dads?"

"Oh, I definitely should, but I don't want to. I can deal with them tomorrow. This, tonight, it might be the only peace we get for a while."

"We'll let future us deal with the fallout."

The idea of a *future us* makes my chest warm, but it's nothing compared to when we climb into bed and wrap ourselves around each other.

I know a shitstorm is coming, but while I'm in Levi's arms, the drama can wait.

CHAPTER SEVENTEEN

levi

I WAKE up to a hard cock pressed against my back and a warm breath in my ear.

"Question. Does anyone at school know where you live?"

I frown. "That's not the sexy talk I was hoping for."

Peyton laughs. "Hey, hot stuff. I really want to get you off, but it all depends on the answer to my question."

"I mean, administration people would know, but I haven't had anyone over other than you if that's what you mean."

"Hmm. The administration building is closed on weekends, isn't it?" Peyton trails his hand down my stomach, but it hovers above the waistband of my boxer briefs.

"Why are you asking this?" And why is his hand not on my dick yet? It tents my already tight underwear, and I wriggle, trying to get him to enclose his fingers around my hard shaft.

He chuckles again. "I just needed to make sure my fathers' threats about hunting me down to kick my ass aren't actually viable. Seems not."

I barely hear his words because finally—finally—he dips his hand inside my underwear and strokes me lazily.

Damn, it feels good. I reach behind me and hold the back of his neck. Peyton dips his head and kisses my shoulder while grinding his equally hard cock against my ass.

I want him to stroke faster, but as I push back and we move together, I decide to let it go. We're in no rush, and somehow, this position feels more intimate than what we did last night. The way I can feel his breath on my skin, his hand caressing, stroking to make me feel good instead of trying to get me off as fast as possible, it's like he's inside me when he's not. He surrounds me, embraces me, and those damn soft kisses along my shoulder send shivers down my spine.

"You going to come like this?" he whispers. "Because it's not going to take me much to get there."

"If you come, I'm going to. Suck on my neck when you're close."

Peyton begins stroking faster, done with taking his time. He grinds against me harder, and when he sucks on my skin hard enough to leave a hickey, I beat him to the punch and erupt all over his hand and in my underwear.

He stiffens a couple of seconds later, and even though he's still wearing his underwear, the head of his dick must have popped out of the top because I can feel his release on my back.

Peyton moans and stills, burying his head at the back of my neck. "I don't know what it is about rubbing off on you like that, but I fucking love it."

"It's probably the orgasm," I say breathlessly.

He laughs against me. "Oh right. That."

It's not just that, though. "I think it's because it's the closest you can get to sex without having to be conscious of prepping and taking your time. It's being in the moment and passionate and ... yeah." I smile. "I'll stop rambling now."

"It's intimate," Peyton says.

"Exactly. What's the time?"

"Almost lunchtime. Weekends are the best. What do you say to cleaning up and then coffee before I need to face the music?"

I groan. "I don't want to get out of bed."

"I've got it." Peyton jumps up and goes to my bathroom. The sight of his boxer briefs makes me pause.

"Are they my underwear?"

"I'm learning. Even though I didn't know last night was going to happen, it must have been gut instinct to reach for the pair you gave me a few weeks ago. This way, I stop ruining my own."

I want to argue, but I don't have the fight in me.

He disappears into the bathroom, but I'm too wrung out to move. Then he's back, naked, passing me a warm, damp cloth on his way to my drawers, where he helps himself to a pair of my sweats.

They're tight, and he's going commando, so his dick print is impressive.

"I'll be back."

"You're not going out like that, are you?"

"Why not?"

"Those pants are obscene."

"I'm just running to get coffee, seeing as I can't make it here without creating a mess."

I grunt. "Fine. I will get up."

"Teach me how to make the good coffee."

I rub my eyes and throw on whatever clothes I can find and

stumble out into the bright kitchen and living area with Peyton on my heels. Though I lose him somewhere between my makeshift art studio and the coffee machine.

I hit the button for the espresso machine to warm up and turn to find him stalled at my latest sculpture.

Fuck. I really should've covered that up.

"What's this?" he asks, pointing at an anatomically correct but small heart that's being squeezed by a large hand.

"An assignment."

"I love it."

"Y-you do?" I'm … sensitive about my art, so I don't know if I want to actually hear his answer.

"Well, it's sad, and I'm guessing it has some deeper meaning than heartache, but it's beautiful."

"At least I nailed the brief." I walk over to him and pick it up. "It was for an assignment where we had to express an obvious emotion without any prompts."

Peyton turns to me, and his stare burns. "You chose heartbreak?"

I could lie here and say it seemed like the easiest one to do, but instead, I go into detail about it. "The heart is actually smaller than that of an average adult, representing someone who was never taught to love properly. They're closed off. Perhaps uncompassionate. The love they have to give is small. The larger-than-average hand tightly squeezing the already small and frail heart represents … life. I guess." Okay, that part is a lie. Not a complete lie, but not the whole truth either. It's not just about Peyton and him running away. It's the heartache of feeling unloved. From having little affection growing up to becoming an adult and not expecting much from others.

I'm not mad at Peyton for running. I'm mad at myself for thinking it was possible for my heart to grow. For it to be full.

"I want to say this must be about your family, but why do I get the sinking feeling this was about me?"

I avoid his gaze as I try to joke but don't quite pull it off. "Wow. There's the Talon genes kicking in. Conceited much?"

"Levi, look at me." His gentle hands grip my shoulders and turn me to face him. "I am so, so, so, so sorry for how I left things the last time I was here."

"It's okay."

"No. It's not. I freaked out because I like you so much, and that hasn't happened to me before, but I should never, and I will never, make you feel used ever again. What I did was horrible, and if you had punched me when I kissed you yesterday in front of everyone, I would've understood."

"I'm more of a bitch-slapping kind of guy."

"Thanks for the warning. But I'm serious. I don't know how to apologize more, but it's owed. And if you make me grovel at your feet, write you a shitty poem about how much I suck as a human being, or ... How can I make things better? Give you a lap dance, maybe? I'll do anything you want until you believe I'm not going to run out on you again like that."

He doesn't need to do any of that because his words are enough. His words are everything.

Without thinking, I press my mouth to his, completely forgetting that I'm holding my art assignment that's due on Monday.

As Peyton wraps his arms around me, I do the same, but it only takes a second to realize my mistake.

Our bodies are tightly pressed together, but the heart slips out between us and crashes to the floor.

It shatters into a million pieces, and we jump apart.

"Fuck!"

Peyton's eyes are as wide as mine. "I guess I'm not done apologizing yet."

"Shit, shit, fucking shit." I scramble to pick up the pieces.

"It's okay. We can fix it. I'll help. I'm really good at jigsaw puzzles, and we can just … glue it back together."

I give up trying and shake my head. "The pieces are too small. It'll be too obvious that it was broken."

"Can we rebuild it? I promise I'll be better at it than making coffee. I'm a quick learner, and I've always wanted to recreate that scene from *Ghost*. You know, the one with the spinny wheel and the clay stuff with the hands and the—" Oddly, his nervous rambling and offer to help ground me, and I start laughing.

"That was pottery clay. This clay is different. But of-fuck-ing-course that happens now. I threw out my first one and changed the concept, actually researched proper measurements for heart valves and the aorta, and it ends like this. Why did I throw out a perfectly good assignment that wasn't in a thousand pieces?"

"We'll fix it," Peyton says again.

"It's sun clay, which means it doesn't need heat to set. It needs two full days to dry, and it's due Monday morning."

"Two full days. We have that. We can make it work."

"It took me ten hours to make the first time." I'm so dejected and … well, heartbroken. Ironic, really.

Peyton slumps and stares at the mess, but then after a while, he rubs his chin. "What if …" He picks up the larger of the pieces on the hardwood floor and then a smaller piece that has most of the small heart still intact. "It's all about being emotionally broken. Not being whole. What if we glue most of it back together but leave out parts like the whole thing is crumbling? You said gluing it will make it obvious that it's broken. Isn't that the message you want to send anyway?"

I immediately go to write off the idea before really thinking about it. The finished product forms in my mind, and I can see it clearly. "Actually ... that's ... actually a brilliant idea."

Peyton smiles proudly. "I have them sometimes."

"You're also a disaster. Every time you've been at my house, you've made a mess, whether it be in your underwear, my kitchen, or now my art corner. I thought athletes were supposed to be graceful?"

Peyton holds up a finger. "First: making a mess of our underwear is fun. Secondly: I'll give you the kitchen thing. But third, and most importantly, this was your fault. You were the one holding it. You kissed me. And you were the one who let it go."

Damn it. "You might make some valid points there."

"Of course I do. I'm a smart jock, remember?"

"Okay, Mr. Smarty Pants. How about you go make those coffees while I start working on this." I take the broken pieces from him.

"Wow. Hit me where it really hurts." He grabs the broken sculpture back. "You make the coffee. I will start on this. I'm sure I can manage gluing things together."

I pause. "Just don't glue yourself to ... yourself. Or to my furniture."

"But if I do that, then I will have to permanently live here, and then I will never have to face my dads about the backlash from last night."

"They'll work out where I live eventually, and then you won't be able to escape."

Peyton's face falls. "You're right. Okay, no gluing my body parts. I promise."

I turn to make my way into the kitchen but pause and turn back. "You're not going to be in a lot of trouble, right?"

For the first time possibly ever in Peyton Miller's existence, he looks ... doubtful.

CHAPTER EIGHTEEN

I'VE PUT off going home as long as I can without my dads calling the police and filing a missing person's report. It's around two o'clock when I make the short walk past campus and head for our house.

Only, when I reach my street, I notice a familiar figure marching up the hill toward home too. "Brady!" I call out.

My brother turns, and I jog to catch up to him.

"Please don't tell me the dads sent out a search party for me."

He blinks. "For you? I thought they'd be sending one out for me. My phone died, and—"

That's when I notice he's wearing the same clothes as yesterday. I'm wearing Levi's, which are way too tight on me, but that's not going to stop me from teasing him about this.

Mercilessly.

"Have a good night?" I waggle my eyebrows. "Who was he? Do I know him? Oh God, it wasn't one of my teammates, was it?"

Brady's mouth opens but then closes again. "It was no one. You don't know him."

I drop it. Brady is kinda private when it comes to his sex life, and if I'm honest, I'm thankful for that. It's like he thinks he has to overcompensate for our dads, who do not skimp on the ins and outs of gay sex. You know, for educational and torturing purposes.

I wrap my arm around his shoulders as we walk. "How much trouble do you think I'm in?"

"I dunno. Probably the same amount as I am?"

I stop in my tracks. "You don't know, do you? You didn't stay for my whole game?"

"I did, but I had somewhere to be. I saw you throw the winning pass, screamed and cheered, and then ran before the crowds could block me in. Why?" His gaze narrows. "What did you do?"

"Uh … nothing?"

"You may as well tell me because if you don't, they will." He points to the house.

"I might have run up into the stands and kissed Levi in front of everyone."

"You *what*?"

The door to our house opens, and even though we're still a few houses away, our dad's yelling could be heard from space.

"Peyton. Brady. Inside now."

Pop stands beside him with his arms folded, and then two other people exit the house.

"Fuck" falls out of my mouth.

Brady starts laughing. "Oooh, you're in trouble." He takes off at a run and goes right toward the person I will be working with for the next few years while I wait for Brady to learn the job.

My future agent: Uncle Damon.

And he does not look happy.

His partner, on the other hand, beams like all the drama is going to be so much fun.

I'm tempted to turn and run all the way to Shenanigans for liquid courage, but I think that might make the inevitable worse. So instead, with false bravado I don't feel, I march right up to my family. "What's up?"

"Cute," Dad says dryly. "But you're not getting out of this that easily. I don't care what innocent faces you try to pull—I know they're all bullshit because you get them from me. Get in the house."

As I walk past the four adults staring at me, Dad and Pop look pissed, Damon appears sympathetic, but when I reach Uncle Maddox, he smiles and hugs me.

"I'm so proud of you, you little manwhore."

I snort. "Thank ... you?"

He keeps his arm around me as we head for inside, and then Brady darts past me.

"I'm getting popcorn." He makes way for the kitchen.

"No you're not," Dad barks. "Come. Sit."

"Why am I in trouble?" Brady asks.

"Oh, I don't know. For staying out all night? For having your phone off? Anything could have happened to you. We thought you were dead!"

Brady looks at Pop. "Why is he always so dramatic when he's stressed?"

"Your dad is *always* dramatic. Period," Uncle Maddox says. "When he's stressed, he just adds a serious tone to it."

Dad turns to him. "Why did you even come? I asked for Damon."

Uncle Maddox sits in one of the armchairs in the living room. "And miss the fireworks? Hell no. Besides, it's the weekend. Looking forward to a Cali getaway after Damon yells at Peyton."

"Hey," I whine. "You were on my side out there."

"Oh, I'm proud of you for staying out all night. So, so proud. Like, if I had ever become a parent, I would've wanted a slutbag like you for a son."

"And that's why we never became parents," Damon says.

Maddox looks at his partner of over twenty-five years. "You said it was because your clients are like your children."

"No, I said they *act* like children."

"Hey," Dad and Pop whine at the same time.

"Are you all done?" Uncle Damon asks.

"Yes. You may get on with your yelling." Uncle Maddox waves a hand and then shuffles to the edge of his seat.

Uncle Damon turns to Brady. "Take notes. This is how you handle athletes who have done boneheaded, impulsive things."

"No yelling?" Uncle Maddox sounds so dejected.

"No yelling." Uncle Damon pulls one of the dining room chairs over into the living room and sits in front of me. "Now. How do you want to handle this situation?"

My mouth opens and closes a few times. "Isn't that a you job?"

"Not yet. I'm still only here as your uncle."

"May as well sign on the dotted line," Dad says. "There's no way your team is going to be selected for the playoff after going viral."

"Says the guy who proposed to his husband publicly after winning the Super Bowl," Brady mutters.

"Key words in that sentence were *winning* and *Super Bowl*. If he'd done it at the final championship, I'd be happy for him. But this couldn't have come at a worse time."

Okay, so Dad really is pissed. It's rare he shows this kind of panic, and the only time I remember seeing him like this is when Brady and I were younger, and I was told to watch Brady at the mall while our dads looked at ... I can't even remember what they were looking at to buy now. I'd say we were maybe six and seven years old, so I spaced out, and Brady disappeared.

I've never heard Dad scream so loud as he ran through the mall trying to find him.

We did eventually find him at the ice cream stand, trying to buy ice cream with a button, but Dad's wearing the same distraught "This is the worst thing that could happen" face.

Pop's there with his arms around Dad's shoulders, trying to calm him down, and now the guilt really hits me in the gut. Though Pop's gaze when he hits mine is somewhat reassuring. He gives me a nod, and I'm thrown back to before the game last night when he told me to follow my heart.

I want to argue that I did what Pop told me to do, but now's not the time to throw him under the bus. "We were all under the impression that if we won last night, we'd make it to the playoff. So, when I made the throw of my college career and we took the win, I got carried away with celebrating. I didn't even think it could put the team's spot at risk. At least, not in the moment."

The win last night should have easily secured FU a spot in one of the two semifinal games, but scandal around a team could make the committee shy away from picking us. Stats can be easily skewed in someone else's favor. They could say that Florida State deserves the spot because they regularly beat Alabama, which is arguably the best school in the south when it comes to football.

Uncle Damon's eyes soften. "In the big scheme of things, a kiss with a boy isn't going to ruin your career."

"Hooray, progress," Pop sings, trying to lighten the mood.

Uncle Damon points to Pop. "Exactly. Because of people like your parents, being gay or bi or pan—however you identify—isn't going to be the thing that holds your team back. It's the behavior and the way you came out that could get you into trouble. It would be the same if your boyfriend was a girlfriend or if you had even been out before this event. Showboating isn't acceptable in college football, and that could definitely be considered showboating. But if I'm honest here, not making the playoff will probably be better for your draft prospects. It will suck for the school and the team, but—"

"How do you figure that?" Dad asks, a little calmer now.

"With the news of Peyton coming out and the little stunt he pulled, he's going to be in the media spotlight more than ever before. He's the son of one of the greatest quarterbacks of all time—"

Dad coughs twice, muttering "*the* greatest" in between.

"Whatever," Uncle Damon continues. "The media was always going to be all over Peyton, but now it'll be tenfold, and if the team does make it to the playoff, all that the media, the NFL teams hoping to draft him, and the fans in the stadium will be focused on is how Peyton is handling the scrutiny. If you go into that semifinal and bomb, it says to future teams you don't do well under pressure."

Fuck. I didn't even think of that. "So that means if we are still selected, I have to play my heart out or lose the possibility of being the number one draft pick?"

My brother speaks up. "Being the first overall draft pick is not the greatest thing in the world."

"He's right," Uncle Damon says. "It's pressure on top of the pressure you're already facing."

"I know, but ..." I really want it. "I can deal with the pressure. I know I can. The only time it's ever gotten to me was this year. When I realized ..." My gaze pings around the room. Admitting my feelings is hard because I've never felt this way about anyone before.

"When you realized ..." Dad hedges.

I take a deep breath. "When I realized that I really do like Levi and I want something with him. A relationship. Maybe a future if we can work out long distance when I'm in the NFL." And now my cheeks are heating up. Fucking great.

Everyone in the room breaks out into "Aww," and I flip them off with both hands.

Dad moves to sit next to me, and he puts his arm around me. It's soft; his face is no longer scowling, and his tone is lighter now. "I'm sorry I freaked out. You deserve to have the type of love I found with your pops, and I shouldn't have yelled at you for it."

"Thank you," I whisper.

"Do I think you could've gone about it differently? Yes. But the others are right. If I had to choose between you being happy or being the number one draft pick, your happiness will win out every single time. Being number one isn't ..." Dad tries not to wince. "Everything."

Gasps from all directions fill the space, and Pop reaches over to put his hand on Dad's shoulder.

"It physically hurt you to say that, didn't it?"

"Where the fuck is my parent-of-the-year award?" Dad asks, and we all laugh.

With the tension in the room easing, I can finally breathe again.

I expected yelling and disappointment, so I realize I'm getting off light, but now my only concern needs to be how the team will handle it if we don't make it to the playoff game because of my actions.

They're going to be pissed. It wasn't just my future I had to think about. A lot of them have NFL aspirations as well, and I should've thought of them first. Not everyone was born into football royalty like I was.

I really hope we make it to that playoff. At the same time, I can spout shit about doing well under pressure all I like, but Brady and I both know there comes a point where it's too much.

I've already hit that point once this semester. I'm worried I'm all talk and that I'll fumble harder than Dad in his first-ever Super Bowl. We've all seen the tape. It wasn't pretty.

But that thought also gives me hope. Dad turned his career around.

I can't let the pressure ruin my future. Pop said to follow my heart, and I won't settle for anything less.

I want Levi, and I want football. Any which way I can have them both.

CHAPTER NINETEEN

I PUT the finishing pieces on what I'm hoping will pass as a "purposefully broken" art project and tell myself to leave it alone and let it dry before I keep fiddling with it and it breaks even more. I've been at it since Peyton left, doing touch-ups, adding clay where I can to make it more stable, and trying to make it work, but as I stare at my phone where the unanswered text from about an hour ago still sits, my mind is no longer on my work.

It's on Peyton.

How did it go?

When I got no answer to that, I followed it up with: *That good, huh? Are you grounded? LOL.*

And now that I'm actually worried, I send: *They didn't kill you, did they?*

About thirty seconds after I hit Send, my phone rings, and his name pops up on my screen.

I answer. "Say *I feel like bananas* if you need rescuing."

He laughs. "I'm all good. Thank you, though. It went …

about as well as can be expected. There was less yelling than I was ready for, so that's something."

"What's the verdict? PR train to famous-ville? Countless interviews and appearances?"

"Nope. The good thing about my NCAA contract is I'm not allowed to talk to the media unless the team and school approve it. They won't be doing that anytime soon. Other than that, my uncles flew in from New York this morning and are here to help with talking Dad down, but surprisingly, he was all right. Not ... great, but could've been a lot worse."

"Wow. I'm happy for you but also kind of jealous. Could you imagine my father acting that way if he found out that I'm not in law school?"

"I'm sorry he's not more supportive. I don't have to talk about my dads if it makes you feel shitty."

My heart thrums at his consideration for me, but it's really unnecessary. "You don't have to do that. At all. I'm thankful you have amazing parents. It's not like I didn't know growing up that my father had dealt with the same generational trauma that he put on me and my siblings. It ... It is what it is, and I've accepted it."

"Have you, though? You haven't told him you don't want to be a corporate lawyer. I'm guessing you haven't shown him any of your art either."

"Fuck no. I haven't shown anyone outside of the art department. Other than you."

"Why not? You're so damn talented."

I shrug, even though he can't see me. "Maybe I'm good enough to do it for a living, maybe I'm not. But the main reason I haven't told him yet is because I'm waiting until I'm twenty-five when my trust fund kicks in. Then I can tell the entire Vanderbilt family to eat a bag of dicks."

"Ooh, right. Take their money first." Peyton's only teasing, but it does kind of hit where it hurts.

"The way I figure it, none of them earned their money either. The Vanderbilt fortune comes from a long line of fat-cat capitalist jerks. At least I'm going to use my money for good and not for evil."

Peyton gasps. "You're going to use it to build a superhero lair? Ooh, I can see you in all leather. Fighting crime. Aww, you'll be my very own Batman. He didn't have superpowers. Just money."

"I was actually thinking of taking enough to support my struggling artist ass and donate the rest to people who actually need money, but sure, let's go with the Batman thing."

"Fine. Be charitable or whatever. Spend your money on worthy causes. Wow, you're so boring."

I scoff. "I might not know how much the Talon-Miller dynasty is actually worth, but I'm fairly certain you would have enough to set up your own bat cave."

"Nah. I already asked, and Brady wasn't down to be my Alfred or my Robin. The NFL was my backup."

How is it that I miss Peyton already? It's only been a few hours, and I want him to come back.

"When can I see you again?" I ask, but before he can answer, there's a knock on my door. "Oh, hang on. Someone's here." I smile. "Is it you?"

I throw open the door, and my face drops.

No, my whole heart, stomach … every vital organ stops working.

"It's not me. Who is it?" Peyton asks down the line.

"It's my father. I've gotta go." I end the call before Peyton gets a chance to say anything else.

Dad looks put together in his casual tan suit and light blue shirt. The scent of his overpowering cologne fills the space and takes up residence. It smells like old dude and money. His graying hair is perfectly in place. His crooked nose that matches my brother's but luckily skipped over me seems more prominent than usual, but that might have to do with the twist of his lips like he's trying not to snarl at me like some animal.

"Are you going to invite me in?"

Where my art is drying and can't be broken again, or I'm fucked? Nope.

"Why don't we go out for an early dinner?" I try to step past him, but he doesn't let me, and then he pushes his way into my apartment anyway.

I hold my breath while I wait for him to do the math, but when I close the door and he turns on me, something tells me he's already been given the answer.

"Really, Levingston?"

I cringe at my full name. It's not that it's a terrible name—okay, it's a horrible name—but Levingston Vanderbilt is everything wrong with the Vanderbilt family. We carry on the family names to honor our ancestors who hoarded money to set us up for life where we have the luxury of choosing to work if we wanted to or live off the wealth we didn't earn. My name represents more than pretension. It represents greed, and I hate it.

"Is this about the kiss?" I ask because I still don't know how much my father knows, but I'm hoping it's only the viral kiss.

"It's about art school."

Well, fuck. "Ah. That." I rub the back of my neck. "How did you—"

Maybe, once upon a time, this is where Dad would throw down a newspaper in front of me to be dramatic. Shoving his phone at me doesn't have the same effect.

On his screen, there's an article about the kiss, and right there in black and white: NFL hopeful Peyton Miller kisses art student Levi Vanderbilt.

"They, uh, got my name fast."

"It's everywhere." Dad grabs his phone back. "What happened to putting your head down while you're out here? You said you were going to study law and live on the West Coast and not ruffle any feathers back home."

Uh, no, that's what he told me to do all because I like dick. "I'm allowed to be gay so long as no one in your inner circle in Chicago finds out about it, right?"

"We had a deal."

"We did. But it was a shitty deal."

He points a finger in my face. "Don't use that language with me. We raised you better than that."

I want to scream he didn't raise me at all. Housekeepers and nannies did. But this is already bad enough. "You also raised me to be straight, and look how that turned out," I say instead. Which, in hindsight, isn't much better.

"You're coming back to Chicago with me. Go and pack your things." Dad crosses his arms. His word is always final.

But I'm not going to stand for it. Not this time. "No."

"What did you just say?"

"I'm not going back to Chicago. I'm not going to law school. I'm not doing any of it."

A confident smile crosses Dad's lips. "Good luck paying

for tuition when I cancel all your credit cards and stop paying for this apartment."

I try not to let my worry show. I'm good for this year's tuition. I paid it in full at the beginning of the semester. But this apartment … food, normal living expenses … I can't cover it all if he cuts me off.

"You've got until the morning to change your mind and come back with me. I've chartered a jet, and we leave at 9:00 a.m. sharp."

Because God forbid he fly commercial.

Dad lets himself out. I close the door behind him and slump against it.

I won't be on that tarmac tomorrow, that's for sure, but making it another two and a half years without my trust fund is going to be a struggle.

There's no way I'd qualify for financial aid when I'm a Vanderbilt. I could look into student loans, but I'm not sure how they work.

Which really only leaves me with one option, and I don't like my chances.

I'm going to have to get a job.

That's not a daunting idea or anything. It's not like I've had everything handed to me—sometimes literally on a silver platter—and I know how to do nothing for myself. Oh, wait. It's exactly like that.

I go straight to my bag and pull out my laptop on the kitchen counter to search the FU forums for any jobs on campus. With my undergrad from Harvard being in political science, I might be able to get a TA position. Though, I know they tend to go to other students doing their postgrad programs. Plus, I don't think it pays well.

I go on to Craigslist, and hey, I could go to some rando's house who's looking to lick another dude's feet for an hour. That's an easy couple of hundred bucks. It should be okay because the ad says, "Nothing gay." That's how you know they're legit and not going to drug you and sell your organs.

The longer I search, the more I begin to think I'll be on that tarmac tomorrow, leaving California and everything I've only begun to create here. My freedom is slipping away with every second that ticks by.

And just when I'm on the verge of tears while envisioning a future of corporate offices and suits and legal jargon, there's another knock at my door.

I hold my breath. If I pretend I'm not here, my father will give up and leave, won't he? I can only imagine he came back to physically drag me after not running after him. But then there's a soft "Levi?" and relief floods every vein.

"Pey ..." I rush to the door and try to school my face, but as soon as our gazes meet, his blue eyes soften, and the empathy they hold does me in.

I step into his arms and bury my head in his chest.

"What happened?" he soothes. "You hung up so fast, I didn't get to ask what he wants."

"He wants me to go back to Chicago." I step back and wipe my nose with my sleeve.

"Because of the kiss?" Peyton swallows hard, guilt written all over his face.

"Not because of the kiss."

He relaxes, and I don't want to tell him this next part.

"It's because someone wrote an article about the kiss. Between you and 'art student' Levi Vanderbilt."

"Fuck. I'm so sorry."

"It's not your fault. I will love that moment between us forever because … Shit, you put everything on the line for it. It was like …" I don't want to say it.

"Like what?" Peyton presses his forehead to mine.

"It was like you were choosing me. I know football comes first, and I get that—"

He shakes his head. "I was choosing you. My pop told me to follow my heart, and it made me realize I want both of you. Football and for you to be my boyfriend."

A smile immediately takes over my face. "Peyton Miller doesn't do relationships, though."

"But he also knows not to let go of something that could be really good for him. And I know we haven't been back in each other's orbit long, and I know that in six months, I'll be leaving."

"I'll be gone tomorrow if I can't find a job," I add.

"What?"

"Those were my options: go back to Chicago with my father tomorrow or be cut off. So unless I can get a job to fund"—I wave my hand around—"this, I have no choice."

Peyton steps away from me and goes to my computer. "Okay, easy. I'm getting you a job." He pauses. "Eww, why does this dude want another guy to lick his toes? And why have you saved it under *maybe*?"

"Well, with each ad, I asked myself which I'd rather do, go back to Chicago or that. The feet licker is borderline."

"I'm fixing this." Peyton searches for a phone number and then puts it into his phone and then dials. "Jerry, hey, it's Peyton Miller." He stands and starts pacing as he talks. "Thank you. It was a great game."

What I've been doing for the last however long is achieved

with five minutes and one phone call with the help of my *boyfriend.*

Is this real?

Yep. Definitely has to be real. This amount of embarrassment couldn't be made up.

"I don't want to say it." I look at my new boss at Bean Necessities with pleading in my eyes, but he doesn't care.

"Whatever name the customer gives you, that's the name you call out. It's policy." Jerry's words and tone are so serious, I don't have the guts to ask if he is.

I think he just wants me to entertain my stupid boyfriend's order name. Jerry's a big bear of a guy and wears a red captain hat. He says it's from some old kids' movie, but I'd never heard of it, so I pretended like I knew what he was talking about. Jerry seems friendly enough. I mean, he was willing to take a chance on me purely because Peyton asked him to.

Considering I thought I was trained for nothing, Peyton knew immediately the perfect job for me: barista. Jerry hired me yesterday, and today is my first day of training.

It was that easy.

The hours aren't much, but they're flexible with my class schedule. Except after seeing the hourly pay rate in the HR forms I signed, I know this job won't put a dent in my monthly bills. It was a shock to see such a low number, and it took everything I had to school my overprivileged reaction of asking, *"How do people even live on that?"* It's not even enough to cover rent.

Which means I'm going to have to move.

Just when I think I'm heading in the right direction, something comes up, I get overwhelmed, and then I think I can't do this on my own and have to go back to Chicago after all. Though to do that now after standing my father up at the airport, I foresee a lot of groveling that might not even work, and that would be the worst thing that could happen. Putting my pride on the line, begging not to be cut off, promising my life to the one I ran away from, only to have my dad reject it anyway.

I won't do it.

I'll figure something out.

Jerry nudges me. "You can do it."

I step up to the counter and lock eyes with Peyton, who's waiting with a big-ass grin on his face. He's here with his entire family. His brother, dads, and uncles. "Large Study Juice with two pumps of caramel for ..." I sigh. "The sexiest quarterback to ever quarterback."

Peyton's smile widens when everyone else in the coffeehouse snickers, but as he steps forward to collect his drink, he's cut off by his dad.

"Aww, son, you ordered a drink for me. How sweet." Talon takes the coffee from me and takes a sip, but then screws up his face. "Holy hell, that's pure sugar." He hands it off to Pey.

Peyton takes a twenty and shoves it in the tip jar on the counter. "That's for actually saying it." He winks and then moves to take a table in the back while I go back to make the rest of their orders, but when I see the next name, I let out a curse.

I make the coffees and give Jerry the side-eye as I put them on the counter and say, "For the men I hope to become my fathers-in-law one day. Jerry, are you sure I have to call out the names like this?"

As straight-faced as he can manage, Jerry says, "We take customer satisfaction very seriously here at Bean Necessities."

"The way I hear it, Levi has the satisfaction part down when it comes to Pey." This comes from one of Peyton's uncles who I don't know. He has graying blondish hair and a cheeky smile, and I'm finally starting to realize the downfall of having such an open and understanding family. No, wait, understanding? I mean *embarrassing*.

I finish off their drink orders with a tinge of pink staining my cheeks, which they all love even more.

When I get to the last order for a Damon, Peyton's other uncle steps forward.

"Thank you for using your actual name," I say, thinking he must be the nice uncle.

But as he takes the drink, he steps closer. "I've already spoken to Peyton about this, but I wanted you to be aware that you can't talk to the media about yours and Peyton's relationship."

That's when it clicks. "Ah. You're the sports agent uncle, aren't you? You don't need to worry about me. I was brought up to say no comment anytime a microphone was shoved in my face." Not that it ever happened to me.

Our family are social elite but not exactly famous. Not like Peyton's parents. But I do remember when my grandfather died, my parents were thrust into the media spotlight because my father and his brother were fighting over the will. Because, you know, the difference between being wealthy and obscenely wealthy is important enough to fight over it. They hired a media coach for us and everything, but we didn't need it. Kind of hard to need it when you're never out with your parents but stuck at home with the staff.

Damon's friendly demeanor is back. "In that case, welcome to the circus that is our family."

With that one sentence, I get a sense of acceptance that I have never once had with my own family. Not even when I was toeing their line.

Even if the job is repetitive and doesn't pay well, I'm doing it for myself. For the future I want.

The hours tick by slowly, but with a steady stream of customers throughout the day, I don't have a lot of time to think about anything else other than coffee. And damn, college students drink a lot of coffee.

When an order comes up for Remy, I glance up to find him with his arm around a guy with lean muscles and wide shoulders. He looks like a swimmer just on first glance. Remy … with an athlete?

I blink at them, and Remy sends me a rare smile.

That's when it dawns on me. I point to his boyfriend. "Your high school 'situation,' I'm guessing?"

The guy grins. "I was a situation? You've been talking about me?"

"Levi, this is Alex. Alex, Levi."

"Aren't you the guy Peyton Miller came out for?" Alex asks.

"Uh, it didn't exactly happen like that, but yes. I'm him."

"I didn't know you worked here," Remy says.

I run my hand over myself, gesturing to my apron. "The consequences of kissing Peyton on ESPN."

They look confused.

"I was cut off," I clarify. "Tips appreciated." I'm only half-joking.

"Damn," Remy says and shoves a fiver in the tip jar. "Are you okay?"

This just goes to prove that Remy has a heart deep down, even if he tries to deny it.

"I will be."

I know it will be tough, but I can't go crawling back to Chicago. I'll make ends meet. I'll move into a cheaper apartment.

I'll do whatever it takes to be free from my old life.

CHAPTER TWENTY

IT ABSOLUTELY SUCKS what Levi's family is doing to him. There aren't enough swear words for how much I hate them.

When Levi didn't turn up at the airport to fly back to Chicago, his dad called the dean and told her that Levi will not be completing the year. Like that would somehow make him say, "Oh, he's taken away my chance to study art, so I may as well go home now." Instead, he spent hours on the phone with administration about the mix-up. Luckily, he got to them in time before they were able to refund the second semester's tuition, and his spot in the art program is safe. For now.

I can't work out the logic behind his dad doing that other than to make Levi's life a living hell. But there's one thing that Mr. Vanderbilt doesn't understand: grown-up Levi isn't the same resigned kid I met on his rooftop four years ago. He's not going to give in just because obstacles are in his way.

That being said, it's only been a week of him trying to work and go to classes, and we were expecting an adjustment period, but he already looks exhausted. He's picking up any shift Jerry will give him, which turns out is a lot. Jerry has a lot of students on the payroll because employees are easy to come by—there's always someone on campus who needs extra money—but the reason he needs so many is because working around classes and social schedules is hard. A lot of the students refuse to work weekends, so for someone who's eager to work, Jerry's going to put Levi on the roster as much as he can. It also helps he makes amazing coffee and needed little training.

But I've barely seen him all week, and the times I have, he's had bags under his eyes and has been utterly wrecked. We've managed a couple of orgasms between us where he's passed out immediately afterward, and I wish I could do something for him.

I've blown off class and come to Bean Necessities today so I can see his beautiful face. Which … is not so beautiful at the moment. His hair is back to his shaggy hairstyle I loved in high school, but it looks like he hasn't had the chance to brush it. He makes coffee after coffee on autopilot, and I don't think he's even noticed me yet.

The line is long, and he's busy, but this is the only chance I've gotten to get away. I'm stuck in my own world of torment while the team trains for the possibility of making the playoff. We're all on edge, and the guys have been pissy with me, which is understandable, and it sucks not knowing how to fix it other than hope we're selected to play. On the other hand, if we are heading for the playoff, I need to be at the top of my game. Which means increased training, practices, and weight sessions. More time where Levi and I won't have a chance to hang out.

I realize if we are going to have any kind of future like I

want, this is what life is going to be like. I'll be focused on football; he'll have school and his art. We won't even be in the same city soon.

So I need to suck it up and take what I can get with Levi. If it's only one or two nights a week, then that's all I'll have.

I finally get to the long line and put my order in with the server at the counter.

"Name?" she asks, and I'm so tempted to fuck with him again, but it's probably too busy in here for that, and it won't be cute but actually annoying. Levi looks like he's not in the mood.

"Peyton," I say, and that finally gets his attention.

Levi smiles, but his eyes don't change. They're still tired-looking. Maybe stressed. And I get it, I really do. This is a huge change for him, and it can't be easy.

I go take a seat by the window that's being vacated so I don't lose it, and instead of calling my name out, Levi walks the coffee over to me.

As he hands me the drink, he slides into the seat opposite me.

"Uh, is this allowed?"

"I'm taking my break. It's been nonstop since I got here to open at five."

"You look tired." I sip my coffee and love that he doesn't skimp on the caramel for me.

"You make me feel so wanted," he deadpans. "We might need to put brakes on this relationship. You're smothering me with too much affection."

I laugh. "I'm worried about you. I thought that maybe it was an adjustment period or because you're working so much now, you're more exhausted, but ..." I almost don't want to ask. "Is it something else? Is it me? Am I demanding too much of your spare time? Not that you really have had any, and neither have I, so—"

Levi's hand closes over mine. "It's not you. At all. It's ..." He glances away and lowers his voice like he's ashamed. "It's everything else. I really don't want to admit defeat, but it's only been a week, and I have no idea how I'm going to pay my rent, let alone tuition next year or for food, textbooks ... anything."

"How long do you have left on your lease?"

"It's technically one of those long-term vacation rentals, so I'm paid up to the end of December, but there's no way I'm going to be able to make enough here to afford next semester. I've been looking at places online to see what there is in my price range for when the time comes."

"Found anything?"

"Yeah, a 2004 Volvo. Can I park my next house in your driveway?"

I get the distinct impression he's not joking. "Shit. That bad?"

"Yep. I asked about the share houses on campus, and of course, they're all full. Dorms have a waitlist."

"Stay with Brady and me," I blurt.

"I can't ask you to do that."

"You're not asking. I'm offering. Brady won't mind, and it at least buys you until the summer."

Levi nods. "Which is the other thing. I'm not going to be able to afford tuition next year. So while it's all good and well to stand on my morals and turn my back on my family, I didn't really think it through."

"Is there any chance of getting your trust fund early? Don't those things have contingencies for situations like this?"

"Not the type I have. I already called."

I try to think. "Loans?"

"I'm still looking into those." His desperation hits me deep in my chest.

"You can't go back to Chicago."

"I don't want to." Levi glances out the window, and I don't think he has once looked me in the eye since he sat down. "But I need to be realistic. I have no idea how people with no money do this."

"Well, they usually get help from scholarships or financial aid, which you wouldn't qualify for."

Levi slumps. "I'm stuck."

I squeeze his hand. "After this semester, move in with Brady and me. And then we can figure something out for next year. Dorms should open up then. Maybe there's an art scholarship you can apply for. We'll work it out."

Stress still rolls off him even if he looks more relieved. "Yeah. We'll work it out." It sounds like he doesn't believe it, though.

"So, you'll move in? If it's too soon, you can take the spare room. That's if my dads aren't still there. They're hanging around waiting to find out if the team will be playing the championship. If we are, you'll have to share my bedroom for the first few days. Aww, what a shame."

Levi doesn't smile like I want him to, damn it.

"Why don't you talk to Brady about it first," he says. "He probably doesn't appreciate you making all these plans without his say."

I point at him. "And that right there is how I know he'll say yes. Because you asked for his opinion first. I'm going to go ask him right now so you can stress less."

Levi huffs. "I don't think that's possible with everything going on, but thank you for giving me options. I should get back to work."

I stand and lean over the table, kissing the top of his head. "Everything is going to work out, so whatever you do, don't even think about going back to Chicago."

He says, "Okay," but I can tell he doesn't have as much faith as I do. I'll just have to change his mind by coming up with a solution that will work without flat out asking my dads to help him financially until his trust fund is released, which is what I really want to do.

And I don't doubt that they'd help. They hate Levi's father as much as we do, and if they knew he was forcing Levi to go back to Chicago to become a lawyer, they'd do anything to help.

I go home to ask them their advice, but I already know they're not there when I see their rental car is missing. When a text comes through from Coach a few moments later, saying there's a team meeting at five, I already know where my dads are.

"The decision's been made," I say to myself and change directions toward the stadium.

I'm still torn between wanting to play and not wanting to play, but all I can do is take it as it comes. If we're in, training kicks up a notch. If we're out, I can maybe enjoy the next month with Levi every chance we get.

When I get to the stadium, I head for the locker room and Coach's office, knowing my dads will already be there.

Coach sees me and holds up his hand to stop me from talking before him. "Can none of you boys read? Five p.m."

"Huh?"

"You're not the first one to call or text since I sent that message out, but it would be unfair of me to tell you if we're in the playoff or not without your teammates here."

Behind him, Dad throws his thumbs up, though. It's not hard to work out what that means.

That's that, then.

Decision made.

I need to make the next two games the best games of my life and prove to the NFL world that I'm more than ready to take my place as their next football legend.

CHAPTER TWENTY-ONE

BECAUSE MY MOVE-OUT date happens to be the same date as Peyton's first football playoff game, Peyton decided I should move all my stuff to his place the day before. It is a cruel, cruel system to make college guys play football on New Year's Day. That's all I'm saying.

Instead of partying it up tonight, it's going to be a quiet night in the Talon-Miller household. Which I'm apparently a part of now. At least for the next five months before Peyton and Brady graduate. After that, I'm still not sure, but I've bought some time, and in the process, I've gotten everything I wanted when choosing to move to California.

I have my dream guy.

I'm studying what I want to study.

I've become independent from my family.

I'm broke as shit and working my ass off to be able to afford the basic stuff I never had to think about before, but it'll be worth it.

Is it really necessary to brush your teeth every day? How did I not know how expensive toothpaste is?

There's still that seed of doubt that this is the right thing. Maybe I should have sucked it up and trapped myself in a life of law school in Chicago until I gained financial freedom and then rearranged my life to go for what I wanted. It's only two and a bit years. I've had Vanderbilt expectations put on me for almost twenty-three years. Two more won't kill me.

It might kill my soul, though.

All of my possessions are boxed up, ready to go. Ready to move to take advantage of my wealthy boyfriend and his amazing family. Maybe that's why it's not sitting right. Because I'm moving from one rich family to another.

Though Peyton's family already appear to like me a whole lot more than my own. Spending Christmas with them was … different. Instead of a stuffy, formal dinner, it was the type of Christmas I've only seen in movies. Santa hats, horrible sweaters, a million presents …

I think that's when the doubt really began to set in. I want to be a part of Peyton's world so much it hurts, and I'm scared that taking advantage of him like this will only drive him away. Not to mention I'll be indebted to him, and then our relationship won't be equal. He will always hold something over my head, and that takes away my autonomy. If Peyton wanted me to do something I didn't want to do, would I feel obligated to give him what he wants?

It's almost like I'm replacing one set of expectations for another.

Instead of familial pressure, it's the pressure of making everything work with Peyton because he's doing me this huge favor.

I'm not like him. I don't take this kind of thing in stride. My mind worries too much about the what-ifs of it all.

What if living with Peyton so soon in our relationship kills it? What if we grow to hate each other? What if he gives me this, takes on my burden of having no money and gives me the things I need, and we don't work out?

Peyton has been used since he was little to try to get to his dads. I saw it all the time at school growing up.

What if he sees me just like them?

I can't be that guy. Which means I can't risk what we have.

The selfless thing to do would be to leave. To go back to Chicago, as much as I would hate it and myself. I'd loathe my family even more than I do now. But I'd be protecting Peyton.

I still haven't decided what to do when he turns up at my building to help move. He has his brother and his dads in tow to help, but as soon as they ask where to start, I practically break down.

Tears spring to my eyes, and I try to hold them back because I will not cry in front of Super Bowl winners. They're big and tough, and I'm assuming they don't cry ever.

"Hey, whoa, what's wrong?" Peyton immediately takes me in his arms and cups my cheek. "Did your dad show up again? Call? What?"

I shake my head. "I … I … Fuck." I step out of his way. "I don't think I can do this."

Peyton frowns. "Do what? Move? You kinda have to. Unless you've suddenly worked out a way to pay for it. I can already tell you, we're going to need to talk about it if you're planning on robbing a bank, becoming a drug dealer, or selling your ass because I'm only okay with one of those things, and I don't think my dads will bankroll a prostitute habit for me."

"I'd be okay with it," Talon says. "Sex workers need to make a living."

Miller backhands his husband's chest. I think it's playful, but it must've been hard because Talon rubs the spot and mutters, "Ouch."

I know they're joking, and I do smile, but … "It's too much. It's just …"

"What's too much?"

Brady says, "Maybe we should let these two talk in private before we start moving stuff."

I think he knows what I mean, and I'm thankful he wants to help. Unfortunately, their dads aren't having it.

"What's wrong?" Miller asks. "Maybe we can help."

"Whatever it is, it needs to be fast because Peyton has a game to focus on," Talon says.

Fuck. Peyton's playoff.

I scratch the back of my neck where it's suddenly itchy, but I can't tell if it's from the stress of everything or because my hair has grown back out now and I'm remembering that it's annoying at this length. In high school, it was worth it to stick it to my dad. Now, not so much.

"I …" My gaze ping-pongs around the room. "I think I should go back to Chicago."

"No," Peyton and his dads say at the same time while his brother literally facepalms.

"It's the most fair thing to do," I say.

"For who?" Peyton growls. "Because it sure as fuck isn't fair on me."

"Especially with the most important game of his career happening tomorrow," Talon adds.

Shit, now tears really are falling. "This has nothing to do with you or us. It has to do with what we'll become if I use you for money just because I don't have it anymore."

"Are you using me for money?" he asks, like it's that simple.

"No, but—"

"Then there's no issue here."

Miller steps forward and puts his hand on Peyton's shoulder. "It's not really that easy when it comes to money."

I nod. "What if we move in together, we fight or we don't get along as well as we do right now, but because I'm so dependent on you, I can't move, and then we grow to hate each other, and it ruins everything I moved here to get. I know it's the wrong time to bring this up—"

"While all your stuff is packed and you're about to move in with me?" Peyton's voice has an edge to it. Not mad, but frustration maybe. "Yeah, I'd say this is shitty timing."

"Maybe that's just it. Maybe it is the timing. Maybe …" I bite my lip and glance at his dads. "You even said yourself that your dads were apart for six years, and they're stronger than ever."

"Six years?" Peyton exclaims.

"Seriously, Dads," Brady cuts in. "We should let them have this out."

Talon holds up his hand to stop Brady from talking.

This is going downhill fast.

"It won't be six years for us. Only two. Then I'll be able to be with you without any financial obligation to you. I need to learn to do things on my own, and if there was a possibility to be able to do that while staying in California, I would, but it's impossible."

Peyton lowers his head. "I don't really understand the difference between being financially dependent on your parents or me other than with me, you get to be yourself. And I can't understand why you'd choose that over me." When he looks at me again, his eyes are glassy, but his jaw is set. "Dad's right. I have more important shit to worry about right now. Have fun in Chicago hiding who you are. Doing everything your dad tells you to. Great life choice, Levi. Fantastic. I can see how that's so much more appealing than living with your boyfriend."

"It's not that," I try to say, but he's already walking out.

Talon follows him, and I expect Brady and Miller to do the same, but they don't.

"I get it," Miller says and steps closer.

"Y-you do?"

"Money is a hard thing to navigate, especially in a new relationship. When Peyton's dad and I got together, he got paid so much more than I did. I moved into his house, he paid for everything even though I had my own money, and it felt like a power imbalance. But those thoughts? The feeling of being inadequate? It was all in my head, and he didn't know he was doing it. But you know the difference between us and you and Peyton? You actually said something. By the time I said something, I was already where you're scared of being. I was growing bitter when all we needed was to have a conversation."

"Thank you."

"I agree," Brady says. "Though I'm going to have to teach you how to handle my brother because that wasn't it."

The knot in my chest tightens, and even though these guys are on my side, I also know I've fucked up.

"How do I fix this so he can understand why I need to go back to Chicago?"

"That's just it," Miller says. "While I see your point, and I commend you for speaking up, I also think you're not exploring all your options."

"What other options do I have?"

"Student loans?" Brady asks.

"From what I read, because I'm still under twenty-four, I'm considered dependent on my parents, so they base the interest rate off my parents' income."

Brady whistles. "Goodbye, trust fund, in interest repayments alone."

"Basically."

"Levi," Miller says, and his tone makes it sound like he's about to say something obvious. "You know more people with money other than your parents. Isn't that why you went to the most expensive school in Chicago? To network with other rich people?"

"Are you suggesting I go ask my high school friends' parents for a loan?"

Miller's mouth opens and then closes, and he shakes away whatever thought is running through his head. "Wow. Okay. I guess I'm going to need to spell it out for you. I would be willing to loan you—"

"Nope. That's basically what I'd be doing with Peyton anyway because you give him money, he gives me money—"

"See, but there's the difference. If I loan you the money, it will be a loan. Not a gift. We can draw up a contract, say interest-free repayments for the first two years, or even no repayments until you graduate or you leave school, and then when your trust comes in, if you pay it all off in one swoop, there'll be no exit fees or anything. This won't be a deal between you and Peyton, but you and me. If you break up with Peyton, the terms stay the same."

It's too good to be true. Too easy.

"I know you're used to strings being attached to nice deeds," Miller adds. "You were raised that way. And while I can say that Peyton would never hurt you or try to control you the way your father has—and we've seen him do it firsthand when you were growing up—it's understandable that you won't want to put yourself in the same position with someone else. Which is why the only strings I have is you have to pay me back. And if your dad somehow screws you over and your trust fund falls through? I really hope your art is good enough to sell, or you might be making coffee for the rest of your life so I can get my money."

I'm still hesitant. "It feels wrong. I claim I want to make it on my own but then need to rely on others to do it. I hate double standards."

"If this offer was coming from a bank, would you be as hesitant?"

"Well, no, but that's different."

"Is it?"

"Yes. I'm not having sex with anyone from the bank. Or their sons."

Brady cuts in. "Wait, do bank loans work like that? Know of any bankers who are hot Daddy types?"

Miller shudders. "Something I didn't need to know about my *child*."

"He has a point, though," I say. "Banks don't work on favors. It's a business."

"You could think of it as an investment in your art. Ooh, what if I commission a piece? Where's that broken heart thingy Peyton showed us on his phone? I want to buy that."

I glance at Brady. "He's not going to let this go, is he?"

"Nope. And if I had to bet, I'd say if you flat out refused, an anonymous donation to your bank account would be the next step."

"Shh," Miller says. "Don't give away all my secrets." Then his brown eyes that are like Brady's meet mine, and he turns serious. "Let me do this for you."

"I *will* need a contract," I say. "And I want to pay interest."

"How about there's no interest until you turn twenty-five, and if you choose not to use your trust fund to pay me back, we can have a low-rate interest tacked onto it."

"That easy?"

"That easy."

I glance between him and Brady, who's nodding encouragingly. "Don't you have to, you know, talk to your husband about it first? I don't think I'm his favorite person."

"What did I tell you before? He pays for everything. I have a nice chunk of cash hidden away for, you know, if he breaks the law and we need to flee and live in the Caymans for the rest of our lives."

"It's scary that I don't think you're joking," Brady tells his pop.

"Your dad's the joker. I'm the smart one."

That pang of jealousy over their close-knit bond hits me like it usually does, and now that I've acknowledged my fear —irrational as it may be—the guilt over bringing Peyton down with my mood is what hits the most. I tore down his generosity and compared it to what my father would do.

Dad has the money, so he makes the rules. And while I still don't want to put that uncertainty and pressure on Peyton's and my relationship, borrowing money from his parents, with a contract in place, takes away all that unnecessary anxiety that has been growing.

It takes away all my doubts about going for what I want.

And what I want, what I've always wanted since that night on my rooftop back in Chicago, is Peyton.

"So does that mean you're staying here?" Brady asks me. "Do we get out of moving boxes?"

"Oh, fuck no. Do you know how expensive this place is? I'll stay with you guys until I can get into a dorm or find cheaper accommodation."

Brady smiles, but it looks sarcastic or like he's doing it through gritted teeth. "Fun for us, then."

I give him a look that screams, *I know your secret, and your pops is right there*. Not that I'd ever do that to him, but he doesn't know that.

Brady claps. "Let's get these boxes loaded up in the car."

Living with him is going to be so much fun.

That's if Peyton will still have me.

CHAPTER TWENTY-TWO

peyton

THE COOL WIND whips at my face as Dad and I hit the beach. He's been following me since I stormed out of Levi's apartment, but he finally pulls me to a stop after five minutes of me kicking at the soft sand with every step.

He grabs my arm. "You cool down enough to talk yet?"

I pull out of his grip and keep trudging in the direction of home. The sidewalk or even the harder sand near the water would be easier, but this is cathartic.

"I'll take that as a no," Dad mumbles behind me.

It's not until we pass campus and are not far from Shenanigans that my muscles start to burn, and I figure I should stop because if I get a knee injury from throwing a hissy fit, Coach will be pissed.

He's been riding us hard since we got the news we were in the playoff, which is probably why I didn't even notice the signs that my boyfriend was unhappy. He has seemed *stressed*, but I figured that was about money. Not … us.

When I slow to a stop, Dad pulls me down, and we sit side by side, looking out at the water.

He doesn't speak, just waits for me to be ready to talk about it, and considering my dad is not known for being patient, I almost want to drag this out to see how long it'll take for him to crack.

"He's not wrong to be worried, you know." Didn't take that long at all, then. "Sure, it was the worst possible timing—"

"Well, that's not entirely true. He could have told me right before I went onto the field tomorrow. With a sign. In front of the whole crowd."

"Okay, okay, so there could be worse timing, but that doesn't mean what he did back there didn't make me ragey as much as it did you. What you need to do is find a way to not think about it. At least for the next few days. It'll be a good lesson in separating your private life from your career, which is something you're going to have to do if you want to make it in the NFL."

"I know. And I'm ready for tomorrow. I was just blind-sided by Levi's idea of a solution. He had a problem, I found a way to fix it, even if it was temporary, and then he ignores it and says he's going to go back to Chicago instead?"

Dad presses his lips together. "If it makes you feel any better, it didn't seem like he actually wanted to go back to his father."

"That's the part I don't understand the most. He hates his dad. He hated his life back in Chicago. And the one he had in Boston. Here … I thought he was finally happy, and stupidly, I liked that I had something to do with that. But if he's willing to ditch it all for money—"

"I don't think he was doing it for the money. You basically offered him a free ride for the next six months, but he didn't want to take it because he was worried about how it would affect your relationship. It would be one thing if you'd been together for years, but you haven't. I can see how it would be daunting for him. You both have amazing futures open to you, and I think he was possibly feeling trapped by needing to financially depend on someone else instead of doing it himself."

That ... makes sense. I guess. "He could have at least picked a better time to tell me."

"I won't argue with that. Just so you know, if you two get married, I'm going to go to Levi the day before the wedding and say I can no longer walk my son down the aisle because it's too much pressure. It will be fun, and I'll get Pop to film Levi's reaction."

"And for that, we're never getting married."

Dad nudges me. "But it made you realize you still want to be with him, didn't it?"

That sneaky bastard.

"I do. I don't want him to leave, but it's not like I can force him to stay. There are laws against keeping someone against their will, you know."

"Oh shit. Are there?" Dad asks. "Totally unrelated note, don't check the basement at home."

"Ha ha."

"I guess we'll have to come up with a solution to get him to stay voluntarily, then." His phone dings in his pocket, so he takes it out. "Huh."

"What is it?"

Dad shakes his head. "Nothing." Yet he types back a response before pocketing his phone again. "So, about this wedding."

I look up at the sky. "Why, God? Why did you give me Marcus Talon as a father?"

Dad deepens his voice, pretending to be the voice of God. "Because you deserve the best, son."

"Sure. 'Best.'" I use air quotes.

But when we laugh, mine dies quickly. Because Levi will never know what it's like to have a relationship with his dad like I do with mine. Both of them. I wanted to give him a taste of my world, welcome him into the fold with open arms, but he's not ready yet.

I can accept that I might have fallen for him already, but he needs more time. It's the giving up part that hurts. The thinking that I could be anything like his father and manipulate him because of money …

Then again, he also said he didn't want me to think he was using me. He was doing it to protect me as much as it was to protect him. I forget sometimes that he was there to see it when people would use Brady and me to get to our dads, when we found out a lot of our friends were fake.

I appreciate him wanting to protect me from that kind of insecurity, but the way he went about it wasn't the best choice.

"Quick question," Dad says. "How important is Levi to you?"

I find the answer surprisingly easy. We've grown close in such a short period of time that it's hard to remember what it was like before he was here. Imagining the next few months before the draft without him makes my chest ache. "Other than football, he's the most important thing in my life."

"Okay, ouch," Dad says, but he's smiling. "But I think that's your answer."

"My answer to what?"

"I wasn't talking to you." He turns his head, and when I follow his gaze and look behind us, Levi's standing there, eyes still shiny from earlier and his nose tinged pink.

"Levi." I stand, but my mouth stops working.

Pop is standing next to him, but I barely acknowledge his existence.

"Let's leave them to it," Dad says and guides Pop away.

I'm thankful they're leaving us alone, while also wishing they could stay and stall for time so I can think of something to say other than *I love you and please don't leave me.*

"I'm an idiot," he says just in time to keep me from blurting something so heavy.

"You're not an idiot," I reassure him. "What you did was idiotic, but you're not an idiot."

"Can I claim temporary insanity for how I acted? That going from having all the money in the world to nothing made me a little crazy?"

I already want to wrap him in a hug and tell him we can work through it together, but I want more of an explanation than that.

"I don't want to make you feel like I'm trying to manipulate you into staying with me."

"You didn't. You wouldn't. Deep down, I know that. I'm just freaking out because I did this amazing thing by coming to California, and I put all my faith on being able to keep this secret from Dad, which was stupid of me because I should've known he'd keep tabs on me, and it would only be a matter of time. My lack of backup plan when I came out here was both exhilarating and my downfall. Because now I have two and a half years of uncertainty, and it's scary. I can't tell you how sorry I am that you were the collateral damage in an explosion of my own inadequacies."

That's such a Vanderbilt thing to say.

Levi shakes his head. "I'm sorry. I'm not as good as you with the apologies. This might be shocking news, but I was never taught how to say sorry properly."

I smile. "You're doing better than you think you are."

"I dunno. It's no public kiss in a stadium full of spectators."

I step toward him. "This is better than that."

"Why?"

"Because it's just us on a beach, our problems unsolved but acknowledging that what we have is worth the fight. I will always fight for you. I will protect you against any Vanderbilt that tries to sabotage the future you want, and that includes yourself."

Levi's arms go around my waist. "I'd say between you and your pop, you can protect me from myself."

"Pop?"

"We came up with an idea that works for me."

I pull my head back so I can look down at him. "You did?"

He nods. "He's going to loan me the money I need until my trust fund kicks in."

"How is that different to me offering to help you? You do know I don't have a job, don't you? Where do you think my money comes from?"

"That's what I said. But your pop promised it would be an airtight contract, so I have to pay it back no matter what happens with us. Whether you're drafted, move across the country and never see me again, or we do long-distance, or I go with you to whichever city you're signed to—"

"That. Let's do that one."

"Let's not get ahead of ourselves. You still have to survive living with me until a dorm opens up."

I squeeze him tighter. "You're still moving in?"

"I'm still going to have to penny-pinch for the next two and a bit years, but yes. Until I can find cheaper accommodation—maybe even in the share house district—you and Brady have me as a roommate."

"A roommate who sleeps next to me?"

Levi leans in. "Every night."

Yes. I close the small gap between us and kiss him with so much force he stumbles backward in the sand, and then I have to hold him tighter to keep him against me.

"Let's make a promise," I murmur against his lips and force myself to pull back. "Next time you're overwhelmed and stressy and I'm not helping, could you maybe talk to me about why before jumping to you're going to leave?"

"Or. *Or.* Hear me out. We call your dads to talk us down and fix all our problems."

"That seems easier. They were surprisingly good at it. And Dad barely cracked a joke during our whole conversation."

"Ah. I had Brady for that."

I shake my head. "My brother likes you more than he likes me."

Levi smiles. "To be fair, it is his job to keep your ego in check."

"True."

"So what happens now?" Levi asks.

"Right now? We move all your shit into my house, and then tomorrow, I kick ass on the field."

"And if you lose?"

"I can't lose. I have to show the world I can handle my personal life blowing up and still be the best damn player on the field."

"No pressure."

I cup his cheek. "What did I tell you about pressure? I thrive on it."

CHAPTER TWENTY-THREE

THRIVES UNDER PRESSURE? That is an understatement when it comes to Peyton Miller. Not only does my man show the entire world what he can do during the semi-final game, but he's totally cool, calm, and collected as we arrive in Santa Clara for the championship a week later.

Peyton thinks it's a sign that it's being played at Levi's Stadium, home of the San Francisco NFL team. The jokes about winning inside me have not stopped. Not even in front of his dads, which is mortifying.

Peyton and his dads go to do team stuff, leaving Brady and me alone for the afternoon. It's only been a week of living together, and while Peyton and I are loving it, I can't help but notice the tension growing between Brady and me already.

I wonder if all the sex noises are getting to him.

There isn't much to do in Santa Clara, so we take their dad's rental car and head into San Francisco for some dinner because we have hours to fill. Hours that feel like days because there's this weird vibe between us now.

We're about forty minutes into the hour-long drive when I can't take it anymore.

"If you hate living with me so much, you're allowed to tell me what's up. Do I chew loudly? Do you hate that Peyton gave me the basement to do my art stuff and all your gym equipment is outside now?"

Brady glances at me out the corner of his eye and then focuses back on the road. "What are you droning on about?"

"Ever since I moved in, you're putting distance between yourself and Peyton and me. Are you worried I'm going to tell him about—"

"No. It's not that. It's ..." He purses his lips. "I didn't realize you'd picked up on it, and that's on me. Peyton is so oblivious to anything that's happening past his own nose, and everyone is always so focused on him that I'm not used to people noticing me. I have nothing against you. Or my brother. Or you two being together. But ... seeing you guys together ... you're just so damn happy."

"Sorry. I'll get right on trying to fix that."

Brady laughs. "Don't get me wrong, I'm happy for Pey, and you're an awesome roommate. I was low-key worried you didn't know how to wash a dish growing up with all the house-keepers you had."

"The last six months were difficult. Did you know that the detergent you put in the sink is not the same detergent you put in the dishwasher to wash dishes? Why don't they teach this stuff at Harvard? Or at least teach you how to clean up a kitchen full of soap suds."

And hey, I get another laugh out of him, which is more than I've gotten the last week. It slowly fades, and then Brady sighs.

"Those guys I was with?"

"The SEALs. How can I forget?"

"Well, yeah, I kinda wish I could forget."

"Didn't end well?"

He shrugs. "It ended fine. We've made a stupid promise to catch up again next year whenever they're on leave and I can get away from New York, but ..."

"But what?"

"I think having them in the back of my mind might hold me back from other possibilities. What if I pass on the love of my life because of these two guys I randomly hooked up with a couple of times? It feels like they're keeping me on the hook. Stringing me along to be their side toy whenever they want me. And the sad thing is I know I'll go running every time."

It's not like I haven't thought the same of Peyton. Come April, he's going to know his future, but until then, it's so up in the air. He could be drafted to somewhere horrible and cold and stupid. Like back home to Chicago. Or the farthest, completely opposite side of the country he can get. Like ... Maine. Wait, does Maine have an NFL team? I don't think they do.

Either way, we're going to have to do the same thing Brady is with the guys he was seeing. Do we try to make long-distance work? Do I defer my art degree and enroll wherever Peyton gets a contract?

These are all things Peyton and I are going to have to discuss closer to his graduation. I'm too scared to bring it up now when we have months left to wait and twiddle our thumbs.

I try to find some reassuring words, but I don't think I have any, so I go with a cliché instead. "I'm sure that when your soul mate … or *soul mates* come into your life, you'll forget all about your SEALs."

Brady smiles over at me. "I really do hope you and my brother work out. I can't really talk to him about this stuff."

"Can I ask why? Peyton will support you always."

"I know, but our dynamic is already shifting. Ever since I quit football after high school, it's like we've stepped into our future roles. He's the athlete, and I'm the person who makes sure he stays in line. Our relationship is all about him, and I'm okay with that. It's what I signed up for when we came up with this plan to be agent and athlete when we were older. But I don't know how to change the topic to talk about me."

"Well, I'm always happy to give you shitty advice when you need it."

"Thanks … future brother-in-law."

"Whoa, too soon for that kind of talk."

Brady scoffs. "It's cute you think our dads aren't already planning the wedding."

I try to hide my smile because that actually sounds like the exact thing I want. Someday. To officially become a Miller.

Goodbye to the toxic Levingston Vanderbilt name. Hello, Levi Miller.

One day.

I let out a hard breath and bounce my legs, and it's not because I'm freezing, which I am, or because the person belting out the national anthem can't sing, which she can't. It's because I'm so damn nervous for Peyton over this game.

When the song ends, Brady grips my shoulder. "Geez, you look worse than Peyton did this morning. You do know you're not playing, don't you?"

"Thank fuck I'm not," I mutter. "Then they'd have no chance, Peyton would blow his shot at the big time, and then neither of us would have a future."

Brady laughs. "You can relax. With how Peyton played in the semifinal, he's more than proven all the media crap about you two didn't affect his game. He could choke tonight and he'll still be okay."

On the other side of Brady, Talon slaps the back of Brady's head.

"Shut your blasphemous mouth."

"It's true, though," Brady complains. "Hell, he could choke and still be the number one draft at this point. He's had a killer year. His college stats rival your own from back in the day, you know, when you weren't over the hill—"

There's another slap to the back of Brady's head.

Brady swats his dad's hand away. "Hey, I quit football to avoid getting a head injury."

"Think positively. You know the game is more mind over matter than skill."

"Yes, but I think that only applies to the ones playing."

Miller puts his head forward and looks past the other two toward me. "We really shouldn't have sat this way because these two will be at it for the whole game." He pokes his husband. "Switch with Levi."

"You don't want to sit with me?"

"I've been sitting with you for too many years already. One of our boys has found someone who doesn't live and breathe football like you do, and I have someone to be an actual grown-up with."

"Fine. Being a grown-up is for boring people anyway." Talon and I switch places, and I have to laugh at Peyton's dad not even fighting his husband calling me more mature.

If anything, that's what I love most about this family. They're unapologetically themselves and see no shame in it. Vanderbilts are famous for being perfect. Anything less than is unbecoming and unacceptable.

Franklin U lose the coin toss, and University of Alabama chooses to receive, which means Peyton isn't even on the field first up. That doesn't stop my nerves from going haywire.

Let him have a good game. Please let him have a good game.

Miller leans in closer to me. "You get used to it."

I flinch. Fuck, I'm so jumpy. "Used to what?"

"Watching. Wanting them to win. The high when they do, the downs when they don't. Peyton's dad played a hell of a lot longer than I did, so I've been in your position a lot."

"This is his dream," I say. "I want him to get everything he's worked so hard for."

"He will. Brady is right in that sense. This game could go to shit, and Pey would still be in a good place. Try to do what I always did and pretend this is just another game."

"Oh, so I should sit on my phone and google what's actually happening on the field?" I don't realize Talon is listening until it's too late.

"That's it. Wedding is off until Levi learns football."

"Wedding?" I croak.

Brady cuts in. "I told you they were already planning it, but hey, there's your easy out. Don't learn football and Dad will never give his blessing."

Alabama fails to score a touchdown, and the ball changes hands. My legs start to bounce again as Peyton takes to the field.

Talon, Miller, and Brady all cheer encouragement from the sidelines, but I'm too busy reminding myself that it's just another game. It's not a big deal. If I'm going to be with Peyton, his pop is right. I'm going to have to get used to this.

I can see the appeal, the adrenaline of it all, but fuck, I'm going to have to find a way to prevent getting an ulcer from the stress.

Unlike the University of Alabama, Franklin starts out strong on offense, and while they don't cross the line, they get a hell of a lot closer than Alabama did.

The score sits at zero across the board for the first quarter, which only makes me more antsy. If Peyton's team could put one away, I might be able to relax.

The second quarter picks up where the game left off, with Alabama scarily close to scoring a touchdown. I learned at the team's last game that the play doesn't reset between the first and third quarters. Only at halftime.

Which sucks for us. Us being Franklin. I've caught the sport mentality when it comes to us being on the field versus players being on the field. The whole school is out there. And if my fantasies of one day becoming a Miller come true, I will have to pretend to like football.

Because the venue this year is closer to Franklin than it is to Alabama, there's a hell of a lot more purple and gold in the crowd, and as Alabama takes the game's first touchdown, it's as if every single person wearing our colors loses a little school spirit.

Beside me, even Miller, Mr. *It's Just Another Game*, starts fidgeting.

It doesn't even pick up when Alabama miss the kick for an extra point.

Instead of the defeat we all feel, when Peyton gets back out there to do his thing, it's like the touchdown against them has renewed his energy. Though he started out strong last quarter too and then slowly faded, getting farther and farther away from scoring with each new possession of the ball.

I pray to the football gods—who definitely exist according to Pey's entire family—that this quarter is better because I don't want to acknowledge the possibility that if he loses this game or any game from here on out, it will inadvertently be my fault. Or that the media, his agent, or the fans will see it that way.

If kissing me in public puts extra pressure on him, if a fight between us gets in his head ...

Down on the field, Peyton passes the ball off on the sly and then pretends to throw it. It takes Alabama only a split second to realize what's happening, but it's a second too late because Peyton's teammate must have rockets in his cleats. He clears all the big guys trying to tackle each other, and even though an Alabama player is on his heels, he doesn't clip him until he's already past the line.

The four of us are out of our seats, cheering like crazy.

Peyton points to his teammate across the field in acknowledgment, but there isn't much of a celebration within the team. Peyton told me once that it can cost them yardage if they don't act professionally after a touchdown.

Which is funny to me because I've seen how the actual pros handle a W, and it's anything but classy or demure.

Franklin's able to secure the conversion, which puts them in the lead, but when I glance at the clock and realize there's still so much game left to play, I make a decision.

"I don't think I'll be able to go to any of Peyton's games in the future. My heart can't take it."

The others laugh at me, but I'm not joking.

"Nah, in the future, you can be in the WAP box and getting drunk while you pretend to watch," Brady says.

"Do I want to ask what a WAP box is?"

"Wives and Partners. It used to be Wives and Girlfriends, but with the changes the league has seen over the years—"

"You're welcome, football," Talon says.

"Yeah," Brady continues. "Because of these two idiots, they came up with a new acronym."

"And something that also means wet ass pussy is the best they could come up with? I have to admit, alcohol would make this better." I could really go for a drink.

"Peyton's got this," Talon says. "Nothing to worry about."

"I dunno," Brady adds. "I'm a bit worried about Franklin's defense. If they keep letting Alabama score, it won't matter how good Peyton is playing."

I groan. "Football is a real form of torture."

Miller throws his arm around me. "Welcome to the club."

I fucking hate football.

CHAPTER TWENTY-FOUR

I FUCKING LOVE FOOTBALL. Nothing emphasizes it more than when I'm deep in the middle of a game with adrenaline pumping, anticipation thrumming through my veins, and the need to win simmering under my fingertips.

It's been a fight, but we aren't done yet. At halftime, we're neck and neck. In the third, Alabama pulls ahead. There's only one touchdown in it, but that could change any second. And as I sit on the sidelines watching them trying to score again in the last quarter, an eerie calm settles over me.

This is the last college game I will ever play, and going into it, the pressure to win was hanging over the team like a dark cloud. For me, it's not so much about winning but making it the game to remember.

Some of these guys will be in the draft with me in a few months. For others, this is the end of the line. So when I told my team in the locker room to go out there and play with their hearts, they all listened.

I reminded them of why we're all here.

For the love of the game.

For the thrill of the win.

And even for the devastation of a loss.

Walking away without the championship will be heart-breaking but not as crushing as never having experienced what it was like to play in a real-life professional stadium, televised for everyone to watch.

This is our glory.

Our legacy.

Win or lose.

And with some divine intervention and a fumble that will haunt Alabama forever, we gain back possession of the ball.

It's my time to shine.

A touchdown and a conversion will put us in the lead, but it has to be nothing less. Alabama managed a two-point conversion with their last touchdown, which means getting it across the line isn't enough. We need the extra point to get us where we need to be. Especially when the clock is running out, and it's now or never.

But I can worry about that when the time comes. I need to do my part.

The play is teed up, ready to go. The team looks strong. And as we take our places in the line of scrimmage, I breathe in deep. I remind my guys of the play. I call for the snap, and we all move as one.

Some plays are textbook, some barely get the job done, and then there are the ones that will go down as the biggest flukes known in football history.

I'd rather end my college career on a play that is so well done that it will be talked about as being the perfect play. Unfortunately, it's as if Alabama know which play we're going to run before we even make a move.

My wide receiver is blocked. My tight end is on the ground. I'm running out of options fucking fast. And while this isn't the play we intended, I wing it and pass the ball off to my running back, who shoots around the scrimmage and goes for it.

Alabama's safeties are on his ass, though, and my breath gets caught in my throat as I glance between the time left and how far we've got left to get in the end zone.

We're taken down at the twenty-yard line. We got way more yardage than we should have for a play we pulled out of our asses on the fly, but it might be enough.

With less than a minute to get us over that last hurdle, the drive to push our limits hits. We have one last time-out in our back pocket, and I call it.

As my guys come and join me in a huddle, I have no idea what to say. "Can I just say *insert uplifting speech here* and let you guys fill in the blanks?"

Everyone chuckles.

"Same play?" Trenton asks.

We're all exhausted, it's so close to the end we can taste it, but we still have so far to go.

"Are we dumb enough to try a play that didn't work the first time?" I reply.

"It's our best shot," Trenton says.

"Are we all happy with that?" I glance around the circle at everyone nodding.

"I can get away this time, I swear it," James, my wide receiver, says from his spot beside me. "I'll get under that ball if it kills me."

I slap his back. "If that doesn't kill you, we will if you don't pull this off."

He knows I'm joking. I think.

"One last thing," I say before we break. "No matter what happens, you're all awesome, and I've loved every second of playing football with you guys."

"Aww, Cap." Trenton sniffs dramatically. "You're gonna make us cry."

I roll my eyes. "How about we put this one away so we're not crying for real at the end of it?"

We get psyched up and break, and as we take our positions for what will probably be the last time, the usual zing skates along my skin. It's a mixture of hope and confidence that will either come crashing down in a minute or soar to impossible heights.

I wish everything went in slow motion like the movies in these kinds of moments, but it doesn't. The play happens so fast I'm barely aware of it. It passes in a blur.

Hell, I don't even pay attention to the rest of the team. My focus is on James and getting him the ball. Even as I'm charged by an Alabama cornerback.

I know he's coming, so I let the ball fly.

The cornerback is too close to pull to a stop, so we tumble to the ground, but then the most heartwarming noise hits my ears. The touchdown horn blows, followed by deafening screams that drown out the school's song.

I'm winded when my teammates pull me back up to my feet, but that's okay. This next part is easy. Getting our kicker out here to win this thing.

My job here is done.

If this were any other touchdown and any other try for a conversion, I might stay on the field to confuse the opposition into thinking we were trying for a two-point conversion, but everyone in this stadium knows what we're going to do.

I take to the sidelines, knowing I've done my best.

If we make this kick, we walk away winners. There's not enough time on the clock for Alabama to score again. If we miss, we go into overtime.

Fucking hell, I can't watch.

Everyone gets into position.

I can't watch, I can't watch, I can't watch.

I wish I had my eyes open.

I can't take it anymore. They fly open to see the ball sail right through the middle of the posts.

Best ending to my college career I could ask for.

The locker room is loud, and by the time media interviews and celebrations are done, my voice is hoarse from screaming so much.

My second college championship win. It's been fucking epic.

But I'd be lying if I said I wasn't ready to leave it all behind me. I'm ready for the rest of my life. Though leaving California and Levi won't be easy.

I'm more than committed to making it work, though. Any which way we can.

When we're all finally dressed and have calmed down a little—only a little because this high is going to last us the next month—we leave the stadium as a team and get on the team bus to take us back to the hotel.

We don't go back home until tomorrow, and I think Coach knows trying to get us to behave tonight will be next to impossible.

The bus pulls up to the hotel, and I can already see my family and Levi waiting for us by the entrance. A few of the other guys' families came too, and they look as eager to congratulate us as we are to get off this bus and start partying.

We try to stand as soon as the bus stops, but Coach puts up his hand to stop us.

"Just … don't get arrested. Underage players, no drinking. And … be responsible. The last thing I want to deal with is a media frenzy where all of you are disgraced publicly over stupid dude-bro actions."

I snort because Coach gave us the same speech last year when we won. And two years ago when we lost. Only then it was tacked on the end of "Don't drown yourself in liquor and end up tits-deep in depression and snow." The game was played in Wisconsin that year.

"Can we go now, Coach? Please?" I beg, and everyone else cheers.

Coach waves his hand. "Go for it." He's so resigned to the fact we're going to do what we want anyway, but his eyes silently plead with me. *Please don't make me drive to the hospital tonight.*

I give him a mock salute as I get off the bus, and even though I beeline it for Levi, my dads and brother get in first, squashing me in a hug from every side.

"You fucking did it," Dad says in my ear.

"We're so proud," Pop adds.

Brady squeezes me tight. "I'm so happy I'm going to be making money off your talent."

I laugh. "Thanks, bro. And as much as I'm loving the family shit, I can hug you guys anytime." I push them all off me and lock eyes with Levi, who's waiting patiently for me. "Didn't want to join in the group hug?"

When I'm close enough to him, he grips my shirt in his fist and pulls me toward him.

"I want you all to myself," he says lowly so no one else can hear.

"Is that so?"

"Mmhmm. I want to congratulate you properly."

"I know you think we can't hear you, but we can," Brady interrupts.

I flip him off without looking back. "We might have to save that for after we're home. I am not getting out of team duties tonight."

Levi pouts, and I relent.

"Okay, maybe some hand stuff when I go drop my bag upstairs."

His hungry look is back, and then I'm waving to my family and telling my teammates I'll be right down.

They don't believe me, of course, so that gives me even more minutes with Levi where they won't be expecting me.

Levi practically drags me through the lobby, but with the team arriving back, it's a full ride to the ninth floor.

"My room is next one up," I say when Levi tries to pull me off the elevator.

"You also have a roommate. I told Brady to fuck off for an hour."

I'm quick to follow Levi down the hall. "I love that you feel comfortable enough to talk to my brother like that."

"We're already like brothers." Levi swipes his key card against the door and lets me in, smacking my ass as I pass him.

"Wait, if your brother is my brother, does that make us—"

His hand covers my mouth. "Don't finish that and ruin this adrenaline mixed with horniness that's pumping through me." He pushes me up against the wall and gets started on loosening my tie and shirt buttons.

"Mm, winning really does it for you, huh?"

"You have no idea. The whole game, I sat there saying I can't watch it, and I hate it, and I had so much damn anxiety from the possibility of you losing that I vowed to never watch any of your games again."

I gasp.

"But then you won, and all those thoughts were suddenly replaced with the need to fuck the quarterback of the winning team. And when I realized I could actually do it? I want to go to every game I possibly can."

"Good." I spin us around so he's the one pinned, and I put my knee in between his legs so he can grind his hard cock against my thigh. "Because I want you there. I know it'll be a while before you can attend every single one of my home games—"

"Wherever home may be," he adds.

"Exactly. With any luck, I'll only be a short plane ride away. Or drive. Who knows? Either one of the LA teams might totally bomb the rest of their season and get to pick me first up."

"I still don't understand how the draft works, but I don't care. I ..." He glances away. "I might have decided something tonight. Something we should talk about."

"There you go making decisions without me again. You're

not trying to run back to Chicago again, are you? Because I'm gonna be pissed."

Levi shakes his head. "The only way I'm heading back to Chicago is if you're signed there."

I cock my head and try not to get my hopes up about what he's saying. "What if I'm signed to Jacksonville?"

"I'll be able to get a tan."

"Mm, Buffalo?"

"Fuck, going back to harsh winters? Guess I'll need to stock up on thermals."

"Are you really saying what I think you're saying?" I ask because I need to be sure.

"With the financial freedom your dads are giving me, I have the flexibility of moving wherever you are."

"You're going to come with me? As in this year. After the draft." My heart flutters, but I tell myself not to get too excited because he could mean in the future. After he graduates here in Cali.

"I'd follow you to the ends of the earth if it meant getting to be with you. I don't want to spend more time apart than we already have."

The warmth in my chest spreads to the rest of my body, and I find myself unable to hold it in any longer. "I love you."

Levi blinks up at me.

"You don't have to say it back—"

"If telling you I'd follow you to the ends of the earth wasn't a big enough hint, I'm in love with you too."

The relief leaves me in a quick breath.

"I know we don't have much time, but I want you inside me," Levi whispers.

"We can swing it. As long as I make an appearance at some point, the team will forgive me."

As Levi pushes past me and shucks off his clothes on his way to his bag for supplies, I slowly lose my jacket and undo my tie.

"Levi?" I croak.

His gray eyes meet mine. He's all the way on the other side of the room now, and I want nothing more than to reach for him because what I have to ask is nerve-racking.

"What's wrong? If we don't really have time—"

"It's not that. I, umm, I was thinking that maybe instead of me … uh, being inside you, it could …" I hesitate and then let the rest out so fast it almost becomes one word. "It could be the other way around?"

A tiny scrunch forms in the middle of Levi's forehead, but his lips turn up in a smile. "You … want that?"

I nod. "I've been thinking about it, yeah. Then I realized I didn't even ask if you do that, and—"

"I do. I will." Levi abandons the supplies and crosses the room, slamming into me. With his mouth on mine, his arms wrapping around my back, and his hard cock pressing against me, the nervousness over asking strips away.

Only then it's replaced with the thought of him moving inside me, and my gut flutters with nerves again. It's not that I don't want to do it—I've been thinking about it since high school when trying to figure out my feelings toward Levi's and my hookup—but I do want it to be good. For both him and me.

My heart thumps, and I swear Levi can feel it against his own chest.

"Are you sure about this? You disappeared just now."

I smile down at him. "I'm so sure, but you're going to have to take the lead on this one. I have no idea what I'm doing."

His lips touch mine again, but it's quick and chaste. "You don't have to do anything. Let me take care of you."

"I want that. I really, really want that."

Levi huffs a small laugh. "Does my big strong football player need some pampering?"

"Always."

It's not all that surprising how easy it is for me to let go and let him take over. Just like that first night we were together. He was so confident, even if he says he wasn't feeling that way, and I had all the trust in the world in him.

Our connection back then was strong, probably stronger than I had felt with anyone before or since. But it took college to realize that. It took that time apart to grow and become the men we want to be before getting here.

For my dads, it took six years; with us, it was four. I only hope that whenever my brother falls for someone, he doesn't have to go through that gap of growing because I have to say, if I could've had Levi for the last four years, I would've spent every single day with him.

Levi leads me over to the bed by the window and pushes me down so I'm sitting on the edge while he gets to his knees. He leans in and peppers soft kisses along my jawline, and his expert hands work open the buttons on my shirt.

Slowly but confidently, he kisses his way down my skin while undressing me.

When he moves to take off my shirt, I instinctively shrug out of it. When he undoes my pants, I lift my hips to help him. It's like I'm his puppet, and all he has to do to make me pliant is touch me.

And like with everything Levi does, he takes the utmost care in getting me prepped, ready to take his cock. I thought it would be awkward, a lot of stopping and starting, but Levi can read me. He knows my tells. So once I'm naked, he doesn't immediately go for my ass.

I lie on my back and raise my feet, mimicking the position he was in the last time we did this.

He explores me, leaves open-mouth kisses all over my skin. From my chest to my abs and down to my thigh.

I shudder with pleasure and need, and only when I'm on the cusp of begging does he move to where I want it. He licks over the base of my cock and trails down, his five-o'clock shadow scraping my sac and sending tingles shooting down to my feet.

He sucks on my balls and strokes my cock, and it feels so amazing I barely notice when his finger presses against my hole, and by that point, I'm writhing with need for more that all I can do is breathe out a loud "Yes."

Levi pushes his finger inside me, and I hate to think it, but all that oversharing by my dads growing up kind of prepared me for this moment. I block that from my mind but remember the advice they gave to Brady when he came out.

I'm surprised I retained any of the information, considering I was laughing so hard at his embarrassment, but I bear down and take a deep breath, concentrating on what his mouth is doing instead of his finger.

My skin burns like I'm too hot, but there's no way I'm going to stop this.

"You're doing so good," Levi encourages. He moves even lower, licking the spot between my balls and my hole. My muscles contract, my ass tightening around Levi's digit, but when he presses his tongue harder against my skin, I relax, and he pushes in another finger.

Then his tongue is gone, and I whimper, but when he lifts his head again and says, "If we're moving too fast, I can slow down—"

"No. Keep going. It feels good."

And maybe that was the wrong thing to say because he turns up his moves.

One finger equals good. Two is … intense. I haven't worked out if it's a good intense or a bad intense yet, but I'm going to let it ride.

His fingers work me open, and his mouth distracts me from it. It gets to the point where my body doesn't know if it's in pleasure or pain, and that feeling is somehow addictive. It even gets to a point where I'm so stretched that I'm begging to feel that pressure and sting again.

That is, until he hits my prostate, and I understand everything I've ever heard about it. I want him to stay right there. He can live there. His fingers belong to my ass now.

"You're almost ready," he encourages.

"I'm ready now. I need your cock."

"If you're sure …"

"If you can hit my prostate like that with your dick, I don't know how I'm going to play in the NFL without you inside me the whole time."

Levi laughs, his breath hitting my skin. "Why am I imagining like a giant baby backpack contraption instead of calling you an idiot?"

"Because you love the idea of always being inside me as much as I do. Please tell me that's why."

"Just wait until your family finds out how much of a cock slut you are."

"One, eww, don't mention my family while your fingers are inside me. And two, we haven't exactly found that out yet, so hurry up and fuck me so we can work out if it's true or not." I regret my words, though, because as he stands, he removes his fingers, and he still has his pants on. "You're not even naked yet? You're killing me. I need you."

He gives me what I want. He lowers his pants and underwear but only to his thighs. He's quick with the condom, and when he lowers himself on top of me and pushes the head of his dick against my hole, my first reaction is to tense.

But then I think of that feeling. That, turning me from the inside-out feeling, while the rest of my body hums with pleasure, I relax enough for him to enter me.

He takes his time, but I'm already addicted.

I'm glad I didn't go out exploring with other guys after my confusing feelings for Levi because I will always share this with him. He's my first and my only.

"I love you," I say to him again. Now that I've started, I can't stop.

I want him to say it back, but he doesn't. Instead, he grits his teeth and kinda grunts.

"Is that caveman speak for you love me too?"

"No. It's caveman speak for 'holy fuck you're so tight, and if I don't get under control soon, I'm going to blow already.'"

"Ah. So it's the sexy kind of caveman speak. Keep talking to me."

Levi leans in and kisses the tip of my nose. "I love you too." Then he kisses my cheek. "I love you." He keeps going, alternating between kissing me and telling me he loves me, and if I'm honest, it's almost as good as the dick in my ass.

Almost.

By the time Levi has kissed nearly every inch of my upper body, he moves in and out of me with ease. I take him, take the sting, take the hit of pleasure every time he brushes my prostate, and when I think it can't get any better, Levi reaches between us and strokes my cock.

"You need to come, Pey. I need you to come."

Like I said, my body is a puppet, and he knows how to play me. I cry out and come hard, covering my abs with my release, and as if holding out for that exact moment, Levi lets out a "Thank fuck" and stiffens on top of me.

He keeps moving in and out of me, slower now, and once we've both recovered and spent, he slumps on top of me.

We're both covered in sweat, I'm covered in cum, but we lie there silently. I stroke his back, and he breathes hard.

That was … perfect. Levi is perfect.

When he lifts up and checks to see if I'm okay, I smile.

"More than okay. How can I not be when I have you? You're everything I didn't know I wanted until I had you. Now I never want to let you go."

"Then don't," Levi whispers.

CHAPTER TWENTY-FIVE

levi

I THOUGHT the energy of a game was high. It's nothing compared to being backstage for the draft. I'm seated next to Brady while Peyton and his dads mingle with players and families from other colleges waiting for this to start.

And here I am, seemingly the only one who's nervous again. How is that possible when this is the biggest night of Peyton's career thus far?

But then Peyton glances over at me, and even the expensive bright blue suit that makes his eyes pop isn't enough to hide the quiver in his confident smile. It's almost invisible, but I notice.

So does Brady. "I'm going to laugh so hard if he pukes onstage."

"You're the worst brother ever."

"Right?" It's not surprising Brady wears that title like a badge of honor because we both know—and Peyton certainly knows—that Brady and Peyton are closer than brothers. It's like they're best friends, brothers, and hell, they might even be closer to each other's perfect half than I am with Peyton.

People might think that's weird, but for them, it makes sense. I know they come as a package deal, so for Brady to give us his blessing, it's a big thing for Peyton.

And I swear it only has half to do with me knowing about Brady's secret rendezvous with men—plural.

"Be honest. Where are you hoping for?" Brady asks.

"I have vowed to follow Peyton wherever he lands, so I do not have a preference."

"Liar."

"Okay, fine. I really, really, really want him to be picked second because Florida sounds so much warmer than Detroit."

Brady laughs. "Understandable. Don't tell Pey I said this, but I hope you get your wish."

"His wish for what?" Peyton drops down beside me and looks at his brother through narrowed eyes.

"My wish that you're drafted first. Duh."

"Bullshit. You want to move to Detroit?"

How do I put this as nicely as possible? "Fuck no. But I would. For you."

Peyton leans over and kisses the top of my head just as the show starts.

Finally, Peyton and his family match me on the nerve scale. We're all jittery and antsy but trying to push through it.

We all hold our breaths as they get ready to read the first name out.

"The first pick in this year's NFL draft, Detroit picks Derek Gardner."

My relief is quick as I squeeze Peyton's leg. Talon claps Peyton's back. He didn't get first, but that's all right.

"You okay?" I ask quietly before they call out the next name.

He nods. "A ton of pressure was just lifted off my shoulders."

For me, that would be a relief, but I know Peyton loves that kind of thing.

I squeeze his leg again and hope with all hope that Florida chooses him.

They don't.

Fuck.

"Is this because of us?" I ask him softly.

He smiles at me, but it doesn't reach his eyes. "Nah. Neither of them are QBs. It's still all good. I swear."

Yet I see the small disappointment in his gaze anyway.

We were all so confident that he'd be first or second that I can't even remember which team is next in line.

The announcer's voice cuts through the din. "The third pick in this year's NFL draft, Arizona picks Peyton Miller, Franklin University."

Thank fuck it's not somewhere cold.

Peyton looks ecstatic as we all stand and hug him. And as he leaves us to go onstage to collect his commemorative jersey and interview off to the side, I look around at Peyton's parents and his brother.

"We're happy, right?" I know they were hoping for first. Especially Talon. So Brady and Miller wait for his response to my question.

"Third overall pick?" Talon says. "Fuck yeah, we're happy." He puts his arm around Miller and kisses his cheek.

"This'll be the farthest we've ever been away from each other," Brady says.

He's moving to New York after graduation next month to

take up a paid internship with King Sports while getting his law degree.

I wrap him in a hug. "Don't worry. I'll be there to keep an eye on him."

"Yeah, but who's going to keep an eye on me?" he jokes.

"Your uncles," Talon says.

"Oh, right. Them. All billion of them."

"If it makes you feel any better, I recently found out football season is only five months. And that's if the team goes all the way to the end. We will have so much time to catch up."

"It is really disheartening that you only recently learned that," Talon says to me. "Remember my rules. No football knowledge, no wedding."

I give my future father-in-law a smartass smile because little does he know, I've spent the last couple of months learning every little detail about football. And sure, the rules still don't make sense because it is the least cohesive sport I've ever watched, but I can follow them.

These guys will be my family one day, I have no doubt about that, and I'm already closer to them than any of my blood relatives.

My mom has called a couple of times to try to talk sense into me, but she knows she would get further talking to a brick wall than to me directly.

I spoke to my brother and sister when all that shit first happened with Dad cutting me off, but they both called me an idiot for turning my back on *all that money*. They've never understood me, just like I've never understood how anyone could love that kind of elitist lifestyle. It's not that they have money; it's that they want to keep it all for themselves and look down on those who don't have it. Even though they did absolutely nothing to earn it.

I'm not going to become a millionaire by selling my art. I already know that. But whatever I do earn, that will be mine. I will have worked for it.

Peyton's the same way with football.

And when he finally comes back and sits next to me again, I grip his arm. "We're moving to Arizona."

"Yes, we are." He leans in and presses his mouth to mine, and he tastes like promises.

Promises of a future.

Promises of forever.

Promises of giving me everything I've wanted since I was a teenager.

We'll start the rest of our lives together right here and now.

I can't wait.

CHAPTER TWENTY-SIX

EPILOGUE

MY ALARM GOES OFF, telling me my time is up. No more lying in bed, sated from the epic morning sex my live-in boyfriend woke me up to hours ago.

I passed back out almost immediately, but the bed shifted with the loss of Levi's weight. It's a game day for me with a 1:00 p.m. kickoff, which means I need to be at the stadium by eleven at the latest.

Even though I'm only the backup quarterback, I'm getting a lot of game time because Tim Warner, the starter, has a shoulder injury. The plan was for me to take over from him in two seasons' time when his contract was up, but his retirement might be coming early. If his injury hadn't happened during a game, I would've sworn black and blue that my dads had something to do with it.

My rookie season is more than I could've ever imagined. I'm getting more field time than expected, my stats for a newbie are off the charts, and our chances to make the playoffs are great. While I'd love to take out the title my first time out, I do have some realistic expectations.

Football royalty or not, no rookie has ever won the Super Bowl their first-ever season.

Still, a boy can dream.

He can also tell his dad to shut up about becoming the first to ever do it because I already have enough pressure on me as it is. Like I found out in college, I thrive under pressure, but some things are just too much.

Everyone from my Franklin graduating class has moved on to their futures. Brady's in New York interning for Uncle Damon and going to law school, but his best friend, Felix, moved to some small town in Massachusetts, so they're still somewhat close. A couple of friends stayed in San Luco, but everyone spread out around the country, and everything we worked for at Franklin is happening now.

This is our future.

And after I drag myself out of bed, have a quick shower to wash off sweat and cum, and get dressed into my suit, I walk to the other end of our house and enter Levi's studio, where I know he'll be.

I lean against the doorjamb and watch him work.

His studio looks out over Arrowhead Lake, and while our house isn't much to look at out the front, the interior and view are worth the obscene amount of money I pay to rent this place.

My dads were insistent I use my signing bonus to put a deposit on a house and get into the real estate market now, but it was too close to jinxing my spot on the team for my liking. I didn't want to buy somewhere and then have to sell if I have a shit season and they release me from my contract.

Even with how good I'm playing, I'm reluctant to take that step purely because anything could happen between now and the Super Bowl. I do love it here in Arizona, and I'd love to stay, but it's not up to me. It's up to the team.

It would also suck to make Levi change schools again. Getting credits transferred from Franklin wasn't as easy as it sounds because Alhambra U in Phoenix doesn't offer the same degree. It all worked out in the end. It was just a pain.

I could see us here long term.

Levi's back is to me, but I can picture the look of concentration on his face as he uses his tools to put final touches on the piece he's been working on for the last week. Sometimes, I know what he's creating because it's obvious, but when he does an abstract piece like the one he's working on now and he asks me my opinion, I freeze up and feel like how my dads must've felt when Brady and I were kids and asked them if they liked our drawings. If I say yes, and then he asks what I think it is, I've learned *a holy mess of blobbetry* is the wrong answer.

"I know you're standing there, by the way," he says, not taking his eyes off his work.

He's only in his boxer briefs, and I love watching his back muscles tense as he makes changes to whatever he's doing.

"Are you complaining?"

"No. I'm wondering why you're standing there and not over here begging for round two." He finally looks over at me, his shaggy chestnut hair falling in his eyes. Even though he hates how annoying his hair is when it's long, he says it's still a reminder that he broke free of the Vanderbilt image. When he takes in my suit, his face falls. "What time is it?"

"I have enough time to make a protein shake to go."

"Oh."

"How long have you been at it?"

He purses his lips. "Well, I woke you at seven. Sexy times. Got up …"

"Have you eaten? It's past ten."

"Umm, no."

Typical Levi. Ever since he walked away from his old life and he has this debt hanging over his head from Pop, he's invested more than ever in his future in art. He's so motivated that he sometimes forgets to feed himself.

"Are you going to remember to get your ass to the WAP box for my game this afternoon?"

"Even if I get distracted, those wet-ass pussies won't let me forget. I'm their favorite accessory. The gay BFF."

"Do they know you call them wet-ass pussies?"

"Of course. I have a rule not to bitch about any of them behind their backs. I'm mean to their faces instead, and they still love me."

"I think it's because they're under the impression you're being funny and not serious."

"Sarcasm is the best. Am I an asshole, or am I hilarious? It could go either way." He jokes about it, but I happen to know he has found a really great group of friends with the WAPs. The ones who know football help him fake the things he's still learning, and the ones who don't know football drink with him. I'm grateful because I was worried he wasn't going to fit in here and want to go back to California.

"Seeing as you haven't eaten, I'll make you a shake too, but then I have to get going."

"No kale for me this time," he calls out.

I'm with him on that one. Kale is gross, but I cover the flavor with berries and fruit. Feeling in a generous mood, after I've made mine, I rinse out the blender and make Levi's with milk and ice cream instead of water and flax seed like I did mine. I'm a thoughtful partner like that.

When I take it in to him, his face lights up, and I lean over to give him a quick kiss.

He lets out a whine when I pull back, but I can't give him more.

"I have to go," I say. "And last time I found you in here to say goodbye, you got clay all over my suit, then I had to change, and I was almost late. Not a good look for a rookie."

"Fine." He huffs. "Thanks for breakfast." He takes the glass and drinks it all in nearly one go.

"Make sure you remember to have lunch too." I kiss the top of his head and then go to leave, but I spare him one more glance before I make my exit. "I love you."

"I love you too." He smiles, and it makes my chest warm in the way it always has when he's looked at me like that.

I can't imagine my life without him, and I definitely wouldn't have been able to have such a good rookie season if he'd stayed in Cali. All I can picture is living in this house alone, getting the occasional visit, constantly thinking about him.

Levi Vanderbilt might have been a distraction from football that I really didn't need, but when life handed me my soul mate at an inopportune time, I had no choice but to embrace it.

I barely remember my first three years at Franklin, and a lot of the time, I forget that Levi wasn't there the whole time.

Because I think deep down, he was always there with me. Burrowed in my heart. Just waiting to reappear and knock me off my feet.

I wouldn't change anything about it.

One day in the future, maybe after I've won that Super

Bowl ring, I'll put a different kind of ring on his finger. Honestly, if my parents didn't joke about us doing it so much, I probably would've already proposed.

This time last year, I was freaking out about choosing between football and Levi thinking it was one or the other, but Levi has taught me I can share my life with both of my loves. That choice would have been impossible because football is my passion, but Levi is my life.

thank you

Thanks so much for reading *Football Royalty*!
We've come to the end of the Franklin U Series, and we all
want you to know how appreciative we are of every single
reader who took a chance on our FUKers.
Missed a few along the way? Pick up the rest of the series
here: https://geni.us/franklinu

Want more from me?
Want to see Peyton's brother Brady fall in love? He's a lot to
handle, but luckily, SEALs come highly trained.
Coming January 2023
Get it here: https://geni.us/cantsaygoodbye

Also from this universe:
Peyton's dads, his Uncle Damon, and Uncle Maddox first
appeared in the Fake Boyfriend universe.
Start with Damon and Maddox's story here:
https://geni.us/fakeoutFB

Or, if you want to jump into Peyton's dads' origin story, you can read that here: https://geni.us/EFBLFBBK4

meet all the couples of franklin u!

Brax and Ty's story:

Playing Games

Marshall and Felix's story:

Dating Disaster

Charlie and Liam's story:

Mr. Romance

Spencer and Cory's story:

Bet You

Chris and Aidan's story:

The Glow Up

Cobey and Vincent's story:

Learning Curve

Alex and Remy's story:

Making Waves

Peyton and Levi's story:

Football Royalty

Printed in Great Britain
by Amazon

33565183R00162